THE ENLIGHTENMENT OF
JUAN BAUTISTA CHAPA

Acknowledgments

The writing of this book would not have been possible without the help of so many. In particular, I would like to thank Nathan Williams and my wife, who were my collaborators and coauthors.

I would also like to express my gratitude to the historians and archivists who so graciously provided their guidance and expertise to ensure that the book hewed as close to historical fact as possible: Richard Boyer, Lino Garcia, Jr., Davide Gambino, Gianni Venturi Luigi F.A. Schiappapietra, Susan Deeds, Hector Jaime Treviño, Israel Cavazos Garza, Gregorio Rodriguez, Francisco Javier Chapa.

Printed in the United States of America

First Printing, 2015
ISBN-13: 978-1517268589
ISBN-10: 1517268583

Quixotic Books
P.O. Box 759
Portland, Oregon 97207
info@quixoticbooks.com

This book is dedicated to my Father, the first and best Chapa I ever met, and to my wonderful cousin, Francisco J Chapa, who introduced me to this fascinating character.

Additionally, I want to give special thanks to my wife; everything that she touches she makes better. Without her significant contribution, this book would never have been finished.

"Literature makes real what history forgot."

Carlos Fuentes

"For us, there is only the trying.
The rest is not our business."

TS Elliott

THE ENLIGHTENMENT OF JUAN BAUTISTA CHAPA

Anonymous

Introduction

The protagonist of this novel, Juan Bautista Chapa, was born Giovanni Battista Schiappapietra in a small Ligurian town near Genoa, Italy in 1627. At the age of 13, he sailed for Cádiz, then emigrated to New Spain at the age of 19. Once in New Spain, he travelled to the frontier region of Nuevo Leon, where he built a long and distinguished career as the secretary and advisor to a long line of Governors and wrote what became the first written history of Northeastern Mexico and Southeastern Texas for the years 1650-1690.

Introduced to the character of Juan Bautista Chapa by a cousin from Monterrey, Mexico, I became intrigued with the man, an Italian emigrant who became one of the defining figures in the history of Northeastern Mexico. After reading a translation of his *Historia del Reino del Nuevo León,* I became fascinated with the arc of Chapa's life and the way it illuminated the development of Nuevo León and Mexico during the 17th century.

Diving into the scholarly works and archives that outline the known course of Chapa's life, I was inspired to take those threads and weave them into a richer tapestry–a novel that could bring the man and his world to life in a more vivid way. To that end, everything I could learn about his life and the era he lived in was employed to try and create a living, breathing person.

Examining Chapa's life through the lens of my own mixed heritage also made me think of how his story could probe deeper truths about how Mexico itself was forged—the difficult and bloody synthesis of Spanish, Indian and African cultures into a new and complex nation. As my interest in the project deepened, it sent me off on a fascinating journey of exploration, one that ultimately connected me with scholars and historians in Italy, Mexico, the U.S. and Canada. I travelled in his footsteps, with visits to Albisola, Veracruz, Cádiz, Cadereyta and Monterrey.

These visits, conversations, and the historical research that sprung from them, all drove me to create a world that is as faithful to truth and history as possible. At the heart of the book is the *Historia* itself, excerpts of which make up the foundation of the narrative. All but two of the major characters are real people with whom he lived and worked, and the narrative of his life is stitched together from historical documents from Italy, Spain and Mexico. While the journey started as a solitary quest, it ultimately became a truly collaborative effort, written with the assistance of my wife, and a young writer/historian, Nathan Williams.

Beginning with a cryptic bequest in his Last Will and Testament, we created a complementary protagonist for my novel, a slave by the name of Francisco. Francisco was in fact a real person, known to us only because Chapa bequeathed a lot he owned to "the daughter of Francisco, slave of the beneficiary priest"–a highly unusual bequest that pricked my imagination. Francisco's voice, and the dialogue that develops between him and Chapa, offered an alternate lens to explore issues of race, religion and governance—giving voice to those whose perspectives were excluded from the official historical documents of that era, including Chapa's own *Historia*.

The conversations that unfold between them over the course of the novel help expand Chapa's understanding of history, morality, and culture, as he battles interior demons born from a lifetime of faithful service to the powers of Church and Crown. Over the writing of the novel, Chapa's story unfolded in a way that pushed me to consider deeper political and philosophical themes that parallel Chapa's personal narrative. In its final form, I hope the novel illuminates more than just the man himself, but also provokes thought on some deeper concepts:

- The interplay of reality, imagination, dreams and consciousness.
- The fundamental question of 'What makes us human?', as viewed from the perspectives of both philosophy and evolutionary biology.
- The meaning of 'Enlightenment'–in a personal sense, yes, but also the philosophical and political movement that had its roots in the 17th century – Chapa's own era.

List of Proper Names Mentioned in the Text

As they were at the close of the year in 1693:

Alonso de León, the elder – A wealthy landowner and mentor to Chapa. Deceased.

Alonso de León, the younger – Mayor of Cadereyta and later governor of Nuevo León. Deceased.

Antonio Fernandez Vallejo – The present lieutenant governor of Nuevo León.

Bartolome Schiapapria – Don Juan Chapa's father. Deceased.

Battistina Schiapapria – Don Juan Chapa's mother. Deceased.

Beatriz Treviño de Chapa, née Treviño de Olivares – Don Juan Chapa's wife. Deceased.

Benito – A driver of mules.

Bishop Juan de Santiago y León Garabito – Bishop of Guadalajara.

Jose Vicencia Ocelo– A trader of Cádiz.

Doctor Alaniz – A physician of Monterrey.

Domingo de Vidagaray y Saraza – A short-tenured governor of Nuevo León. An enemy of Chapa. Deceased.

Padre Joseph Guajardo – The young priest of Monterrey.

Padre Luis – Padre Joseph's predecessor. Deceased.

Padre Mateo – Personal secretary to the Bishop.

Francisco – An indentured servant working in Chapa's house.

Gaspar Chapa y Treviño – Don Juan Chapa's eldest son.

Josefina – A woman born near the Kongo River, now a slave. Possibly deceased.

José-Maria Chapa y Treviño - Don Juan Chapa's second son.

Juan Bautista Chapa, the younger – A retired councilor in the frontier province of Nuevo León. Born Giovanni Battista Schiapapria.

Juan Bautista Chapa, the elder – Don Juan Chapa's uncle. A trader in Cádiz. Deceased.

Juan de Olivares – Father of Beatriz. A great landholder of Nuevo León and the subject of rumors. Deceased.

Juan Pérez de Merino – The present governor of Nuevo León.

Luisa – Francisco's daughter. A serving woman.

Manuel Astorga – A merchant of the Monterrey market. A seller of luxury goods.

Martín de Zavala – A long-tenured governor of Nuevo León. Deceased.

Masina Schiapapria - Don Juan Chapa's grandmother. Deceased.

Maria de Chapa – Don Juan Chapa's elder daughter.

Nicolò Chapa – Don Juan Chapa's elder brother. A friar. Born Nicolò Schiapapria. Possibly deceased.

Rodrigo Ulias – Secretary to Governor de Merino. Successor to Don Juan Chapa.

Santiago de Treviño – Brother of Beatriz. Witness to a miracle.

Sister Maria – A nun in the service of Padre Joseph. Friend of Luisa

CHAPTER 1

The Mirror

*So old and frail, your withered body mocks the young man who
came to this dusty corner of the world. The world no longer needs you
and will soon forget you were ever here. All the hours spent writing
and rewriting, preserving the truth as you wanted it remembered; all
wasted now. From now on, the only story that remains is the one you
tell me, and I am far more critical than those blank sheets of paper. The
deft hiding, the cautions of a lifetime are pointless now. Face the man
in front of you. Before you put your very life to the torch, there are
questions to answer.*

This mirror. Of all their mother's baubles, my children left
just this one, this little polished oval. It has been my close
companion these last months, the unsentimental truth of its
reflection a last gift from my love. If only it looked at me with
the forgiving cast of her loving eyes. But no, my sins require
God's own searing gaze.

*Placate the Bishop with your burnt offering. Save your children
and free yourself. Abandon your defenses, your denial and too-
convenient forgetfulness. You recall more than you admit, and far
more than you ever recorded. Your dreams, though, they speak the
truth. Open your mind to the wisdom torn from those nightmares.*

I see it now: the compromised ideals, the broken promises, a life devoted to the ambitions of selfish men. So dedicated, but to what end? A life played out in the shadows of petty men, pursuing their stupid quarrels, papering over ugly sins, cementing the power of tyrants. Grease on the axles of power. How did I end up here?

This is home. You belong here, in this landscape of haunted beauty; rooted in this sun-beaten soil, the dirt that holds Beatriz' lovely bones. Nuevo León, your children call it, in reverence for a Spain they will never see. She gave you prestige, land and family. And in return you gave her . . . everything. What crimes have you committed in her name? How many lies have you told to cleanse the story of her creation, to absolve yourself of the crimes of her birth?

My *Historia*, born from the pursuit of truth, is crippled with lies and distortions. Will torching the past, the lies along with the truths, finally give me peace? In my mind, the book was like my *hacienda* records—double-checked, copied, sorted, and tagged. Accuracy, transparency, thoroughness. Truth. Love of truth drove me at every step. How did falsehood invade so easily?

Through you, Giovanni. Surely you see that. Your vanity, your unquestioning deference to powerful men, your smiling acceptance of moral blinders. But your dreams show you the truth; your servant has challenged your lies. In this mirror, you have watched imagination challenge reality, then listened as reality answered back. Soon your children will bury you; your last will and testament will be read, your few possessions meted out. Ashes to ashes, dust to dust. Your Historia, *the passion of your life, for which you sacrificed a thousand peaceful evenings, is your final offering before God. Pray that it is enough to make amends for the sins of a lifetime.*

I beg forgiveness of all whom I have wronged. Will any still hear my apology? God, perhaps. He forgives those who truly repent, doesn't he? Will He forgive me?

You will find out in God's own time. But for now, let us finally honor the truth. Don Juan Bautista Chapa. Giovanni Battista Schiapapria. At long last, are you ready?

I am. Ready to speak truth to this old mirror, but also to let the truth turn to ash. Ready to sacrifice what I must, in the hope of a peaceful life; in the hope of a reconciled death. Goodbye, my friend.

CHAPTER 2

Paper, Ink, Bread, and Wine

Francisco carefully poured boiling water into the earthen bowl, the dry cacao grounds rising to the top and then slowly sinking again as they absorbed the swirling liquid. He placed the scalding iron pot on the shelf above the *fogón* and twirled a wooden spoon between his palms to mix the cacao and water. In his great-grandfather's day this had been a drink of warriors and priests, mixed with *atole* and *chile* to create a bracing drink in service of strength and courage. But times had changed, Francisco reflected, as he added two shards of dark brown *panela* and a sliver of cinnamon bark. Sweets of all kinds were now loved by Spaniard and Indian alike. The old servant, hands still steady and strong despite his age, set the bowl on a polished wooden tray next to a porcelain cup and a short wooden ladle, and crossed the patio towards his master's study.

Francisco was entering his seventh decade on this earth but still stood tall, his shoulders and back strong. Perceptive eyes shone in a dark face, complemented by a strong, broad nose and cheeks dusted in black stubble. His woolly hair was cropped short, cut with a knife by Francisco himself on the first Sunday of each month.

The door was ajar, and Francisco glanced in before entering. At a battered old writing table sat his master, the esteemed Don Juan Bautista Chapa. Now retired, Chapa had served as attorney, secretary, and councilor to three generations of governors in this kingdom of Nuevo León—the far northeastern frontier of the Spanish crown in this new world. To the north and east, beyond the great Rio Bravo, roamed only savage Indians for hundreds of *leguas,* until one finally reached the tiny, scattered settlements founded by the English, Dutch, and French along the Atlantic coastline. True civilization in the Americas existed in only one place: New Spain, with Nuevo León a lonely outpost clinging to its furthest edge.

The old councilor sat hunched over his desk, finely crafted out of local pine but worn and scarred from years of use. His hair had not been cut in some time and was rather wild from his habit of anxiously running his free hand through it while deep in thought. The fingers of his right hand were already smudged with ink after only two hours writing—the old scribe's once-immaculate penmanship was now slow and shaky with age. Intelligent eyes were set in a square face of ruddy, pale flesh— Chapa saw little sun these days. His prominent nose was balanced by a thick mustache that had gone mostly white. In recent years younger men of good families had begun to adopt an entirely clean-shaven appearance, but Chapa still wore a mustache and chin beard in the manner of the late Phillip IV.

There were worse masters, Francisco knew, and he allowed himself a measure of fondness for this eccentric old man of letters, in spite of the condescension and short measure of patience he was often granted. Would he act any differently if he had enjoyed Don Juan's life of privilege? Francisco suspected he might not. All men have the same weaknesses. Francisco knocked and entered in one fluid motion—the knock was pure formality, like so many of the perfunctory rituals of the *peninsulares* in this frontier. He set the tray down on a small table next to the writing desk.

Only then did Chapa look up from his writing. "Ah, Francisco, how nice. The sun is already well up and I still haven't shaken the chill from waking."

Francisco ladled the sweet *xocolatl* into Chapa's cup and stole a quick glance at the manuscript over which his master labored. "I would be happy to set your desk by the fire in the front room, Don Juan, to spare you from working in this drafty study."

Chapa took a small cautious sip of the still-steaming beverage. As he leaned over, his hair fell into his eyes, and he brushed it back behind his ears," I would need to move all my bookshelves and papers and various other effects to make that a practical solution." The drink too hot for his lips, he blew across it to cool it. "No, I don't mind working here. It has been my study since Beatriz and I were given this house over forty years ago, and it will remain so until I die. The cold bothers me, but too much warmth lulls me to sleep. With the time I have remaining, I prefer a little discomfort while I work."

Francisco nodded, smiling at the old man's notion of discomfort. Chapa sipped his drink, lost in thought, thinking of the house in those early days, Beatriz's birds hanging in the patio, the children's laughter as they played in the garden with their *amas*. A sharp knock from the front door echoed across the patio, startling him out of his reverie. "That would be Padre Joseph," said Chapa. "Please let him in and offer him a chair in the front room. I will join him in a moment."

Chapa set down his pen and began to rise, but the long woolen blanket resting on his shoulders became caught on the back of his chair, creating an awkward tangle.

"Don Juan, let me . . ."

"No. I can manage," the old Don said, his voice frustrated and touchy. "Just go and see to my guest."

Francisco nodded and quickly exited, happy to escape his master's small irritation before it became a great one. When Don Juan emerged, Francisco knew the old scribe would do so with a restored state of composure and benign humor.

***

Francisco opened the door gracefully, as he had long ago been instructed, and offered the guest a short bow without making eye contact. As Chapa had predicted, it was the young priest. "Francisco, my son, is your master at home?"

"Yes, Father. Please come in. Don Juan asks that I offer you a seat, and he will join you shortly."

Francisco stepped aside to let the priest pass by. Padre Joseph carried a small, ornate wooden box in his hands and a rough leather satchel over his left shoulder. He dressed entirely in black: the traditional cassock of the priesthood, a woolen cape, a simple felt hat with a low crown, and a pair of well-worn boots. The priest was short, and though young was already losing much of his hair. Though the day was not especially warm, his pudgy face was damp with sweat.

Padre Joseph cradled the box in his right arm and shifted the satchel from his shoulder. "Francisco, please take this from me."

"Of course, Padre. I will retrieve it for you when you leave."

"The contents are for your master. But wait to give it to him, as we first have more pressing matters."

By touch, Francisco guessed that the satchel contained either some sort of large book or a large quantity of paper. The hard round glass bottle inside indicated that the second guess was most likely correct. He carefully placed the satchel on a chair in the corner of the room.

"You are serving Don Juan well?" Padre Joseph asked. The priest's eyes scanned the room, glancing over the outdated furniture, the worn boards of the floor. "This room doesn't see much use, does it? Where does the Don spend his time? I heard he has quite an extensive library. Does he still occupy his days with writing?"

"I hope my service pleases him, Padre. And you, of course," Francisco answered. "Don Juan Chapa spends most of his time in the little study on the other side of the patio. He keeps busy, writing and reading for most of each day. What he writes I cannot say."

"Is that so?" said Padre Joseph. The priest started to say something else but then thought better of it, hearing the first sounds of Chapa's steps on the patio stones.

"Don Juan," Padre Joseph said, smiling, "You look well."

"Thank you, Father" answered Chapa, "Be welcome in my humble home."

Chapa dressed in understated clothing for a man of his status. While simple, the garments were carefully tailored, and of fine materials still scarce in this corner of New Spain. He wore the low-cut shoes now in fashion and appropriate to a man who would never again find himself atop a horse, but he also maintained the traditional boothose of thick Cambrai linen worn over his finer silk stockings.

He still preferred the loose-fitting rhinegrave breeches of his older generation and a simple shirt tied together with a narrow auburn cravat. Over it he wore a subtly patterned broadcloth waistcoat, long-sleeved for warmth in these colder months. In the intervening time, he had managed, Francisco noticed, to run a comb through his unkempt hair, creating at least a semblance of order.

The old man extended his arm towards the priest, grasping his shoulder as the priest returned the gesture, ostensibly out of affection, but more to subtly steady the old scholar. "The Lord's blessing on you, my son. Do you recall what I have come for?" The priest's inclined his head towards the box cradled in his free hand.

"I suppose it has been quite some time," Chapa answered, his voice revealing the slightest edge of reluctance.

"It has been nearly a year according to my ledger, Don Juan. The good Doctor Alaniz is charged with the tending of your body, but it is my duty to care for the health of your soul."

"Yes, of course," Chapa said, remembering himself. "It pains me greatly to no longer be able to attend Mass in your beautiful church."

"You should sell this house," the priest answered, "and move closer to the *traza*. You could then easily walk to church for daily Mass."

The *traza* was Monterrey's central square, a large rectangular plaza exemplifying Castilian ambition and Roman geometry. On one side of the *traza* stood the *reino*'s administrative building, once more familiar to Chapa than his

8

own home. Around the other sides stood the governor's palace, Padre Joseph's *Iglesia de San Francisco*, and looming over it all, the unfinished, still-unnamed cathedral. A few fine private homes owned by well-to-do *peninsular* and *criollo* landowners and merchants filled in the gaps around the square.

The fine facades ringing the *traza*, however, were just that, masking the insignificance of the frontier city. In fact, were it not the seat of government for Nuevo León, Monterrey would hardly merit the designation *ciudad* at all, with a population of just a few hundred Spaniards (no census bothered to count the Indians). Most of this tiny band of *primeros pobladores* actually worked and lived out on the *haciendas* and *ranchos* scattered across the valley, keeping houses in town mostly to maintain their rights to participate in government and to give them a place to stay when they rode into town for the Sabbath and festival days.

Chapa nodded slowly, as if to convey his sincere regret. "If only I could. But this house was a gift from my father-in-law and so beloved by my Beatriz. I could not bear to leave it, as each little object reminds me of her."

"I understand, Don Juan. But I do hope you will reconsider. In the meantime, let us proceed."

Chapa knew there was little point in hedging any further. "Would here suffice, Padre? Before the crucifix on the wall?" Beatriz' mother had given it to her when we moved into the house, and made sure it was hung directly across from the front door, the first thing anyone saw on entering the home.

"Yes, of course. That will do well. Perhaps you would be more comfortable in your study, however. If your chairs there give you more comfort, I can attend you there."

Chapa demurred quickly, "No it is too cold and the room too untidy to serve such a sacred purpose."

"As you wish. Francisco, please give us privacy for a little while. Your master must confess before he receives the Eucharist. To listen would be a sin."

"Yes, of course," said Francisco, and retired to the garden behind the kitchen, where he was far out of earshot. As he walked through the small garden, Francisco noted the weeds that had crept into the beds and the grape arbor that was starting to buckle. Even in such a small house, there was far more work than one servant could ever complete. Given the *don's* age and ill health, he had so much more work than an ordinary servant. Still, he felt healthy and strong, even though he could count on one hand those in town who were older than him. He knew better than to feel sorry for himself.

***

"Is there anything else, my son?" the priest asked after Chapa had confessed only the mildest of sins, most of them simple matters of impatience or discourteousness. Chapa shifted in his seat, uncomfortable at the forced moment of introspection. Looking at the round, self-satisfied cheeks of the plump young priest, he sensed an expectant energy as the young man leaned forward to hear his confession.

"My life is long, Father, and certainly each day I have lived I have also sinned. I am quite sure there are sins here and there I have not recounted, but I cannot recall them," said Chapa, truthful after a fashion, but guarded, opaque. He felt in that moment the same twisted pangs of guilt that haunted him each night during his nightly prayers. He longed for the anonymous confessors of his youth, cloistered priests bound by vows of silence and seclusion, disconnected from the politics and intrigues of the outside world.

"You were involved in many of the Indian wars, were you not? Did you ever kill a man, Don Juan?" the priest prompted, clumsily trying to prod the old man into deeper revelations.

"No, thank God. I never did," said Chapa, sidestepping the priest with the agility of a lifelong public servant. He spoke truthfully, in that he did not directly lie. Such legal distinctions meant little to God in the final reckoning, and his was a calculated gamble, staving off a public confession while he prayed for some kind of private bargain with God himself.

"Now, killing an armed man while at war is not necessarily a sin," continued the priest, leaning in.

10

"Of course not. But in any case, I did not. However deft I was with a quill in my hand, I was equally clumsy with a sabre or harquebus," said Chapa, "I served on many campaigns, but I was less danger to my fellow campaigners with an astrolabe in my hand."

The priest shifted in his chair and realized he was getting nothing more. He blessed the old man, stifling the urge to lecture him on his stubbornness. "Then for your penance I assign you . . ."

***

After assigning penance and leading Chapa in the Act of Contrition, Padre Joseph called for Francisco to return and move the small table away from the wall, centering it before the crucifix. Francisco complied and then watched as the young priest, surely no more than twenty-five, set down the ornate box and carefully removed from it a folded square of silk cloth and a small jar. The old *don*, who deferred to very few, stood patiently awaiting the priest's instruction. He had been told once that a priest's cassock always bore exactly 33 buttons—representing each year of Christ's earthly life. He tried to count the padre's buttons as he moved, but found himself losing track and being forced to start over.

"Let us begin," said Padre Joseph.

Chapa nodded. Realizing he could not stand unaided through the entire ceremony, he reached a hand out to the wood mantle, steadying himself. Francisco noted this and moved to a spot just behind him, ready to come to his master's aid should he become weak and begin to sway.

"*Pax Dómini sit semper vobíscum.*"

Chapa answered, "*Et cum spíritu tuo.*"

"*Orémus. Præcéptis salutáribus móniti, et divína institutióne formáti, audémus dícere,*" the priest continued.

Francisco listened in silence and mused to himself: Latin was so close to Castilian in many ways. And closer still to the Ligurian he had heard Chapa use on occasion. Over his long life he had also heard French, Catalan, Aragonese, Milanese, Tuscan, and Portuguese, all bearing remarkable similarities. Could the *peninsulares* not have settled on one language and saved themselves a great deal of trouble? And then how to explain that strange tongue of the Basques?

"*Pater noster, qui es in cælis: sanctificétur nomen tuum: advéniat regnum tuum: fiat vóluntas tua, sicut in cælo, et in terra. Panem nostrum quotidiánum da nobis hódie, et dimítte nobis débita nostra, sicut et nos dimíttimus debitóribus nostris. Et ne nos indúcas in tentatiónem...*"

On cue Chapa answered the final line obediently: "*Sed líbera nos a malo.*"

Padre Joseph reached down and unfolded the fine silk with his fat, soft fingers, revealing a single wafer. He held it high. "*Accípite, et manducáte ex hoc omnes, hoc est enim corpus meum.*"

Chapa nodded and opened his mouth.

The priest held the wafer above Chapa's head. "*Corpus Christi.*"

"*Amen.*"

The priest set the wafer on Chapa's tongue. Chapa quickly chewed the thin, tasteless wafer, trying with all his might to imagine it was indeed the flesh of mankind's savior.

Padre Joseph unsealed the lid off the jar, revealing the small volume of red wine within. "*Sanguis Christi.*"

"*Amen.*"

The priest offered the small vessel to Chapa, who took it and drank from the jar. There were fine wines now made in the North, but this—or, he mentally corrected himself, what this had been before transubstantiation—was not one of them. He returned the jar to Padre Joseph.

The priest carefully set the jar down beside the box. "*Et vos omnes, qui hic simul adéstis, benedícat omnípotens Deus, Pater et Fílius, et Spíritus Sanctus.*"

Chapa nodded one last time. "*Amen.*"

"Good. It is done." Joseph returned both the cloth and jar back to his little box. As he closed the box he turned to Francisco. "Francisco, I will stay a while and speak with your master, but please make sure not to touch this box. This vessel may only be cleaned in the sanctuary."

"I understand, Father. It is not for me to wash the blood of Jesus Christ."

As they spoke, Chapa wandered to the front window, drawn by the sight of the street now bathed in sunlight, a refreshing contrast to the overcast morning. "Would you like to join me in my garden, Father?" he asked without turning. "I circumnavigate my garden path ten times each day. While it may be taxing, the Doctor believes it strengthens my constitution."

"Of course, Don Juan," the priest replied.

"Good," Chapa turned back to the priest and began to lead him out through the patio door, across the patio to a little wooden gate next to the kitchen. Opening it, he motioned the priest to enter the little walled garden. "Be so good as to take my arm and support me if I should waiver."

They passed the small, orderly kitchen—well kept by Francisco—and into the garden. To say Chapa was proud of his little garden would be an overstatement, but he found frequent solace there, the tranquil sort of pleasure he never would have appreciated in his frenetic youth. Tall plastered adobe walls extended from the house and wrapped around the small *huerta*, blocking out the dust of the street.

His garden contained the holy trinity of Spanish trees that graced each garden in Monterrey. Near the entrance stood the three trees planted and especially beloved by Beatriz: an *oliva* tree, now twelve years old and bearing good fruit, the *higuero*, and the *granada*. Ranged along the south side of the garden were other trees that belonged only to this new land, *aguacate*, *papaya* and *guayaba*. His *limón* tree had grown rapidly and now dominated the southeast corner of the garden, providing ample shade in the afternoon. This time of year, however, the only fruit he could hope for were pomegranates.

In a few months, he—or Francisco, rather—would plant various vegetables in the beds: *calabacitas* and *tomates*, *chile* and *cebolla*, along with herbs for seasoning and medicine. A small path circled the perimeter of the garden, and a few wooden chairs, partially bleached by the sun, were placed under the lime tree, near the flowering cacti, hibiscus and rose bushes hugging the east wall. At the very center stood a circular brick fire pit, useful for burning fallen leaves and other debris. The window of Chapa's study looked out on the garden, and he often took solace at the changing of the seasons as he labored at his writing table.

The young priest turned to ensure they were alone and then asked, in a solicitous whisper, "How has Francisco been? I know the circumstances of his service are . . . uncommon."

"There are no concerns, Father. He is diligent and loyal. I have few possessions of worth—few that would have value to anyone but me—so I don't worry myself about his past. I thank you again for the loan of his services. I don't know what I'd do without him," said Chapa.

"Think nothing of it, Don Juan. He belongs to the parish, not my own personal property. And while my predecessor might have missed him, I am young and need nothing beyond the care given by the kind sisters of Pobre Clara." the priest said.

"How is your parish, Padre Joseph?" Chapa asked. Most men were happiest when talking about themselves, Chapa knew. When he found himself pressed on matters he would prefer to avoid, Chapa almost always found that vanity made an easy fulcrum for diversion.

"It is kind of you to ask, Don Juan. With God's grace we are thriving. My flock here is so spread out on distant *haciendas* that I spend most days on my mule, little Clarita. Just yesterday I gave last rites to an old woman on the *hacienda* of Don Jose Saenz, a *meztiza* who had cared for the *don's* children when they were young. After tending to her, saying a mass in the family chapel and enjoying the midday meal and a little siesta, I rode back nearly three *leguas,* barely arriving before darkness fell. We studied a great many subjects in seminary, but none would have been as useful as the art of riding mules."

Noting the rotund figure of the priest, Chapa felt sorry for poor little Clarita. Stifling a smile, he remarked, "The distances in this land can indeed be punishing. On the last expedition I undertook on behalf of the Crown, just three years ago, my bones were so rattled by the end of the journey that it took a week of bed rest just to unknot the kinks in my back. A man of my age feels every one of the ten *leguas* each day that such journeys require, especially as the weeks drag on." He thought to poke a little more at the priest for his complaints, but decided it was better to change the subject. "It has been too long since I dined with Don Jose. I hope he is well."

"He is well, although troubled by the continuing Indian raids in his part of the valley. It is difficult in that area, since the *haciendas* butt up against the mountains where the devils take refuge."

"And that *hacienda* is close to that of my son, Gaspar, isn't it? You didn't stop in and visit with him on your return?"

"I am afraid not, as I feared the approach of nightfall. I don't recall seeing him since I blessed his ranch last August, but I am sure my memory eludes me and he has since attended Mass. How is he?"

"Gaspar?"

"Yes."

Chapa paused for half a step, uncomfortable, then quickly recovered his gait and replied casually, "Oh he is well, I'm happy to say. Would you like to take a few pomegranates back to your rectory? They are just coming into season."

"Thank you, Don Juan, but I am well fed by the generosity of our parish."

"Of course."

The priest fidgeted. "I would ask, Don Juan . . ."

"Yes?" Chapa replied.

"Would you mind if I smoked while we walk?" The priest gestured to the pocket of his cassock. "I have my own tobacco in case—"

"Of course," Chapa said, "I am a poor host for not having already offered. Please, though, try a little of my tobacco."

"No need to apologize, Don Juan. I could not have accepted earlier even had you offered. Did you know, so prevalent is the habit in our native lands that His Holiness felt it necessary to forbid smoking before and *during* Mass."

Chapa laughed at this notion and when they reached the kitchen window, called for Francisco to bring them two cigars and a candle. The two cigars lit, the servant nodded and retreated to the house.

Chapa savored his first shallow inhalation. "I find the local tobacco grown in continental New Spain to be of poor quality. This tobacco comes to me from Cuba through Veracruz. Although it's expensive, I have few guests these days and smoke very little, so a parcel lasts me a great while."

Padre Joseph exhaled, examined the cigar and nodded in agreement, "It is a very fine tobacco, Don Juan. Thank you."

They reached the kitchen door again and began their third lap around the small garden path, Chapa surreptitiously tossing a pebble into a small bowl to mark the circuit.

Padre Joseph could no longer restrain his curiosity at this ritual. "Don Juan, why do you mark each lap around your circuit? Is it a form of meditation or prayer, like the beads on the rosary?"

Chapa flushed, caught out on his little habit. "It is just a little eccentricity of mine, I suppose. I am a creature of habit, and from the time I was little I kept track of each little journey. You know, it took me 1,647 steps to get from my house to the beach where I played when I was a young boy, 165 steps from my house to the front of our family's church and 275 steps to my grandfather's inn from my home. I have always counted my steps," Chapa said with a self-conscious laugh, "Just a little tic, I suppose."

Chapa coughed, first a small cough, but it was followed by another and another still, until it became a brief fit. He halted and bent at the waist, his hands on his knees, struggling to recover his breath as Padre Joseph extended his hand to Chapa's back. After a moment or two, the old man stood up straight again and, eyes somewhat dampened, he nodded to the priest to signify his recovery. "My apologies, Father."

"Not at all."

"Doctor Alaniz urges me to smoke more often in service of my health, but I find it difficult in my present state."

"Perhaps, like any medicine, it must merely be taken more slowly," the priest offered.

Chapa nodded, unsure but unwilling to debate the matter. "You are surely correct." He drew a shallower breath of smoke from his cigar and moved to continue their walk.

***

Inside, Francisco set the bowl of *xocolatl* on the *fogón* so it would be hot when Chapa returned. He slid the tray into its place and set the ladle and cup aside for washing. He glanced out the kitchen doorway to see Chapa and Padre Joseph still in conversation, strolling in slow clockwise circles around the garden. They seemed to be without immediate need, so Francisco left the kitchen and once again made his way across the patio to his master's study.

He examined the quill pen Chapa had been using and discovered that the split in the nib had begun to separate from over-pressing. Francisco wiped the pen clean of ink on the hem of his rough tunic and took his knife from his belt. He cut off the pen's frayed nib and began to shape a new one from the freshly cut end.

As he worked this delicate task, one he had performed hundreds of times, Francisco allowed himself to gaze at the paper over which his master labored. Instead of another detailed account of Nuevo León's recent history, he was surprised to discover words that suggested an unfinished poem.

Mournful and sad place
Where gloom alone attends you
Because ~~misfort~~ sad fortune
Gave your inhabitants a beastly death
Here I only ~~observe~~ contemplate
That you are a fatality and a sad example

17

Of the ~~fickle~~ ~~cruelty~~ inconstancy of life
Because the wild and murderous enemy
So cruel and inhuman
Discharged his ~~er~~

Francisco wondered if this was an original creation of Don Juan's or an existing work he was transcribing. His eyes searched for an original that Chapa might be copying but he spotted none. The only other paper on the table was an old one, yellowed and brittle, titled "Battle of the Cacaxtle, 1665". He scanned the poem once more and wondered about the context. Where was this "mournful and sad place"? His eyes lingered on the word "inhuman."

Just then he heard Padre Joseph's urgent shout: "Francisco! Come quickly."

Francisco quickly set down the pen and knife and rushed out into the garden. It seemed Chapa had become too weak to stand and had collapsed, slowly and without violence, onto the garden path.

Assured that his master was still breathing steadily, Francisco threw the old man over his sturdy shoulder and carried him back into the house. Chapa protested, repeating several times that he had only made six turns of the required ten. He was so agitated that Francisco had to promise that he could make the final four as soon as he awoke from siesta. Under Padre Joseph's somewhat fussy and unhelpful direction, Francisco set Chapa down in a chair in the front room. Still light-headed, Chapa made a weak gesture of thanks but did not speak.

Padre Joseph handed his still-lit cigar to Francisco and bent before Chapa, making the sign of the cross on his forehead. "My visit has tired you, my son. I will take my leave. I bless you. *In nómine Patris, et Fílii, et Spíritus Sancti. Amen.*"

"Wait a moment, Father," Chapa said, weakly. "Did you bring with you . . .?"

The priest suddenly remembered. "Yes, of course. It nearly slipped my mind. Francisco, please fetch me the bag I gave you."

Francisco returned and retrieved the satchel from the nearby chair. He handed it to the priest and stepped back, closely observing his master's state.

Padre Joseph opened the bag and removed from it a thick sheaf of paper. He held it up for Chapa to see. "Paper, Don Juan, from the mill in Ciudad de México. The quality is still poor, but they have brought in a Genovese master and he is beginning to make improvements."

Finding his breath and his voice, Chapa said, "Yes, thank you."

The priest set the paper down on the table next to Chapa and reached into his bag again. He removed a jar, about one *cuartillo*, of thick, purple-black iron gall ink, and held it high so that Chapa would see it plainly. "Ink, Don Juan, that the merchant made for me just yesterday."

"Thank you, Father."

The priest turned and retrieved his small ornate box and stepped through the door that Francisco had already opened in anticipation of his leaving.

Chapa gestured to the table again. "So it is, surely."

"May God watch over you, my son."

Shortly after, Francisco helped his master to his bedroom for his siesta and fetched his woolen blanket from the study. Chapa lay in bed, exhausted but dreading sleep, knowing it would bring him no peace. Of late his sleep was plagued with nightmares, which were worst at those times when he most struggled with his conscience. His thoughts drifted back to the work he had tried to bend his hand to this morning – a reworking of an important part of the *Historia*, an old battle, one that lived in his mind as if it had happened yesterday. In the end he had been unable to concentrate, and had dawdled instead, working on a little poem he had started some weeks ago. It was the battle that lay heavy on him when the fat little priest had pressed him for confession, needling him with the same insistent guilt that had followed him ever since that day.

He struggled to stay awake, watching the tiny lizards chasing each other around the frame of his window, fearful of what waited for him. As he lay there, though, his eyes grew heavier and finally he drifted into an uneasy sleep. After Chapa dozed off, Francisco retrieved the paper and ink, and returned to the study, placing it on the writing table next to the yellowed papers already lying there, pausing to study the account sitting on the corner of the table.

***

La Historia del Nuevo Reino de León, Chapter 11

The Indians continued to gather near Saltillo. This obliged the lord mayor of Saltillo, Don Fernando de Azcué y Armendariz, to form a company and ask the governor of Nuevo León for another. The companies were organized to enter the enemy's land and to eradicate, in one fell swoop, the settlements of the Indians who were causing so much damage. A war council was convened in Monterrey and, as a result, assistance was given to Saltillo. Thirty soldiers were enlisted, with Juan Cavazos as captain. The Monterrey troops joined Don Fernando, who came to Nuevo León with 103 soldiers, 800 horse, and 70 loads of supplies.

The companies marched out in very good order, and in six days they arrived twenty-four leagues beyond the Rio Bravo in search of the warlike Cacaxtle nation. It had been announced that an Indian named Don Nicolas el Carretero who was peacefully settled in Saltillo would gather Indians loyal to him to support the Spaniards. He collected more than three hundred Indian troops; the majority were of the Bobole nation. Although the Bobole were suspect, they behaved very loyally on this occasion and fought bravely.

The enemy was hidden in some woods, but they were surrounded at dawn and could not escape. The Indians resisted valiantly. Because the woods were very thick and Spaniards could not penetrate them, the troops shot the Indians they could see. An enemy Indian urged the Spaniards to cease the struggle because the Indians wanted to make peace. But the Spaniards recognized this as a ruse to allow the Indians a chance to regroup, which they did, to build a protective enclosure of tree limbs, prickly pears, and branches. When the diversion and feigned peace were recognized, our men continued their attack, and the fight lasted until the hour of prayer. One hundred Indians were killed and seventy small and large weapons were taken.

During the battle, an old Indian woman played a flute to give the Cacaxtle courage. She was at the time a Spanish captive, and the friendly Indians asked if they could eat her. The Spaniards would not allow this, nor any similar cruelty that would serve as vengeance against her. However, the Indians knew that a boy among the prisoners was a relative of hers. That night the Indians secretly managed to secure <u>him</u>, and they ate him, for which there was no remedy.

In this great battle, twenty-two Spaniards were wounded, although none were killed. Two friendly Indians died, and others were wounded. When the enemy had no more arrows they fought us with clubs.

This expedition was very successful because many of the enemy were killed and their settlement destroyed.

Excerpted directly from <u>La Historia del Nuevo Reino de León,</u> by Juan Bautista Chapa

CHAPTER 3

The Game

While Francisco quietly hovered over the writing table, reading the account of the battle, he heard muffled sounds from the bedroom next door, Chapa plagued as always by the mysterious nightmares that disturbed his sleep. He wondered what could possibly be tormenting the old man so. Even though his own life had been hard and often dark, he had never suffered from nightmares in the way this old scribe seemed to. What could haunt him so terribly?

***

"Cavazos, Chapa! Take your men and close off the south side of the ravine!" We circle the rocky hillside, the anxious horses sliding on the skittering stones, their hot breath sending out white plumes in the frigid air. My God, it's cold. I shiver–from the chill, or out of fear? I don't know.

We know there are Indians hiding on both sides of this ravine–by sealing the exit on the far side, there is no way out of the barranca except through the mouth where we now stand. I feel their eyes upon us, and my mind vaults to their perch–I see us as they do: monsters, half flesh, half metal, hairy arms and legs with cold steel chest plates and bronze helmets. I am a clumsy Sancho Panza, but the criollos are centaurs, fluid unity of man and horse. I don't see the Indians' fear, but I can feel it on the back of my neck.

At our side are two hundred Boboles. They are Indians we have tamed and made our subjects (in their language they call us "allies,"). Usually quick to retreat or abandon a long campaign, today their blood is up. These Cacaxtles before us are their ancient enemy – with terrible crimes to their name going back generations.

Those Cacaxtle fools should never have fled their village. They're usually smarter than this, often craftier than we are. Why take such a dangerous position and then drag their old, their women, and their children along with them? They're up there. I know it. They're hiding up on the canyon ledge, but we can't see them. Riding into the canyon from this narrow north entry, I feel their eyes as my horse picks its way down the path. Where are they?   We could starve them out easily; but we don't have the time or the food to wait it out ourselves. In my ears I still hear the echoes of their women wailing and their children crying as we ran them down yesterday. Their men still hear those echoes, surely, and they want to kill us now.

After the heathens fled, the Saltillo soldiers put the Cacaxtle settlement to the torch. The dark smoke from the fire billows on the horizon. It must be driving these heathens mad to see it. It's everywhere, choking us, blinding me. I can't see anything. I'm scared, but I put on the face of a man who has been on a hundred such terrible campaigns. Can the men sense how weak I feel inside?

Behind me sits the old woman José dragged along with us. Why on earth did he take her? She must be at least eighty – tiny, hunched over and toothless, but with the evil eye of a witch. She turns towards me, spits and casts a spell. My horse stumbles and throws a shoe. I wheel my horse around, pulling my bronze pistol and leveling it at her head. She laughs and squints her eyes, daring me to shoot. My hand is frozen, my fingers curled around the gun. I can't move, but can't look away from the grinning skull of the old woman. She puts a tiny bone flute to her lips; the strange melody makes my hair stand on end. I pull on the reins to ride away, but the horse is now a statue, a bronze, in thrall to the song.

A Cacaxtle slides down the steep rocky slope in front of us, a makeshift crucifix held high over his head. Cavazos has ridden off, so the men look to me; is this a trick? Is he mocking God with this crude depiction of his suffering, or is he a believer after all, a savage child of God?

"Llamo Jorge. Jorge yo." I can barely understand his Castilian, but his meaning seems clear. He's asking me to accept his surrender, and let his tribe swear allegiance to the Crown. Don Nicolas shakes his head, as does José Maria, but the decision is mine. I swing down from my horse and take hold of his cross. Fighting *without need is stupid and I am not risking my neck. I have nothing to prove here.*

Jorge whistles a signal, calling his people down from the hill; they creep down, weapons abandoned, hands and feet bloody from their frantic flight up the craggy hillside. They are starving and weak, many of them sick, their faces marked with bloody pox. They are defeated now, but how long until the next savage uprising? We might convert some of them to Christ, but more likely they will just spread disease and treachery among the already domesticated tribes.

A scream pierces the air behind me; my horse rears and pulls the reigns out of my hand. The Boboles rush past me, a mob rather than an organized charge. They are too many; we can do nothing to halt their vengeful tide. They hack with knives and spears at the Cacaxtle kneeling in front of me. The Cacaxtle men throw their women and children upon the ground and turn to fight, but they have no weapons. I stand mute, frozen. Finally, I run, my mouth screams to Cavazos for help, for action, but he does nothing. Pulling him to face me, I command him to stop them. He ignores me, looks past me, stone-faced as the slaughter continues, blood and flesh spattering us both.

I stand mute witness to a hatred that predates us by centuries. A group of Cacaxtle children break free from the Bobole onslaught and charge our line, screaming as if they have let go of life. My men lift their guns. A quick retort cuts them down easily, the bullets shattering their thin, naked little bodies. One of the Boboles decapitates a young girl, the blood spurting from her neck like a fountain in Hell. My stomach heaves – I turn and vomit, trying to hide my weakness. The walls of the canyon swirl around me, the shapes and colors of the Indians just a blur.

A boy staggers up towards me. He can be no more than twelve years of age, his eyes revealing shock and grief so great they verge on madness. To meet his eyes is to stare into the heart of pain itself. He is weeping, pleading, falling on his knees before me, his eyes fixed on mine. I move to cover him with my arms, but my feet are rooted to the ground. José Maria comes up from behind me, his eyes cold, indifferent, his arm raised, his harquebus looming over both of us. I turn to stop him and we are suspended for a moment in silence, mute challenge in his body. I step forward to stop his arm, but falter, a coward. My body pivots, turning its back to the boy while I float, slowly drafting in the hot air like a hawk. Looking up at me, José Maria calmly swings the butt of his harquebus and smashes the boy's skull. The boy falls forward, his blood splashing the breast of my horse, and lands in the dust, pink matter oozing from his left temple, his gaze trailing me as I float above him. Jose Maria wipes his weapon on his breeches and grabs my arm, pulling me out of the air, pushing me onto my horse.

As I ride through the screaming and the rending of flesh, a strange sound weaves in and around my head, lilting and sad in its savage key, the old Cacaxtle woman pulling at me with her flute, playing as she watches her people, every soul she knows on this earth, butchered like savage beasts, the Bobole carving their flesh.

Stopping amid the carnage, I do nothing, say nothing. My soldiers turn away from the scene, spurring their horses towards the mouth of the barranca, *leaving the Bobole to savor their revenge, reminding each other that we Spaniards are fighting to bring His grace to this land.*

I stand alone on my horse; now it is just me and the old woman playing her flute. I look at her. She has death in her eyes, and levels them at me once again. She owns me, the witch owns me, freezing this moment forever in my mind, to be revisited over and over again. Her flute and its otherworldly music will echo in my ears forever. She smiles, mad, and returns to her song of death.

My God, are they eating them?

Pe amô de Dîo.

***

Chapa woke from his afternoon siesta with a sharp gasp, the curse of the old woman ringing in his ears. The sun had crept around the window frame and its direct light warmed his face, calming him enough to slow his pounding heart. The days were growing shorter and the sun was ever lower in the sky. Still shaken by his dream, Chapa wondered if the coming winter would be the last he would ever see.

Francisco had not expected his master's sudden waking, though it should not have surprised him. Hardly a night went by without Francisco hearing a hoarse shout echoing from Chapa's bedchamber.

Without urgent chores and with his mind as troubled as Chapa's by today's visit, he had taken up a weathered tome from Chapa's library, Quevedo's *Los Sueños*. Chapa's troubled sleep reminded Francisco of the strange and vivid vision of the afterlife depicted by the famous Madrileño poet. Momentarily startled, Francisco recovered his composure quickly and closed the book with the simplest of gestures, as if it had never been in his hands.

"I was just about to wake you, *patrón*. Would you like to dine in your study tonight or by the fire where it is warmer?"

For the moment, Chapa chose to hide his surprise at finding Francisco with his Quevedo and agreed to eat by the fire. Though the autumn days in Nuevo León were still mild, the nights could be clear and cold; it took little for an old man to be chilled.

As the day faded into dusk and the flickering light of the fire filled the room, Francisco served his master a simple meal of beans stewed with chiles, onions and a handful of *machaca*, the pounded shreds of dried cured beef that seasoned the *guisados* and *revueltos* of the region. Alongside it were a few tortillas—the last of the small batch delivered by the *mestiza* girl who stopped by daily with her little basket—and a cup of wine. After serving, Francisco as usual stood in attendance a few feet away as the Don ate in contemplative silence.

The earlier incident, unmentioned but very much on both their minds, at last prompted Chapa to break that silence. "Francisco."

"Yes, *patrón*?"

"Earlier today, as I was waking. Was I dreaming still or did I see you sitting with one of my books in your hand?"

Francisco took a breath and thought before answering. "I was concerned for your health after you collapsed, and while you slept I kept watch. Waiting for you to wake, I sat with one of your books, as I sometimes do. I hope it does not trouble you."

"It is no great sin, Francisco. But I wonder, what interest could you possibly have?"

"It was the subject. *Los Sueños*. Your dreams seem so vivid and violent these days, and it made me curious about them. I have often taken counsel from the wisdom of books."

A jolt of realization shot through Don Juan. The old *mestizo* could read. Had Francisco read the letters he often left lying on his desk? His mail when it arrived? He could not, at least, have delved into the private papers he kept carefully under lock and key.

"Francisco, am I to understand you can read Castilian?"

Francisco nodded, "My father taught me letters as a young boy. He read both Castilian and Latin, and he passed that knowledge to his children. Later, after I . . ." Francisco hesitated, searching for the delicate words necessary to avoid mutual embarrassment, "after old Padre Luis, God rest his soul, brought me to serve the parish, he learned of my literacy and shared the books he owned. He was a kind and thoughtful man, and I learned much from him. In that time, I learned not just to read but to love books themselves. I can write as well, but my days allow me little practice. It is a harmless thing for an old servant."

"Your father was a *peninsular*?" asked Chapa, "Or a *criollo*?"

Francisco shook his head. "He was not."

Don Juan had long ago observed that Francisco possessed some unmistakably *peninsular* features, even though his skin was quite dark for a servant who spent no time in the fields. By far the most common pairing that led to this mixture was a Spanish man taking an Indian bedmate (or, less often, wife).

"Am I to understand your Spanish mother married an Indian? You are of course *mestizo*, aren't you, Francisco? I believe I read as much when perusing your trial records."

"Not according to Spanish law, Don Juan, no."

"I confess that surprises me. Can it be you are a full-blooded Indian then? I have never in all my life heard of a full-blooded Indian who could read."

Francisco had generally tried to avoid any discussion of his *casta* status. He had served Chapa for nearly three years without any inquiry into his parentage and found little meaning in the absurd categorizations of race the ruling *peninsular* class imposed on the continent. If he truly wished to avoid the matter he could have simply accepted the *mestizo* designation and pivoted the conversation in another direction. Instead a kind of stubbornness—which some would call pride and others dignity—forced his hand.

"No, I am neither."

Chapa found amusement in this little mystery. "How can this be? You say you are not a full-blood Indian. You are no *peninsular*, like myself, nor a *criollo*, like my sons. And you are certainly not a *negro* or a *mulato*. So you must be a *mestizo*," Chapa said, reasoning each step out aloud.

"I do wish there were so few classes of men," said Francisco, with a bitter smile, "It would have made my long life much easier."

"Oh yes, yes," said Chapa, "*quinterón* and all that, a quarter of this and a little of that. Even we *peninsulares* find these fine distinctions between different mixed races hard to follow, and honestly, somewhat trivial."

"It may be convenient for *peninsulares* to use terms like *mestizo* and *castizo* with little care. But you know, Don Juan, the rules of the *casta* have very real consequences for men like me."

"I grant that. So what are you? Or, wait—" said Chapa, seized by a sudden and uncommon playful impulse. Was it fueled by loneliness and boredom—the long absence of play in his life since the loss of Beatriz? Or did part of him want to remind Francisco that literacy in no way meant true intellectual equality. "Indulge your master and let us make a game of it. Like you, I consider these categories somewhat comical, but they provide a good subject for a guessing game. Tell me your family history, starting on your father's side, and I will guess your *casta*. If I cannot guess, you will enjoy the last cup of wine tonight. If I do guess, it will just be for my own satisfaction. So there you have it, you cannot lose. What do you say?"

"I cannot say no," said Francisco.

"Good. Then begin by telling me about your father's side of your family."

Don Paulo in nearby Parras de la Fuente made an excellent wine from Spanish vine cuttings, although Francisco still preferred the native *pulque*. Francisco turned for the bottle, which he had kept close at hand, knowing the Don's propensity for several cups before retiring. As he poured the wine, Francisco reminded himself to tread carefully with his narrative. History and identity were vital matters of power and authority, deciding who would rule and who would serve; the distinction between a slave and a nobleman could be but the difference of a great-grandparent or two. He would speak truthfully on these matters; his conscience insisted on it and his advanced years, he felt, allowed him that liberty. But the difference between simple fact and the way a fact is presented could be very meaningful, particularly for someone in his position.

"To tell such a tale I can only rely on the family history passed down to me from parent to child. If it should be false, know that I tell you honestly what has been passed down to me. And if, in telling my story, I say something that might be considered heretical, please stop me before I speak further. I am a good Christian but a simple one, Don Juan."

In Francisco's own lifetime the Inquisition had executed twenty-nine people and driven many more into exile. They typically paid little attention to Indians, instead focusing on "crypto-Jews," alleged homosexuals, and those heretical souls distributing banned books or criticizing the church. But even to a poor slave far beneath the Inquisition's notice, there was nothing more terrifying than a court with unrestricted power, so viciously single-minded that it had been known to dig up and try the bones of the dead.

Chapa reassured him, "You needn't fear the *auto de fe* for some story about your ancestry. But if it soothes you I can promise that your account will not leave this house."

"Thank you," said Francisco, pausing only briefly to collect the facts in his head before embarking, "To begin, I have Indian blood. My skin and face tell the tale before my mouth opens. My grandmother's father was a minor noble of Tlatelolco. He was born in the Christian year of 1515, six years before Cortés conquered the Aztec Empire. His birth name was Xipil, and when he was baptized his name became Xavier. His family did not own land but produced many important priests. They lived a life of privilege and ease before Cortés arrived."

29

Many Indians falsely claimed descent from noble blood—as, indeed, did many Spaniards. But nothing in Francisco's demeanor suggested boasting or deceit to Chapa. "So, you are descended from a nobleman. Not many Indians can claim that, and few *peninsulares*, though they may try. Your noble blood, however savage, gives you honor. As does, I might add, your ancestor's prudent early conversion to Christ."

"Thank you, Don Juan," said Francisco. "When the friars came to the Valley of México they founded a college—the first in New Spain I have been told, though you may know better. *El Colegio Imperial de Santa Cruz de Tlatelolco*. It gathered students from the Aztec noble classes. My great-grandfather was one of their number. Because the true goal of the *colegio* was to make priests of these noble Indian boys, Xavier was taught Latin letters, and Spanish, along with music, philosophy, and other important subjects. Xavier nearly became a priest. If that happened I would not be here with you today, so I suppose I should be happy he was not. Quite suddenly the Crown, in its wisdom I am sure, banned Indians from the priesthood. The students were released and the *colegio* fell into ruin."

Chapa had often wondered what that time was like, the early years more than a century before his own arrival, when there were millions of Indians and just a few thousand Spaniards, and such a grand, ancient empire was toppled with such little force. Would the world ever see its like again?

Francisco continued, "Xavier was told by a kind Franciscan friar, a disciple of de las Casas, that he could keep two books—one in Latin and one in Castilian—if he promised that he would teach his own children to read and write. Soon after, he married an Indian woman—whose name I do not remember—who bore him six children. Their third was my grandmother, Xochitl. I knew her in my youth, a tiny Indian woman with white hair, who told me stories of her father, and how he taught all of his children to read and write from those two books. He yearned to teach them more about theology and mathematics, but the poor man worked long hours and could not lead the life of a scholar. After the closure of the *colegio* he was forced to become a common laborer, since as a noble's son he knew no skilled trade."

30

"My own father worked very hard," Chapa told him. "I know how he must have felt."

"I'm sure you do, Don Juan."

Chapa rarely spoke of his father, Bartolome. What would he think of his boy Giovanni living so far from their ancestral home? Adopting the name of Chapa and the manner of an *hidalgo*. Would he be proud of the status his son had achieved on this distant continent, or would there be disappointment at the way he had wielded that influence? At that moment, the sharp pang of memory hit with force, and Francisco and his story receded as Bartolome's lined face rose in his mind's eye.

***

Father's thick arm wraps around my skinny shoulders. Together we lean over the ledger I have been keeping for him, peering down in the dim candlelight. He has been working since before dawn and is exhausted. He takes the time to double-check the ledger but mostly I think he is staying up so he can spend time with me.

"These are very good, son. I do not see a single mistake. I am very proud of you. I never had a head for figures. You have been given a great gift; make sure you honor God in the way that you put it to use."

"I like numbers most of all, Pápa. When your work is right it's always right, when it's wrong it's always wrong. It feels good to know that something is so right it is true forever."

My father laughs and holds me even closer. "You already think like a friar!"

I smile and, greedy for more praise, offer a suggestion: "Father, I think there is a way to make a little more money."

"Your mother would be happy to hear that. What do you suggest, Giovanni?"

"I see that you sell our wheat to the merchant for one quarter ducat per bushel."

"Yes, that is the agreed upon price this harvest."

"But here," I say, pointing to the figure, "You sell the same bushel of wheat to the Sisters for just one fifteenth of a ducat. If you sold the wheat at the same price, we would make at least four more

ducats this harvest. In seven years, if we saved those, there would be enough to buy the parcel of vineyard land Don Locatelli wishes to sell, right?"

My father nods soberly, his eyes suddenly clouded with concern. I thought my discovery would bring him joy but it seems to only increase the weight that always presses down on his shoulders. I don't know why, but I can tell I have erred.

"You are a clever boy. And no one works harder." (Which is a lie because nobody worked harder than he.)

"But I'm wrong somehow, aren't I?"

"Your figures are right but yes Giovanni, you are still wrong. Do you know why I sell the wheat so cheaply to the Sisters of the convent?"

"Because they are poor and have dedicated their lives to God?"

"Yes. The poor Sisters sacrifice so much that we sinners might find salvation. Each day they rise at dawn to bake bread and feed the hungry. If I could give them my wheat for nothing I would, but they insist on paying me. I don't want to embarrass them so I take the money."

"I should have thought of that. I'm sorry, Pápa."

Pápa paused, seeming to search for the right words. Finally, he looked at me and asked, "Has Father Enrico ever told you how, as a young priest, he sailed with the Portuguese trading ships?"

"Yes, he talks about it all the time. Just last week he told us all about the heathen religions of India. Of men who worship fire and such things."

"The good father is a very wise man, and once he told me of a parable he heard from an old man in Goa. This old man told him that the flesh is an elephant and the soul is the elephant's rider. The rider thinks he controls the elephant, but really, most of the time the elephant goes just where it wants. When the elephant moves to the river, the rider just convinces himself that he really wants to see the water flow by. Only a strong rider, aware of his own weaknesses, can truly control the elephant."

I lift my hand and then drop it again, testing my body's compliance to my mind's commands. But something tells me this is not exactly what my father means.

"It is the nature of a sinner to act selfishly, Giovanni. Your desires will steer you to selfish deeds and the easy path will be to follow and then build a story that satisfies your conscience, no matter what your true intention was. You must pray for the strength of soul to set your own course. Always step back and ask yourself, is the elephant leading me or am I guiding him down God's righteous path.

I nod, trying to grasp the meaning of his words.

"I know you understand, my son. Someday you will understand even better than I." He ruffled my hair, and said, "Now go to sleep before your mother gets mad at me."

***

Chapa realized his mind had drifted from Francisco's story and he guided his elephant back to the conversation at hand.

"By then, there were many Spaniards in this country, but nearly all of them were men, as you know. My grandmother was educated, and from an Aztec noble class, so she was very desirable in those days to Spanish men. She was known as a particular beauty, even though she had the brown skin and small, square body of an *indígena*. She was taken by a Basque, a man by the name of Ramiro Iñárritu, and the two moved to Jalisco, where he owned a mine."

"Ah, let me stop you there, Francisco. I think I can win this game now. You say your grandfather was Basque, which is to say a *peninsular*. So that would make you a *cuarterón*, or a *cholo* as it is called in some parts."

Francisco shook his head, "I am afraid not, *patrón*. But you are getting closer. Don Ramiro never married my grandmother, because Spaniards almost always waited to marry a Spanish wife, sometimes even preferring to marry a Spanish prostitute rather than settle for an Indian woman. They did, however, live together long enough to produce a son, who was my father."

"Your father's lineage is clear to me, Francisco," said Chapa, interrupting Francisco with little thought, "You don't need to elaborate any further. The key to my winning this game must lie in your mother's side. We have established your mother is neither Indian nor Spaniard, and she could not be a simple *mestizo*, since that would make you merely the breed of two *mestizos* and thus one yourself."

"That is so."

"So I deduce that your mother must have been a *cuarterón*, which would make you a *quinterón*."

"Wrong again, I'm afraid," Francisco said. "Or rather, not yet right. But I am sure you will get it right in the end. Should I continue?"

Chapa nodded, "Go on, but pour me some more wine first."

Francisco refilled Chapa's cup and continued, "My mother's mother, my dear grandmother Leónór, was an African slave, the property of a good family from Veracruz. She bore a child by the head of this family and was freed upon his natural death, but was forbidden to ever speak his name. She travelled north to Jalisco in the paid service of another family and raised my mother there. My mother, as an illegitimate *mulata*, with no hope of education or dowry, was very lucky to marry my *mestizo* father; but he was young, she was beautiful and so it goes. And there you have it," Francisco said, "I am Castilian. I am Basque. I am an Aztec. I am an African slave. So, what am I?"

"Your origins are so convoluted that you may have won this game, after all, Francisco. I believe the word escapes me. *Chino* comes to mind but surely that is not it. *Barcino*, perhaps?"

Francisco shook his head, "According to *casta* law I am a *coyote*. But I am sure that would have been your next guess."

Chapa shook his head ruefully, "Since you are the winner, Francisco, you get the final cup of wine tonight." Chapa stood up, and with an exaggerated bow, filled his cup and handed it to Francisco. The old *mestizo* — or, rather, *coyote* — nodded to his master and dutifully took a small sip as Chapa sat back down.

"I wonder," said Chapa, after a moment's contemplation, "Of all the books that Padre Luis owned, which gave you the most pleasure?"

Francisco did not need to wrack his brain for the answer.

"There was one. A book of stories about a foolish old knight," he said, "who was maybe also a very wise knight, though he did not know it."

Chapa smiled, "So, old Luis had a copy of *Quixote*! I wish I had known, I would have enjoyed discussing it with him before he left us."

Memory is mysterious. In his old age, the Don could not always remember what he did the day prior or even that same morning, but the mention of *Don Quixote* somehow brought forward in vivid detail the day he left Cádiz to set out for New Spain. His old second-hand trunk, a gift from his uncle and namesake, was short on supplies but full of books—most more serious than *Don Quixote*, as young men foolishly value serious subjects over more frivolous ones. *Quixote*, though, he could not leave behind.

With a heart full of ambition, an old bronze pistol and a brittle *espada ropera*, he felt himself an heir to Cortés as he boarded the ship. But minutes after the weather-beaten carrack weighed anchor, his boldness—and his breakfast—quickly left him, and his thoughts for the next three months careened wildly between speculation on the life that awaited him in New Spain and rumination on the life he had left behind. With its stories of adventure and mystery, longing and sadness, *Quixote* had been the perfect companion for that long and tedious voyage.

"Isn't that a dangerous book for you to read, Francisco?" he continued slyly, "Especially since it features a servant who is cleverer than his master."

"Cleverer perhaps, but in the end no wiser. It is just a story, like the fanciful ones I used to tell my daughter. Do you remember the old Aztec story about the eagle landing on an island with a snake in his talons. It doesn't mean a thing beyond its telling." Sancho Panza was promised his own *insula*, but was he the snake or the eagle?

***

As he lay in bed that night, Chapa turned over in his mind the events of the day. Part of him was still uneasy at the fact

35

that Francisco had concealed his literacy. With all of the time they spent together amid his books and writings, he could easily have mentioned it before. Why keep it a secret? It reminded him of the uneasy intimacy of master and servant, and the fact that such relationships must always be founded on suspicion.

His mind was taken with his servant's story and what it revealed about this strange land, now his home for nearly fifty years. The strangeness of the *casta* system, its artificial chopping and slicing of human families into rigid categories was now laid bare in the roots of a single man. The Spaniards, so precariously perched on top of this fluid and diverse mass of humanity, went to great extremes to hold this babel at bay, even though with each generation their families became more intimately entangled with the polyglot population of this new continent. He thought back on his father's words about the elephant and thought about the Spaniards' fears, their need for separation, for dominance. The elephant wants what it needs, and the rider just makes it all up as he crashes along on its back.

Wasn't it all just a lost cause? How long can the few *criollo* families continue to intermarry? Already here and there, from one generation to another, a third son or a homely daughter is settling for a *mestizo* or a *morisco*, a *torna atras* or an *albina*. Not to mention the little families created on the side, the children a few shades lighter than their Indian or *mestiza* mothers. His own son married the favored daughter of one such family, the father making up for the tawny cast of her skin with a hundred head of cattle and a couple of house slaves. In time, Chapa wondered, won't we all end up as one great mongrel people?

As Chapa tossed and turned, these thoughts, and many more besides, churned within him until at last sleep crept in and bore his mind away.

CHAPTER 4

Open the Trunk

I know her well, this ravine, this cañon. *I've walked her a hundred times and a hundred times before that. She is old and has known men before me. And she will surely know men after. But, for now, she is mine alone.*

I know the feel of her walls, how my songs echo through her heart, the steady pulse of her little stream, the way each arm and finger bends and twists. But today my canyon feels different, uneasy, reticent. Someone else, a stranger, is here with us, silent and unseen. Did God warn her first?

Rusty chains pull me along, dragging me further into the ravine. My shadow follows me along the wall of the cañon, *so full of fear that it has drifted out of step. Halting, hesitant, it stumbles along a half step behind me. Why are we so afraid?*

I am dreaming. This can only be a dream. My steps echo – one, two, three, four; each foot cold, dry, and brittle, the echoes out of synch. I count every step, but the echoes are too early, then too late. Standing still, I wave my arms and snap my fingers, trying to follow my shadow and echoes since they refuse to follow me. My head buzzing with the disparity.

Water. I must've gone too long without water, old fool. When did I last drink? I can't remember.

Poison. A damned Indian *must have poisoned me. He's watching me, I know he is. The stranger in this* cañon.

I cup my hand and slip it under the cool, clear stream, my fingers dragging through rust-colored pebbles. The small rocks sparkle. They're beautiful. I coax a little water out of the stream and splash it on my hot dusty face. I feel nothing. I reach down again and drink. The water is cold in my hand, but yet I cannot taste it. So frightened.

The stranger gazes up at me from the river, his face lined and weathered, eyes deep under creased lids. Me, but not me. I move my right hand and he moves his left, but slowly, his face twisted in pain. My heart pounds, echoing in my ears. Talk to me, stranger. His eyes look back, blank. An empty void.

Me, but not me.

O mæ Dê. Tell me. What? Tell me something.

He says nothing.

He feels nothing.

***

Chapa shuddered, his eyes opening to a dark room. The sun was still hidden beneath the horizon, but the sky announced its coming—star-pocked black giving way to expanding sheets of charcoal, silver-blue, and purple. He lay for a moment, considering the dream and its meaning, picking at the loose weave of reality, illusion and distortion. Why did he keep having this same dream, or some variation on it? What did it mean?

A man of rigid habit, Chapa woke each day at precisely the same hour and began his work promptly without breaking fast, pushing aside the night's turmoil with neat lines of writing. But today was different. Jolted to life in the dark, he was forced to relive the night's terrors without the soothing distraction of pen and paper. Trapped, he scanned the room in the dim light, his eyes drifting to the door that opened onto his waiting study, his mind coming to rest on the old trunk waiting silently in the darkened room. As always, it weighed on him, following him like a loyal dog, one he could kick and beat and yet knew would always return.

It was his last unfinished business, the only thing left to do — if he was honest with himself — before departing this earth. For months he had struggled even to find the courage to open it.

Chapa sat up in bed, removing his nightcap and running his hand idly through the thinning strands of hair upon his head. He thought again about his game with the old *mestizo* (or, what was he again? A *coyote*? How absurd. *Mestizo* would do.) He turned the image of Francisco over in his mind, the old man who served him and shared this small house with him. Francisco was now his closest companion — no one since his wife knew him so intimately — but until now he had been all but invisible.

He imagined Francisco's father — what did he say his name was? The humble, bastard *mestizo*, never recognized by his Basque father, poring over two tattered old school books, summoning the full vigor of his Spanish blood as he struggled to inspire a small brown boy with the spark of learning. To elevate his boy's mind if he could not elevate his birth.

What would his own father, Bartolome, say about this strange *casta* system? To him, each man walked under the same sky. The blue Mediterranean brought many strange faces to Genoa — Greek and Savoyard, Moroccan and Sicilian, Levantine and Crimean. But could Bartolome have imagined a land as wide as this New Spain, vaster than the ancient Roman Empire, or creatures as alien as these Indians who worshipped the sun and ate the flesh of men? Could his egalitarian smile and warm, outstretched hand have survived the shock of the truly unknown?

And how had Beatriz felt? His lady of the *hacienda*. Chapa often caught her laughing with the servants, listening to their talk of *novios* and *niños*. He admonished her on more than one occasion not to forget that which separates those born to rule from those born to serve. It was just an amusement, she assured him, the sharing of simple human pleasures. Had he erred in steering his wife's heart from its nobler instincts?

Each of these thoughts troubled him. Still more crept in, one by one, until he could no longer hear his own voice above the cacophonous crowd. To silence them, he realized what he had to do.

***

Francisco roused slowly. The embers in the hearth glowed softly, their warmth embracing his body coiled on the simple mat. The rough blanket of boiled wool was too short to cover his fully outstretched frame but just sufficed when he drew his knees up to his broad chest.

The sky outside was dark. The town's many roosters still slumbered. His ears, still quite good for a man of his age, could hear nothing stir in the small house. And yet he knew somehow, without a doubt, that his master was awake.

Francisco rose to his feet and folded up his blanket and mat. He set them to the side of the fireplace and raised his arms for a quick stretch. His joints creaked and groaned, and his back reminded him to take matters slowly. His belly, long accustomed to being ignored, made a half-hearted request for food. But on the whole he felt good—God had graced him another day. He opened the front door quietly and walked through the dim light to relieve himself in the shallow gutter along the street. The morning air was chilly and crisp. The east glowed red to welcome the sun.

***

Chapa heard Francisco make his way across the patio. The old *mestizo* walked with uncommon softness for a man of his size and strength, but the early morning was so still that even his careful steps were conspicuous. Before the servant reached the bedroom, he heard Chapa's voice call out to him from the nearby study, "Francisco, come in." Francisco stepped into the study, betraying slight but unmistakable surprise at Chapa's abnormally early rising. Chapa was already dressed and sitting behind his desk, pen in hand.

"Good morning, Don Juan. I'm sorry I overslept," said Francisco. He entered with a small candle in his hand, which he used to light the dozen or so larger candles placed in clusters

40

throughout the study. Within moments the room began to glow with warm light.

"Don't be, Francisco. You and I both know the hour is quite early, even for me. And yet I don't dare return to sleep," said Chapa.

"Are you well?" Francisco asked, setting down his candle and dropping his arms to his sides.

"I hope so," Chapa replied. "I'm not sick, if that's what you mean. At least, no sicker than I have been lately. But my mind and heart are agitated and ill at ease, with so much work left undone. It occurred to me for the first time this morning that you might be able to help me."

"Of course," said Francisco, wary at the strange mood that had overtaken his master, "I am at your service. "

"Please go to my bookshelf and find a book in Spanish. It can be any book. Pick one out and come sit by me. I want you to read for me."

"*Sí*, Don Juan. As you wish." The old servant stepped towards the solid old bookshelf and looked for a book that might please his master. There seemed no safer choice, and no better one, than that which they had discussed the previous night.

Francisco scanned the dusty leather tomes. Over the years, Francisco had observed his master arranging and rearranging the books, lining them up exactly with the edge of the shelves. Francisco often wondered why Chapa spent so much time aligning his books so perfectly, sometimes seemingly moving books around simply so that he could reorganize them again. He often spied Chapa just staring at the precisely arranged bookshelf with a contented look on his face. If his master had a methodology for this ritual, it was beyond Francisco's ken. A moment later his fingers found the worn binding of the book and he pulled it from the shelf, leaving a single neat gap in the perfectly aligned row.

"I have chosen the book we discussed last night. *The Ingenious Gentleman Don Quixote de la Mancha*," said Francisco.

"Francisco, the book you're holding in your hands is very special to me," Chapa said. "It was given to me by my mentor, Don Martín de Zavala, when I served under him during his last years as Governor of Nuevo León. My own copy of *Don Quixote* was stolen shortly after my arrival in Ciudad de México, and when Don Martín urged me to revisit it as a more mature man, he lent me the copy you hold in your hands. We spent many happy hours debating the many layers of Cervantes's tale. I am pleased you chose it," said Chapa.

Francisco set the book down on his lap and turned the book over in his hands, "From which page would you like me to read, Don Juan?"

"Please read me your favorite passage. As you've read it before, I'm sure there must be some part that you find especially amusing," answered Chapa.

Francisco began leafing through the book, unsure of his destination. There was plenty of wisdom in this book, and humor too. But there was also much that eluded him. Spanish law and culture permeated every corner of life in México, but Spain itself — at least as Cervantes described it — seemed such a different world from that which Francisco and Chapa inhabited. As he leafed deeper into the book, passing into the second volume, he wondered if he should have picked something simpler than this dense and convoluted tale of stories within stories.

"Don Juan, since you are visited by so many strange and disturbing dreams, perhaps I might read the passage when the squire leads his master to the Cave of Montesinos, where Don Quixote dreams of the legendary heroes and the beautiful Belerma. Shall I begin there, Don Juan?"

"That sounds perfect. And don't worry if you have trouble with the pronunciation of some of the heroic names, as many are ancient and obscure even in Spain itself," replied Chapa.

Francisco nodded, wetting his lips before commencing, "Thank you, Don Juan. I will begin with Don Quixote already speaking about his dream:

"And so, to proceed – the venerable Montesinos led me into the palace of crystal, where, in a lower chamber, strangely cool and entirely of alabaster, was an elaborately wrought marble tomb upon which I beheld, stretched at full length, a knight, not of bronze, or marble, or jasper, as are seen on other tombs, but of actual flesh and bone. His right hand (which seemed to me somewhat hairy and sinewy, a sign of great strength in its owner) lay on the side of his heart; but before I could put any question to Montesinos, he, seeing me gazing at the tomb in amazement, said to me, 'This is my friend Durandarte, flower and mirror of the true lovers and valiant knights of his time. He is held enchanted here, as I myself and many others are, by that French enchanter Merlin, who, they say, was the devil's son; but my belief is not that he was the devil's son, but that he knew, as the saying is, a point more than the devil."

It was immediately apparent to Chapa that Francisco read exceptionally well. His voice was strong—in spite of his advanced age—and his enunciation confident. He read slowly but at the natural pace of thought, rather than the rushed recitation of a student eager for his ordeal to reach its end.

Francisco continued, relating Don Quixote's strange dream:

How or why he enchanted us, no one knows, but time will tell, and I suspect that time is not far off. What I marvel at is, that I know it to be as sure as that it is now day, that Durandarte ended his life in my arms, and that, after his death, I took out his heart with my own hands; and indeed it must have weighed more than two pounds, for, according to naturalists, he who has a large heart is more largely endowed with valor than he who has a small one. Then, as this is the case, and as the knight did really die, how comes it that he now moans and sighs from time to time, as if he were still alive?

As he said this, the wretched Durandarte cried out in a loud voice:

'O cousin Montesinos!

'T was my last request of thee,
When my soul hath left the body,
And that lying dead I be,
With thy poniard or thy dagger
Cut the heart from out my breast,
And bear it to Belerma.
This was my last request.

Francisco paused a moment, weighing whether to continue, and then looked up to his master, stretched out at full length in his chair, though this was surely no palace of crystal.

Chapa smiled with unexpected pleasure, "Francisco, that was better than I expected. You have a natural cadence that cannot be easily taught."

"Thank you, Don Juan. I am sure your learned presence has inspired me to read so well today," Francisco said, closing the book.

"Perhaps," Chapa answered, a little irritated with the overt flattery in Francisco's words, but also with his own obtuseness in appraising his servant. How else, he wondered, had he underestimated this *mestizo*? "There was a reason I asked you to read for me, Francisco. And now that I know you were not boasting last night—indeed, you were too modest. I know you are equal to the task. The chest that sits against the wall there. I imagine you have long wondered what was inside."

Francisco understood that Chapa valued the chest almost beyond measure, beyond his books and his lands, beyond his cattle and his bronze helmet. Francisco knew only that it contained a mountain of paper, sheets old and new that Chapa would peruse at length and then suddenly lock away, to avoid again for weeks—paper that surely held immense value to his master. Did it hold the same value to others? Francisco looked at the trunk and then shifted his gaze back to Chapa, waiting, his hands a little unsteady as he wiped his palms quietly on the sides of his trousers.

Chapa studied his servant for a moment, the *mestizo's* sudden discomfort giving him a moment's pause. Why was Francisco suddenly so uneasy?

"You may have even found a way to open it before," Chapa said, wondering if Francisco's old habits were working on his mind again–the locked trunk perhaps a temptation. "I know you are resourceful," he said.

Francisco shook his head soberly, "No, *patrón*. As I have said, I have read from your books, because they sit on the shelf for all to see. I have never tried to open your trunk."

"Well today you shall. Here, around my neck is a key. Take it and open the chest for me," Chapa said, leaning forward. Around his neck was a key hanging from a tarnished silver chain, alongside a crucifix and small gold ring.

Francisco complied cautiously. He took the key gently off his master's head, making sure not to catch the chain in Chapa's stray locks of hair. He then turned and knelt down at the trunk and pushed the key into the simple lock. He turned the key, the lock sticking just a little. The chest was musty and showed water damage on one side. One hinge was a bit stiff but the lid swung open easily.

The contents were laid out with obvious care, each bundle neatly tied, small notes attached to the strings. All of Nuevo León knew of the *don's* meticulous nature. The archives of the city, the legal accounts, the tax records of the many *haciendas*, all had been constructed and organized in perfect order. Beleaguered royal inspectors, often dreading their visits to this crude outpost, sighed with relief when they inspected Don Juan Chapa's accounts, surprised at their clarity and beauty—if bureaucracy can indeed be beautiful.

And yet even with careful organization Francisco could detect the chaos of life through the sudden diversity of colors, textures, and even odors. In a rush he could smell countless nights of sooty candles and tobacco, cattle farms and wheat harvests, salt water voyages and rooms packed full of too many human bodies. Don Juan's accounting made order of the world, but life always struggled to break free.

"There, at the top," Chapa said, "The large manuscript bound with red string. Bring it to me."

Francisco spotted a bundle quite a bit larger than the others, comprised of papers of different sizes and thickness, some curling and yellowed, others still crisp and white. The little tag attached to the red string carried a single word, 'Historia'. Francisco placed the large bundle on top of the writing table and Chapa gazed down towards it, feeling its weight before he even touched it. It had not always weighed on him so. Not so long ago it gave him joy and contentment; it was a pleasure to sit quietly, alone with Beatriz, entirely consumed with the work of its writing. Whole days were swallowed by it, and he gave into this passion willingly.

"I want you, Francisco, to read what I have written. Before I die, I must decide its fate. The task feels too heavy to me now and there is no one left in this *reino* on whose silence I can depend. Strange as it is to say, you may be the only one I can trust." Unspoken but mutually understood was that this trust rested on Francisco's powerlessness. Any public testimony against Chapa would effectively carry no weight at all.

"*La Historia del Nuevo Reino de León.*" As my days began to draw to a close, I decided to continue the great unfinished work of Alonso de León the elder. He was a hero to me, truly a great man. Don Alonso's written history of this *reino* began in 1620 *anno domini* but was cut short in 1649, and it has languished unpublished and unknown ever since. Working in the same silent obscurity, I set out, in his shadow, to pick up the task for the years since, recording the history of this region before all those who experienced it are gone."

"Please begin reading it today and we will discuss it when you have finished. You are the first and only soul to lay eyes on it. This territory is as vast as Iberia itself, but at the same time it is as small as the tiniest village—and I fear that one cannot speak truthfully about these chaotic events without risking accusations of insult or heresy. For this reason, I fear that my account, labored over for so many years, may never be published or read by men of generations to come."

46

Francisco considered Chapa's words for a moment, emotions flickering beneath his impassive face. There was pride in this moment, to be finally recognized by his learned master as a man whose mind could be as valuable as his shoulders and back. But that pride came with a small but painful wound, the understanding that he could be trusted only because of his insignificance. Most of all, though, he was curious. He had lived through the same years, hadn't he? Chapa's version of events would be different than his, but the prospect of reading and talking over those old, wild days would make for more interesting conversation than either of them had enjoyed in a while. Underneath it all was a deeper thrum of anxiety, caution and unease, as he felt himself pinned, as always, between worlds.

"Don Juan, I am honored by your trust. I will read as quickly as I can."

"Better to take your time and read once thoroughly rather than twice in haste." The decision made, Chapa felt easier than he had in months, a strange relaxation unwinding his knotted spine. He stretched and turned to face the sun streaming through the window. Francisco set the manuscript carefully on the writing table and turned back to close and lock the trunk. Standing over it, he glanced at the tags on the other bundles: *Jornada – Cádiz, Cartas – Nicolò, Jornada - Veracruz, Documentos – Albisola.*

"Shall I close the trunk now?"

"No, I have more use for it," Chapa said, "And after you return my key you may go. I dressed myself this morning, so that you may find more time to begin your reading."

Francisco carefully closed the lid of the trunk, and then handed the key and chain back to his master. "Don Juan," he said, "your children are very lucky – they will have the whole history of their father in this trunk, with your very thoughts recorded for them to relive as if your life were their own. I carry the story of my father only in my head, and those memories are now faded scraps, mixed up fragments of his days on earth. My own daughter will carry an even smaller portion of that when I am gone." He took up the *Historia* in his hands, nodded to Chapa, and then left, closing the door behind him.

Chapa sighed, knowing his sons would care little for the dusty manuscripts in the trunk. They were children of this frontier, expert horsemen and ranchers, crack shots with the new flintlock muskets, overflowing with a love for life on the *hacienda*. Like Beatriz, they were rooted in the mountains and high desert, full of her joy and energy. They were closer to her, he knew; she gathered everyone to her.

He chastised himself once again for the impatience he had shown as the children dawdled over their lessons, his sharp criticism over their lazy handwriting and careless sums. The tender moments near the fire, holding them close and watching them toddle towards their mother—these he remembered and cherished now. At the end, too much of his time with them had been wasted in useless struggle, working to instill in them lessons that had little meaning for them and even less practical value. They loved and respected him, he knew, but at a distance. How he ached for a way to break through that reserve; with Beatriz gone, it felt like the family had lost its center.

He considered the bundles in the trunk. These were very different from the *Historia*, which was so carefully written, with one eye always towards the Inquisitor. These papers carried his uncensored thoughts, recorded just for himself. Would his children fear their contents? Condemn them as heresy to protect themselves? Perhaps, at long last, it was time for him to revisit the past.

CHAPTER 5

The Savage Indian

TO THE RIGHT AND PIOUS FATHER NICOLÒ CHAPA, CÁDIZ, ANDALUCÍA

My dearest Nicolò,

I pray this letter finds you in sound health. I do hope my previous two correspondences of 12 Dec. of 1647 and 8 Aug. last have found their way into your hands. If they have not, know that I have written to you twice since arriving here in New Spain.

You are often in my thoughts, beloved brother. I miss your steady and fatherly advice. (Would our own father take offense at that characterization?) Too often on this adventure I feel my feet leave the ground; I know were you here that you would hold me down to the good earth. If you receive this letter, please write back to tell me if you are still living in Seville or have moved to the monastery in Cádiz and pass on any news you might have from our uncle Giovanni or any of our other family in Albisola.

Nicolò, it may surprise you, but I have left the Ciudad de México. *It is a great and prosperous metropolis, but it is a more hospitable place for men with good family connections, or those who came earlier in its history and have already made their mark here in New Spain. For those whose only resource is ambition, it is hard to gain a foothold there, even more so if your speech betrays a foreign birth. After just a few years, I realized that my future lay out on the frontier, helping to build a new kingdom for the glory of God and Spain.*

I have attained the position of secretary to the town of Cadereyta in this northern territory of Nuevo Reino de León, a region administered under the Audiencia of México and the diocese of Guadalajara, though it is so distant from both as to be almost beyond notice. The governor's seat is in the city of Monterrey, which lays about 180 leguas north of the capital, and seven leguas west of here. I serve as Secretary to the noble Chief Justice Don Alonso de León, a learned man and captain of the local militia. I live and work on his hacienda, a vast property with huge herds of cattle and sheep. The scale of everything here is so vast you could scarcely imagine it.

The struggles of life here in this wilderness keep me so busy that there is little time to think, much less the leisure to daily record the events of each day, as has been my habit since my youth in Albisola. Please forgive my ragged penmanship and the cramped nature of this letter, but paper here is quite precious, since it must come from Spain and its distribution is tightly controlled. Even though I am the official secretary of Cadereyta, nearly all of the writing I do, even the daily accounts of the de León hacienda, are recorded with charcoal on the whitewashed walls of my little office–to be transferred to paper, if a permanent record is required, whenever some paper arrives with the mule trains.

Yesterday, however, was a day that cries out to be recorded. And so I take pen in hand on this solitary sheet, the last of the paper I brought with me from the Ciudad, to recount the events of the fateful day to you, my beloved brother.

I must first explain how dangerous matters are here on the frontier. There are many savage Indians here. Unlike the more civilized and settled Indians in the Valley of México, almost none of the Indians in these lands have converted to our holy Catholic faith. Several tribes are friendly, trading with us Spaniards; some even respond willingly to the summons of the repartimiento, the system by which the Crown is endeavoring to civilize the indigenous peoples of this land, wherein a landowner is given the governance of indigenous people and the right to their labor in return for taking on the sacred responsibility of bringing them into our true Catholic faith.

But we can never trust them completely; deep down these savages are cunning, cruel and duplicitous. They steal and kill and eat the very flesh of their fellow man. They make treaties only to buy themselves the time and position to attack again. When I perish here in this distant land, it will surely be by the arrow of such an Indian.

After most of us on the hacienda retired for the night and were deep asleep after a long day of labor, one of the mestiza women here on the property heard strange sounds. She soon realized that the local Indians were sneaking up on the estate from the small river below and roused Don Alonso to warn him that Indians were preparing to attack the hacienda and slaughter us in our beds. Don Alonso sounded the alarm and the entire hacienda sprang to life.

I share a little cabin on the hacienda with Don Alonso's crippled brother, Joseph, and his wife and four children. As soon as I heard the alarm, I leapt out of bed, still in my white undergarments, dressing quickly and readying my harquebus. I was still weak from a terrible three-day fever, but somehow was seized by uncommon strength as the fear and excitement shot through me. I led the poor cripple and his family to the main house, the only stone building on the hacienda, where all were gathering to defend against the attack.

By the time we reached the house, Don Alonso and Antonio Cortinas were already on horseback. The rest of our little band of able bodied men huddled in the great stone house, determined to protect the women and children — Spaniard, mestizo, and Indian alike, locking them in the inner rooms as we manned the doors and windows with our guns and swords.

The attack began almost immediately with a rain of arrows. Because of the protection of the house the arrows of our attackers did little harm, thank God. We fired back into the night with our harquebuses, but because of the darkness we could not easily repel the Indians. The stalemate continued for some time, and Don Alonso counseled us not to fire too eagerly without sight of our enemy.

Fearing that we would soon run out of powder and shot and be forced to defend ourselves with cutlass and spear, Don Alonso ordered his eldest son, Juan de León, to mount his horse (bareback, because there was not time to saddle the horse) and ride to Cadereyta to raise the militia. Don Alonso's mother staunchly opposed this, fearing the Indians would lay in wait and kill him.

I confess to you and you alone, Nicolò, that it was not courage which overtook me but a kind of madness when I volunteered to go in his place. I, a scribe who once aspired to be a priest, riding into danger

51

through a band of attacking Indians? It was as if someone else's voice spoke in my mouth when the words were uttered.

Don Alonso embraced me like a son and set me astride a horse at the back of the house, where the Indians had not yet positioned themselves. He took my bronze pistol — very difficult, of course, for even an expert marksman to fire from horseback — and handed me his beautiful schiavona, a sword surely worth more than our father's farm.

As I sheathed the don's sword and spurred my horse forward, I felt sure I was going to die, but somehow became more alive than ever before. At the same time, I felt tranquil, absorbing the very sensations of living, knowing they might well be my last. Time moved very quickly and yet felt slow at the same time.

I rode out into the night, arrows tearing through the air around me, while a hellish fire from a burning shack illuminated the dark and smoke-filled courtyard. Everyone's eyes were wide with fear, even my horse's eyes shone with terror in the firelight.

Don Alonso fired his gun to clear the road ahead of me and somehow I escaped the hacienda safely. I still don't understand how an arrow didn't strike me, exposed as I was on the back of the horse, but God surely protected me. I rode the half-league to town as fast as I could, pushing the horse beyond his usual paces. As I approached the town, the horse finally rebelled against the pace and threw me to the ground.

Fortunately, I landed without damaging Don Alonso's sword and ran the rest of the way on foot. I shouted myself hoarse as I entered the town and by the time I arrived at the plaza, breathless, a few dozen men had assembled in various states of dress. I told them of the attack on the hacienda, and the small militia saddled their horses and rode out to relieve Don Alonso.

By the time we reached the hacienda, the Indians had withdrawn, as help had already arrived from Don Alonso's neighbors Juan Lopez and Luis de Zuniga. At least one Indian was killed, and when morning arrived, more than a thousand arrows were picked up from around the house. The only serious injury was suffered by Don Alonso's wife, Josefa, who was struck in the throat with an arrow while helping the men re-load their weapons with powder and bullets. The door, thanks be to God, deflected the arrow — otherwise it would surely have killed her.

Nicolò, I write to you today to bear witness to you how God, in his infinite mercy, prevented the barbaric and depraved Indians from fulfilling their murderous intentions. God called Don Alonso, who had been away for weeks on a journey to Zacatecas, to return to the hacienda far earlier than he had planned. As God ordained, he arrived on Santa Catalina's Day, only two days before the attack. Without his leadership we would surely have fallen to the savages.

I also write to record, in some fashion, how I acquitted myself that night. I feel myself now truly a man. Everyone speaks of my courage, but I know it was God's grace and your prayers that moved me to act. I had never before been in so much danger – and privately hope never again to be – but I didn't cower in the presence of fear. I feel finally worthy to be named a conquistador. *I hope that you are proud and wish that you had been here with me. With this letter, I somehow feel as if you were here to witness my entrance into manhood.*

I love you, Nicolò. If by some miracle you see our uncle Giovanni, please give him my love and respect. I hope to receive a letter from you soon, and I expect to be at this same house for some time, and so hope you will do me the favor of a return letter.

May God preserve you.
Your devoted brother,
Giovanni
28 November, MDCLI
Cadereyta, México - Nueva España

Faithful copy of original letter – made 29 Nov. 1651 – GBS

***

The rain began that afternoon. It came first as a light shower and then in great sheets. The wind rose from the southwest and battered the house with wet gusts. Francisco rushed to shutter the affected windows, including the windows in Chapa's small study. The rain—the first in months—revealed a small leak in the clay tile roof in the main room, which Francisco labored to patch from the inside. Water dripping around his hands, he filled the crack that had opened up between two of the handmade tiles, using a mixture of water, clay, sand and horsehair.

Chapa sat in his best chair, a warm blanket wrapped around his shoulders and a wool knit cap over his head, offering advice as Francisco stood on a small stool and applied the wet mortar to the hole above his head. They were close in age. (Did Francisco even know the year of his birth?) He ruefully considered his own withered frame, which had so easily made the taxing journeys from Italy to Spain and then the 70 day journey across the great Atlantic—the same body which had survived dozens of skirmishes against the treacherous Indians here in Nuevo León and bore several wounds, that body which only a few years earlier had ridden with Alonso de León the younger on the great expedition across the wide Rio Bravo into the land of the Tejas Indians.

But now? An abiding fatigue had overtaken him. His chest, shoulders, and legs were all still strong, but beneath it all crept a growing emptiness that sapped him of his vigor. His ankles and feet had become strangely swollen; the doctor could only offer that his humors were out of balance and that he ought to walk more often and smoke more tobacco. He still had his wits about him and, thank God, was in no great pain. But he sensed somehow that he had already begun the long slide from health, one that would hasten with each passing month. He had seen it happen again and again, most recently with his beloved Beatriz, and in his bones, Chapa knew that his grave would soon rush up to meet him.

Francisco had surely lived no easy life, but the years somehow rested more lightly on him. His journey had taken him from the place of his birth in Jalisco to the dusty city of Monterrey, and as a *mestizo* laborer he would have toiled many hours each day under the hot sun, enjoying rest only on the Sabbath and the great festival days, with a few tortillas at the start of the day and a meager bowl of beans at night. Francisco had also survived the fighting during the great uprising in the San Antonio Valley in 1671 and surely many other attacks as well—this tumultuous land scarcely saw two years go by without armed raids by the Indians.

And, yet, here was Don Juan Bautista Chapa, the *conquistador*, a thick blanket over his waistcoat to fight the chill, able only to tender limp suggestions while Francisco stood, arms above his head and sweat dripping into his eyes, toiling as if he were a man of twenty. Chapa tipped his bowl all the way back and let the last dregs of his *caldo de res* drip into his mouth. Then he set the bowl down on the small table Francisco had placed in front of his chair. Francisco finished applying the clay mortar and allowed his arms to drop to his side as he loosened his shoulders, knotted after so much effort. He gazed upwards, ensuring that the mortar had plugged the leak.

Chapa took this moment to break the silence. "I am sure that the challenges of this weather will impede your reading of the *Historia*. I only ask that you find what time you can."

"Thank you, Don Juan. I have begun to read and think on it," Francisco replied.

"Does it make sense to you, what you have read so far? Which chapter are you currently reading?" Chapa asked, immediately recognizing in himself an over-eagerness unseemly in a master.

Francisco stepped down from the stool and sat on it, wiping sweat from his eyes with his shoulder—his hands still wet with mortar. The seat of the three-legged stool stood only a foot or so off the ground, setting the tall Indian's eyes well below Chapa's. Francisco thought for a moment, guarding his words as carefully as always, and responded. "Do you write this *Historia* only from memory, Don Juan, or do you seek the memory of others?"

An insightful question, Chapa thought. Francisco was no fool. "For those events I experienced first-hand, I write of course from my own memory and the personal papers I have from those times. I don't know of anyone else who took the time and care to note the historical importance of these events as they transpired. For better or worse, I had the privilege of bearing witness to so many of the events in this *reino* over these last four decades. On those occasions where I write of events I did not experience, I have consulted important men like Don Alonso de León *el mozo*, as well as the official documents of our *reino*."

Francisco nodded, "Sometimes I think about the past and wonder about the things I remember and those that I forget. Talking with other old men—not men of such high rank and character as you, of course—I speak with other old men and find sometimes we remember things differently."

Chapa chuckled at Francisco's elliptical comments. "Are you trying, in your own deferential way, to suggest I might misremember some of these events?"

"Not at all, *patrón*. You are a wise man and a great scholar. I am too clumsy with my words," Francisco said. He paused a moment to think and then continued, "Let me make a crude example, if you will allow it. Let us say you took two men, equal in sight and thought, and placed them on opposite sides of a burro. One at the front, by the burro's head, and one at the back, by his tail. And let us say they were men from a distant land, perhaps Japan, where men had never seen a burro before."

"Like Indians in our own land before Cortés came with horses and pack animals," Chapa interjected.

"Yes, like those men," Francisco said. "So you might ask the first man, by the head, to describe what he sees. He would answer, 'I see two large eyes, set wide, and a strong nose with big nostrils. I see ears which point upward like a rabbit's.' The man in the back would say, 'What are you talking about? This creature has two powerful legs and a long tail of hair. It is not the least like a rabbit.' But of course both men would be right, even though they felt they had encountered two completely different animals."

Chapa smiled at this childish example. "So, Francisco, you suggest that while I remember these events accurately, perhaps I do not see them completely?"

"I am only curious about how a man writes a history, Don Juan. I could never judge your work. Perhaps I let my mind wander too much as I read," Francisco said.

"In the pages you have read so far, is there anything that strikes you as incomplete? Have you read as far as the second chapter, of the treacherous night attack on the elder Don Alonso's *hacienda*?" Chapa asked.

"Yes, Don Juan," Francisco replied.

"I described that event quite thoroughly, don't you think?" said Chapa. "That night, even though it happened long ago, is still so vivid in my mind. In that chapter, for example, I describe the background to the attack, the parties who were present, the various injuries, and the precise progression of occurrences. Even the reason, as far as any Christian man can say, for the Indian attack. If you consider that chapter, for example, what do you think is lacking from my account?"

Seeing Chapa's color rise, Francisco reconsidered his candor, "I would not say anything is lacking, Don Juan." He turned and started gathering his tools, hoping to exit the room and end the conversation.

Chapa shook his head in frustration. "Sit down, Francisco. Speak freely and stop being so obtuse. I have worked at the mercy of many governors, and am quite used to having my work critiqued. I can see quite plainly that you have your own criticisms to offer. Get them out, man."

Francisco sat down and leaned a bit to one side, as if to acknowledge the eccentricity of his perspective. "There are simply several mysteries, to someone as uneducated as myself. For instance, the alarm is first raised by a *meztiza* woman, who you do not name."

"Yes," Chapa said, "that's right. What about it?"

"You write that all were asleep apart from this woman. This woman was by herself, awake and alone, and somehow heard a party of Indians stealing through the trees by the river."

"Yes, thank God that she was awake. She raised the alarm and saved us all, I am sure."

"And I have no reason to doubt this, Don Juan. What puzzles me is how this woman could have heard the raiders at all. The river, as you know, makes a great deal of noise as it flows through the rocky terrain by the de León property and I know that along that stretch of the river it is almost always windy, especially at night," said Francisco.

"Yes, it might have been windy," said Chapa, his mind reaching back to recall that night. He remembered the fear first—the stab of fear still hit him in his gut just as it had so many years ago. He recalled the thrill of mounting Captain Alonso's horse. The feeling of the sword in his hand. The whistle of the arrows flying by him. Yes, there had been wind, he realized, because he recalled how the crosswind carried the arrows wide of his head, their intended target.

Francisco continued, "I don't know these Indians, and I wasn't there. And of course Indian warriors are always a poor match for an armed Spaniard. But the only area where they excel is the way they can sneak silently across broken ground. This lady must have had very sharp ears to discern their movements and report them early enough for Don Alonso and the rest of the men to dress and arm themselves before the attack."

Chapa smiled, Francisco's point finally becoming clear. Although he bristled at being challenged, in truth he was enjoying having an audience for this story, as it had been years since he had spoken about that night. Francisco surprised him with his forthrightness, and he started preparing his riposte to Francisco's thoughtful but misguided critique.

"Ah, but you forget one key detail, Francisco. This was no small murder party of a dozen Indians, but a host of maybe 600 warriors, representing ten Indian nations," Chapa said. "Even the stealthiest Indians cannot move silently in such large numbers."

"That was my mistake, Don Juan. It seems I was confused about the number of Indians, since later you tell how just two Spaniards, Don Luis de Zuniga and Don Juan Lopez, were able to rout the whole party of Indians alone."

"That was no copyist's error. I took great care to make sure every fact was recorded accurately," said Chapa. "The number of Indians both verifies the woman's story and increases the fame of those two brave men." He fell silent then, fidgeting in his chair and twisting the fringe of the blanket between his fingers. He struggled to his feet and walked over to the window, looking out on the muddy street as if he hoped for some kind of distraction. "It's right there in the text, Francisco. You should read more carefully. We counted their arrows the next morning. In fact, I personally recounted the arrows three different times. I am an exact person, Francisco—I even know that it was exactly eighty five paces from the house to the river—I counted them each time I went to draw water. My point is that so many arrows could only have been fired by a great war party."

"Thank you, Don Juan. I now understand it better," said Francisco, somewhat unconvincingly. Francisco genuinely found the history quite interesting, and he could see that this document would be of great value to future generations. But having lived through those times himself, he felt an almost irresistible urge to help shape this *Historia* while the clay was still wet. His command of numbers had never been his best skill, but even he could not understand how six hundred Indians would have fired a mere thousand arrows.

His mind was drawn to another, unusually vivid passage that had clearly left its mark on the writer in a very personal way. "I was also wondering about another battle with the Indians that took place some years later. On an expedition across the Rio Bravo."

"The sally in 1665 against the Cacaxtle?" Chapa's breath quickened just a little. "Have you really read that far, or were you just perusing the manuscript? I don't want to discuss a chapter unless you have really read it. And I want you to read the thing in logical order."

"Yes, I have read it," said Francisco, "I am not a soldier and know little of the trade, but again I wonder how a hundred of the enemy might be killed without the loss of even a single Spanish life." Chapa's demeanor surprised him, and he sat silently for a moment, appraising the situation. He was enjoying the conversation, and risked prodding Chapa a little, as long as it was cloaked in the deference that convention required.

However, Francisco sensed that here he should tread even more cautiously. Chapa had already turned his body away from Francisco, staring silently at the glowing coals of the fire. A little pocket of resin in the *piñon* log exploded, startling them both and sending a shower of sparks onto the hearth.

"On this subject," said Chapa, "I can tell you first-hand the numbers are not false. I myself witnessed the battle in the cold light of day. Not a single Spaniard was killed, though a handful were injured."

"Then surely the allied Indian tribe, the Boboles, must have done the bulk of the fighting."

Chapa nodded gravely, "Yes."

"Then they must have been a very brave people."

"Some were," said Chapa quietly, reflecting on that bloody day. For years, he had kept thoughts about that battle buried. Immediately after it happened, he suffered terribly with nightmares, to the point that Beatriz prodded him to consider visiting Father Santiago, thinking that a confession, or perhaps even an exorcism, might free him from the nightly torment. In time, however, and with Beatriz' loving care, the memories faded and life returned to its normal rhythms. It was not until he began writing the *Historia* that he again had to face the events of that day. The writing of the story of this battle brought the return of those awful nightmares, so vivid that they hung over him like a cloud all the next day. During that time he lived in such a surreal state that he could no longer separate what was real and what was a dream, whether he walked in the present day or in the dusty canyons of the past.

During the fortnight he spent working on that chapter, he was visited every night by the old woman, her curse flowing like a wisp of cigar smoke as it curled out of the little bone flute held to her lips. After he finished, he didn't pick up his pen again for several months, and when he did, it was to record a dry account of the rapid succession of governors that began in 1664.

"Thank you for illuminating me, Don Juan," said Francisco, even though Chapa had done nothing of the sort. Realizing the conversation was over, he picked up his stool and bucket of mortar, and prepared to leave the room, also preoccupied with his own thoughts. Almost unconsciously, he turned to Chapa as he approached the door. "Oh, I almost forgot to ask. Whatever happened to the woman with the flute?"

Chapa was lost in his thoughts and didn't even hear the question. "What?"

"The woman with the flute, Don Juan. The one who played during the battle. I have never heard of such a thing. What became of this remarkable woman?"

"We took her with us on our journey back across the river, but two days later she died, likely from thirst, as she refused to eat or drink even a mouthful of water. I think she was mad."

"Ah, poor soul. You did the best you could for her, señor."

"I suppose we did," said Chapa.

Francisco gave a quick bow and left the room.

***

Chapa listened to the rain drops pounding the roof above him and the wind gusting against the adobe walls and rattling the oak shutters. He stared up at the drying mortar and ruminated again on the events he had recorded. He had no reason to doubt his own account of those years, had he? His memories were corroborated by his own letters and journals, and the recollections of many prominent men in the *reino*. Why then, could he not rid himself of the small seeds of doubt this inquisitive servant had so casually planted? The more he told himself he was sure of the account, the more the doubt of being wrong haunted him. He wondered if he had fooled himself about that day in order to make himself feel better about what he had accomplished.

Chapa sat in silence, ruminating on the battle with the Cacaxtles, the guilt of that day again weighing down on him. For years he had delayed confessing those sins, fearing the repercussions from such disclosure, and making the calculated gamble that there would be time later to absolve his conscience of the deeds of that day. Now, he realized that the opportunity for a face-to-face confession was gone forever; this smug young priest could not be trusted, not in the changing atmosphere here in Nuevo León. And yet for Beatriz's sake, he could not let those sins go without absolution; if he failed to obtain forgiveness he would surely never join her in the next life. The thought of once again sitting beside her was all that had kept him going since her death.

He pondered the dilemma in silence; he knew that death would visit him soon, in one guise or another, and going across with this sin still staining his soul was unthinkable. If a face-to-face confession were impossible, perhaps God would hear his confession even if it were written and sent to one with the power to forgive his sins. God sees and knows all, and is not the act of seeking absolution that which matters most? His brother Nicoló was a priest if he still lived. Couldn't he confess to him?

The mule train would be leaving at first light; he must deliver the letter to them before nightfall. He picked up his pen and began to write.

***

Francisco finished cleaning the bucket of mortar and then washed his hands and arms. He took two large pieces of firewood and some kindling and added them to the now diminished fire in the kitchen hearth. On this cold and dreary meatless Friday he would prepare a favorite of his master, a yellow *pipian* made with carrots, pumpkin and the little potatoes that he had dug out of the garden. The *pipian* was a fairly difficult one, a complex paste of pumpkin seeds, sesame seeds, chiles, and peanuts, all roasted and ground on the *metate*, and then cooked with onions and garlic and then thinned with the stock that simmered on the back of the *fogón*. It was a great deal of work, but the richness of the ground seeds gave a heartiness to the dish that made up for the lack of meat. He put on his gardening straw hat—intended to ward off the sun and not this driving rain, but it would be better than nothing—and walked briskly out to the storehouse and grabbed a small pumpkin and the potatoes, then walked to the garden and pulled a few late carrots from the saturated soil.

Francisco would never admit it, but he loved cooking. He learned the craft from his grandmother, who told young Francisco that the secrets she passed along came from his Aztec ancestors. He often wondered why the Indians had such a greater appreciation for cooking than the Spaniards. He supposed that it was because Indians were so much more patient and rooted in the land. They worshiped the land and its seasons, and celebrated its gifts by creating a dizzying variety of dishes, all so much more complex and satisfying than the simple rustic meals of the *peninsulares*. The Spaniards always seemed in a hurry, more interested in taking from the land than investing in it, although in truth the *criollos* had already adopted the tortillas, chiles and vegetables that were staples of the *indigenas'* diet.

Back in the house, he removed the hat and shook the cold rain from his body, feeling fortunate to be laboring for the next hour in the embrace of this warm kitchen. He stoked the growing fire again and set a large *olla* filled with water onto the *fogón*. He felt a sudden chill as a gust of wind whipped past him through the door from the kitchen to the garden and into the house. Curious at the source of the cross breeze, Francisco walked into the front room and discovered that the front door to the house was wide open, swinging back and forth in the steady wind.

Francisco chastised himself for not barring the door earlier when the weather turned — he would have to mop up the considerable water on the floor — and he went to the door to close it. As he did he glanced down the street and noticed a lone figure trudging wearily through the storm. The poor soul leaned into the wind, hand up against his hat, his feet almost ankle deep in the thick mud that had once been the dusty street. Entranced by the sight of this figure, somehow both courageous and pathetic, Francisco lingered in the doorway. It took only a moment further for him to realize with a shock who the figure was.

***

"My letter," Chapa protested. His voice was desperate but very weak.

The merciless rain pounded on them as Francisco hauled the old man — heavy in his waterlogged clothes — over his shoulders. "There is no time. You must write another." To stoop into the mud for the soggy paper now would be senseless, the script already bleeding into the dirty water soaking the letter as it lay in the mud, Francisco concluded. His obligation was to bring his master to shelter and warmth as quickly as possible. All else would have to wait. The letter disappeared under Francisco's sandal, sinking into the mud, its fate sealed.

Francisco picked his way back through the slog, avoiding the deeper water in the wagon ruts and hugging the dryer earth under the eaves of the little buildings lining the street. He finally made his way back to Chapa's house and entered through the front door. He set the old man down on a chair, stripping off his clothes and hurling them into a sopping pile in the corner. Cradling the shivering man in his arms like a child, he carried him into the kitchen, setting him down on the floor next to the fire now blazing in the hearth.

"Stay here, Don Juan, while I fetch dry clothes and light a fire in the fireplace of the *sala*."

Chapa mouthed an inaudible word of thanks and reached out to touch Francisco's hand. Francisco nodded and pulled away, hurrying out of the kitchen and across the patio to Chapa's bedchamber for dry clothes and a wool blanket. Hair and body drenched, a vicious chill cutting him to his core, Chapa sat and stared into the crackling flames, naked, inert, mute.

CHAPTER 6

Dreams, Illusions and Realities

A crowd of friendly Indians stares at us. Silent, their eyes follow us with caution, their faces obsidian masks. General . . . what is his name? Why can't I remember his name? The General brushes past them, barely registering their existence. So careless, I think as I walk behind him, a half-stride back. The peninsulares *come here so confident, thinking the Indians are like the peasants back home, easily cowed, easily beaten. He doesn't see them as the killers they are, a people who worship murder like we worship God's love.*

His breastplate glints in the low light bouncing off the canyon walls; the dark steel takes on a bronze cast in the dying light. The hilt of his sheathed sword clanks against his belt buckle, marking an odd and discordant rhythm as we walk. I am quieter, observant; skirting the group and counting their weapons, sizing up their movements, my fingers nervously playing with the harquebus slung over my right shoulder, my softer boots making a more muffled sound on the sandy soil beneath us.

The trees ahead bend and sway in front of us, as if they bear some impossibly heavy fruit. Blinking, I steal glances back at the Indians from under the brim of my hat. The trees move again, bowing to us, their branches sweeping towards us like ladies at a dance. Why do they lean towards us, so seductive, so graceful? I can't make sense of it all – the General with no name, the Indians, they don't belong here, the trees that are so, so heavy, so heavy with fruit. Mango, aguacate, guayaba, peach; I love them all, but these trees are too big, too old to carry the fruits we know. My legs, I can hardly drag them through the sand and the General is well ahead of me now. So quiet, that soft breeze, fluttering across the grass and ruffling the leaves of the trees, what are those trees? Their branches are so heavy. I can't hear the sound of our footsteps any more, not even the General's heavy rhythm because the breeze is filling my ears again, buzzing as I watch the lips of the Indians, barely moving in their silent masks.

The branches of the trees, so close now I can almost touch them. So heavy, they are so heavy with fruit. Cottonwoods, they are cottonwoods. Twenty-two bodies hanging, strange fruit indeed, swaying and twisting from the branches like wayward pendula. Cottonwoods don't grow here, not like this; I've never seen a grove like this before.

The General slows and I walk past him as we reach the grove. I still can't remember his name, but it doesn't matter — he doesn't matter. The silhouetted bodies are not human any more, skin darkened, their eyes and tongues swollen, you can no longer make out their individual faces. The breeze dies and a suffocating stillness comes over us. My chest feels like it is underwater, laboring just to breathe. Their heads somehow are all now turned towards the west — are they looking towards the setting sun or just defiant, turning their heads away from us and the land of the Quetzalcoatl that arrived over the waves? Only one looks elsewhere. His head faces north. Why?

These merciless beasts. Cruel and godless. They chose this fate. We gave them every chance to avoid it. The light of the dying sun lends them a kind of beauty somehow, a sight I won't forget. The General doesn't see any of this as he inspects the bodies. I don't know why I show him so much deference. He is a thorough man, but he doesn't really see. He cares only that justice has been meted out, without error and without mercy.

The bodies begin to twist again in the wind, each at its own rhythm, as if this dance were a final illustration of each man's unique character. But beyond this there is nothing left. Chief and warrior, priest and slave, they are all equal now. What bothers me is the feeling of peace they share. How long did these murderers suffer? Not long enough.

***

66

Chapa awoke with a start, breathing heavily, his hair matted with sweat. He felt both hot and cold. His bones ached. Was he dying, was he one of those hanging bodies? No, just another dream. He rolled over onto his side, a sharp pain as he took a deep breath to calm himself. He turned his dampened pillow over. Those days were gone, part of a past that built the foundation on which they stood. There was no changing any of it now, he reminded himself, nor should one wish for it. The world moves according to God's own reason. He closed his eyes, licked his lips and forced himself to listen to the raindrops fall outside his window.

Pâxe.

***

A crowd of friendly Indians stares at me as I walk slowly towards the trees, their faces a mix of intrigue and disgust. The General acknowledges them with a nod of his head and walks forward, his one foot dragging a little, his sword knocking against his thigh, his stiff boots marking hard time against the soft earth. I walk beside him, a half-stride back, watching the Indians, counting their weapons, listening to the murmur of their voices. Someone needs to be watchful, someone needs to pay attention.

The General's cutlass bounces with his steps but strangely doesn't make a sound. I can't hear anything, just the rush of my own blood in my ears. My own footsteps, my very breaths, the wind that whistles across this vast plain, I can't hear anything. Have I gone deaf?

The trees ahead bend as if pressed down by a great being's hand, splaying the branches out like long fingers, pushing towards the earth. If He can bend those strong oak branches, He could flatten me in an instant. I take a breath and walk on, small and insignificant next to that General, just hoping to escape His wrath. Hoping that he goes for the General.

We are closer now, and I can see that they are not oaks, they're cottonwoods. And it is not God pushing those branches towards the earth. Indians are dragging the limbs down. It has nothing to do with God. Twenty-two Indians, hanged by the neck until dead. And now they swing, lazily, a clear warning to their fellow pagans; defiance of

Spanish law means annihilation. "Justice," says the General. "That is what this is. They belong to the devil now." Nodding, I keep my eyes on the last one, a young man, round-faced and soft-skinned, barely old enough to sire a child. Did he ever feel the touch of a woman before we hoisted him up into this tree? Too late now.

They look so peaceful, so quiet. I envy them their repose. Most of them face west towards the setting sun, but a few others gaze out to the south or back to the east.

The world is silent, so utterly still. But in a rush they come alive again, surrounding me, their faces open and filled with hope, fear, and the thrill of that last, final violence against our authority. Another moment, and their faces fall, eyes empty with the futility of their last moments.

I can't stop staring.

Where is the General?

***

Chapa woke again, a growing pain in his throat and a pounding ache in his head. He shivered, soaked through with sweat. That dream again. The rain continued to pound his garden outside, the lush leaves beaten into the earth. His poor pomegranates surely lay smashed upon the ground. Would he live to see them coming to fruit in another year's time?

He rolled over again and let his mind drift to pleasant thoughts of green and beautiful things. Of the great garden at Pienza. How little he knew of his own homeland. Perhaps one day he would return to Liguria.

Beléssa.

***

The crowd of Indians stare at me, faces blank, but I ignore them and walk on alone. I left the General behind me a half-mile ago. You can feel their eyes, like a hand on your shoulder, but it's better not to return their gaze.

The trees lay ahead, cottonwoods, unusual for this area. Each tree has a hanged man, pulling the branches down, each one a great weight

68

on the tree's conscience. Was the wood of the cross that bore our lord Jesus just as weighed down with guilt?

The people of Nuevo León have sent me to ensure justice has been done. Actually they sent the General, but I don't think he has the stomach for it. We pardoned many, most of them, but these two-and-twenty were the worst. An example must be made. Christ's peace can never reign in this land as long as these fractious savages resist our rule of law.

As I reach them, the breeze picks up a little, and I move to stand in the center of the grove. Their feet dangle, darkened, rough and dusty, almost at the height of my eyes. They are all barefoot. I reach out and touch one, why I don't know.

An old man. His knees are knobby and swollen with arthritis and his toes twisted and stunted. A little push against his leg sets his body swaying and I look up at his face. He stares back, plaintive and sad. Most of the bodies face in a single direction, as if pulled by a lodestone towards the west. Only four face east, east--back to Liguria. I circle back to the eastern edge of the grove, and face them.

One is my brother Nicolò. My uncle Giovanni, my namesake, hangs to his left, my father and my mother on his right, their eyes all sad, mournful, accusing. "Giovanni, why did you leave us?"

Nicolò speaks, but I don't see his lips move. "Why did you leave us all?"

Who spoke? Was that my father? I haven't heard his voice since I was eleven. "Why did you let me die? Why did you leave Mama?"

My Nonna, how I miss her.

"How could you let us die? Giovanni, how could you do this?"

***

Chapa woke, the veins in his head pure fire, the room spinning around him. He shouted for Francisco.

Amô.

***

69

Chapa opened his eyes, and tried to swallow, his tongue sticking to the roof of his mouth. The sun was high, and he felt himself wrapped in fresh sheets, wearing a clean, dry nightgown. He put his hands to his chest, feeling the rough wool of the blanket, the slow rise and fall of his chest. He looked around his room, at the bodies clustered around him. Had the Indians come off the trees? Was their revenge finally at hand?

His mind returning slowly to lucidity, the figures come into focus. Closest to his side sat Doctor Alaniz, a small set of spectacles at the end of his nose and a book in his hand. On the table by his side sat a small basin, with an inch or so of dark red blood already congealing. Chapa flexed his hand and felt the bindings around the wound on his forearm where the doctor had bled him. Standing behind the doctor, in quiet conversation, he saw Padre Joseph and his eldest son, Gaspar. Francisco was nowhere in sight.

The doctor looked up from the small volume in his hand, noticed Chapa's waking and stood up, peering at him over his spectacles; he gave a short, sharp cough, just loud enough to draw the attention of the two other men. Gaspar and the priest turned at the noise.

The doctor spoke first: "Don Juan, do you know where you are?"

Chapa was weak, but still managed to feel annoyed. "Yes. I'm in my bedroom. And I know you three gentlemen quite well. What are you all doing here? I am not at death's door."

"No, Don Juan, you are not, thanks be to God. But you've had a very dangerous fever, and you shouldn't take it lightly," the doctor said.

"Father," said Gaspar, "your slave tells me he found you out walking in the storm. What on earth were you – "

"Am I confined to this house?" Chapa retorted. "Is there any reason I can't go out and do as I wish?"

"Your son didn't mean to say you weren't free, Don Juan," the priest said, playing peacemaker. "Only that it wasn't wise for your health."

"Where on earth were you going?" Gaspar asked.

Chapa looked over at his eldest son and felt that familiar mixture of love, pride, irritation and consternation. Gaspar was always so direct and forward when he addressed him. The younger *criollos* had already dispensed with many of the deferential manners and traditions of Spain—and, in truth, Chapa himself had probably helped to bring about the change—but he had to admit that Gaspar's bluntness still rubbed him the wrong way. Chapa shook his head, "It's not important."

Gaspar turned away, his shoulders betraying the frustration he felt. He had spent the last two days at his father's bedside, with the doctor and priest hanging on his elbows like vultures, their tongues wagging with their stupid pieties. That first night, sitting beside his father, holding the basin while Francisco wrung out rags and laid them on his father's forehead, he felt ripped open by the love and tenderness he felt for the old man. All the prickly difficulty of the last fifteen years fell away, and for that one night it was all so simple. Once these two showed up, though, the intimacy evaporated, and the resentments and anxieties of a lifetime crept back in.

"Don Juan, you need to stay in bed until this fever is completely gone," the doctor said. "If you need something, send Francisco to fetch it. If you need spiritual comfort or have something to confess, I know Padre Joseph would be happy to attend you."

The young priest nodded, although his manner was flat and tired. "I would be more than happy to, Don Juan. When God calls you, he will call you. But until then please don't act recklessly."

"I promise I'll listen to the doctor," Chapa said, ignoring Padre Joseph. "I can see I am ill, although I doubt it merits this kind of assembly."

Gaspar turned back, "You're an important man, father, whether you like it or not. Your life and your health have consequences to this community, and to your family."

Chapa took a deep breath, feeling the heaviness at the bottom of his chest. Leaning back on the bed, he looked around him, "Where is Francisco? I'm so thirsty."

Gaspar moved towards the doorway to the patio and shouted, "Francisco! Bring your master some wine."

"Wine cut with water,"said the doctor cautiously, "and make sure the water is fresh."

Gaspar, not hearing a response, yelled again to Francisco. "Wine and water. Be quick."

***

After giving Chapa—and, by extension, Francisco—careful and thorough instructions on how to treat his fever in the coming days, the doctor gathered his implements and left. Padre Joseph offered Chapa a simple blessing and a final friendly admonishment about his stubbornness, and then too took his leave, promising a return in the next few days. All the while Gaspar moved restlessly around the room, interjecting occasionally, clearly impatient for the others to depart.

When they were finally alone—apart from Francisco— Gaspar settled onto the chair by Chapa's bed. He relaxed a little, picked up his father's fragile hand, still faintly stained with ink, and turned it over, his gaze penetrating but his voice a little softer now.

"You can surely see, Father, that you may not have long to live," said Gaspar.

"I have a lot less of my life ahead than I do behind," said Chapa, "but no man knows when his last day will come."

"You are my father and I cherish you. And you are a great man in this *reino* besides. But you need to think about the real problems that could follow your death."

"My last will and testament, you mean?"

"That should be a relatively simple matter, although it should have been taken care of long ago. I will ask Alferez Don Pedro de Almandos to draft one for you."

"No," said Chapa firmly, "I will draft it. There have been many great men in this frontier. Far greater than me, no doubt. But if there is a better attorney in this valley I have not met him," Chapa said.

72

Gaspar sighed. "In any event, it's not your will that concerns me."

"You will receive a fair portion, do not worry," said Chapa.

"Father, I just said that's not what I am worried about. You could leave me everything, far beyond my fair portion, and it would be a small addition to my estates. What concerns me is not your material wealth but your immaterial works," said Gaspar.

"There are hundreds of documents in that hall of administration that I have drafted. They do me, and you, honor, and are a testament to the authority of the Crown here. They may not bring us glory, but they won't bring us shame either."

"Father, why do you have to make this so hard? You know I don't mean those either."

"Then what?" said Chapa, knowing he was being mule-headed but still resentful of Gaspar's peremptory tone.

"When I was a boy, you used to have a large chest full of papers that you kept in your study. I know you were always writing and I once overheard you say to mother that if the Church or Crown ever knew about your journals we would all be tried and locked away."

"My son, I was only joking with your mother. I do of course have many papers in my chest. And I am sure you have taken a look into my study and seen it still there."

"I did. I found it locked," said Gaspar.

Without needing to raise his hand to feel for it, Chapa suddenly realized the key around his neck was missing. If Gaspar did not have it, then who?

Gaspar continued, "You must realize that these papers, your legacy, are not merely a matter for your pride; they could put at risk the safety of your children and your grandchildren here in Nuevo León. Remember, it has only been ten years since you were almost exiled from the *reino* for your stubbornness and your Genovese birth."

"My principles, Gaspar, not my stubbornness."

Gaspar jumped out of his chair, full of agitation. Chapa looked at his son's face, and thought, not for the first time, about how strong the Treviños' bloodlines were. They were brilliant, but nearly all of them were nervous creatures, beset by anxiety and too easily tipped out of balance. Beatriz seemed to have inherited her mother's temperament, but her brothers were so nervous that they could not bear to leave the security of their *haciendas*. Gaspar was a very successful rancher, and a steady husband and father, but he still struggled to contain his nervous energy.

"You only escaped exile because your accuser died suddenly in the midst of the Royal Court's decision."

"He ate too many melons one night, as I recall," Chapa smiled and laughed in spite of himself, setting off a small coughing fit.

"Father, this is no laughing matter," Gaspar said.

Chapa took a moment to recover himself, looking for a way to calm his son. "No, it is not, son, and I am sorry if I treat it too lightly. But I will remind you that I was vindicated by a charter from none other than our gracious king, His Royal Highness Carlos II."

"Be that as it may," said Gaspar, his tone now softer and more thoughtful. "The affair should remind you that your presence here as a foreigner and a man of difficult opinions has always been precarious. I have the utmost respect for your life's work, father, and I am full of pride in all you have accomplished. But I know you realize that your sons and daughters here cannot thrive under such a cloud. We own land here, and have children. We are grounded in the soil of Nuevo León. An exile for you might have been an adventure. For us it would be a kind of death."

"So you fear that there are writings in my chest that are controversial? Or worse, treasonous?"

"I don't know, father. This is what I'm asking you. I know your good friend Governor Zavala owned books on the *Index Librorum Prohibitorum*. Works by that Protestant Cartesius for instance."

"Descartes was no Protestant." Chapa retorted.

"Then why did he take refuge among the accursed rebellious Hollanders, and then with the blasphemous Queen of Sweden?"

"I cannot tell you, Gaspar. I never knew the man, though to be honest I wish I had. But I have it on good authority he is buried in consecrated ground in Paris."

"Well if he was not a Protestant he was an atheist, because his works are still banned by the Holy Father. And you yourself told me your friend Zavala read his impious writings openly."

"I did. And I also told you that as he neared his death, from that cancerous growth in his leg, he asked me to destroy them," said Chapa.

"Then I only ask," Gaspar said, "that you take the same consideration for those you leave behind that Don Martín did."

Chapa did not reply, lost in thought.

Gaspar continued, "If you won't let me look through your papers, please do it yourself while there is still time. And when you do, think about your children and grandchildren. Don't leave us vulnerable to the whims of an unfavorable governor or a capricious *comisario*."

Chapa nodded, recognizing the wisdom of what his son was saying. Once again, he was full of regret for all he had put his children through during that difficult time. He put his hand out and patted his son affectionately, his hand lingering on his shoulder. "My dear son, of that you have my promise."

Gaspar squeezed his father's hand. Clearing his throat, he said huskily, "Thank you, father. You're tired now, I should leave you to rest. But first try to eat at least something."

He crossed over to the little kitchen to tell Francisco to bring Chapa his evening meal. Francisco fetched Gaspar his hat and cloak and then finally brought in the soup that he had been long delayed in serving.

***

TO THE HONORABLE SECRETARY OF NUEVO LEÓN, DON JUAN BAUTISTA CHAPA

Father,

Please. You must see reason in this matter. The Governor has formally asked you to file a report to the Viceroy. You are the Secretary of this reino. You must obey. If there is injustice in it, it will be sorted out in time.

If you do not file this report he will exile you and it will be great stain on our family. Our sister Juana's marriage has already fallen through because of your stubbornness, leaving her in the most dire and shameful straits. Everyone remarks on it. Our mother is too gracious and too loyal to say so, but it pains her too.

Again, Father, all of us understand the unreasonableness of Governor de Vidagaray but you must comply.

Your son,
Gaspar
5 May, 1681
Saltillo, Nuevo León

***

TO SERGEANT GASPAR CHAPA Y TREVIÑO

Gaspar,

Understand that I have been the Secretary of Nuevo León for nearly twenty years. I have managed its affairs under good governors and poor ones.

I cannot let a rascal like this Vidagaray draw a sword on his own Lieutenant Governor, seize the man's belongings and sell them at auction. He is a brigand and has no authority to bend the law to his own whims.

Know that I act according to my conscience and my best judgment. I will do my utmost to protect my wife and children but I must act according to what I know to be right and just.

Your loving father,
Juan Bautista Chapa
18 May, 1681
Monterrey - Nuevo León

Faithful copy on 19 May, 1681 JBC

***

BY ORDER OF THE GOVERNOR OF NUEVO LEÓN, Don Domingo de Vidagaray y Saraza

The Governor of Nuevo León, through the power invested in him by the honorable Viceroy of Nueva España and His Royal Majesty Carlos II, hereby, immediately, and irrevocably orders the <u>banishment</u> of one Juan Bautista Chapa from this reino.

Juan Bautista Chapa, born Giovanni Battista Schiapapria, is ordered to depart Nuevo León immediately and remain no less than <u>200 leguas</u> from its borders for the remainder of his life. Failure to comply with this order will result in indentured servitude in the Captaincy General of Las Islas Filipinas *in His Majesty's Colonies of the East Indies and a fine no less than <u>1,000 pesos</u>, to be paid by him or his heirs.*

Let it be known that Juan Bautista Chapa is seditious and provocative of strife and divisions and many other evil proceedings in this reino. *Moreover, he is a Genovese* extranjero *in illegal residence in New Spain, in direct contravention of His Majesty's Ordinance of Foreign Exclusion.*

Any inhabitants of Nuevo León caught harboring Juan Bautista Chapa, whether peninsular, criollo, mestizo, *Indian, or otherwise, will be fined no less than <u>200 pesos</u>.*

Signed and enacted immediately, this day of 6 June, 1681

Governor Don Domingo de Vidagaray y Saraza
Monterrey, Nuevo León, México – Nueva España

***

La Historia del Nuevo Reino de León, Chapter 26

In 1681 General Don Domingo de Vidagaray entered the governorship. His Majesty gave him the office because of his merit and prior service; these are evidence from his papers, which reflect that he served forty-four years in naval operations and the army. He was a native of Vizcaya and somewhat rigid in disposition, as will be soon seen.

He visited the house of Juan de Echeverria, a settler in Saltillo who was also a native of Vizcaya. Echeverria entertained his fellow countryman for eight days. All the settlers went to visit him, among them Don Pedro de Cajigal, who had been lord mayor of Saltillo and at the time was Nuevo León's lieutenant governor. The governor did not honor Cajigal as expected, remaining seated without coming to the door and following the same style when he bid Cajigal goodbye. The governor had an excuse, however, because he was crippled. This must have been the reason.

Don Pedro, however, was very offended. When the governor, in a large coach went to pay him a visit, Don Pedro did not go to the door when the coach arrived. For this reason the governor became irritated, called out to him, and reproved him. At that, Cajigal came outside with sword and buckler at the same time that the governor was alighting from his coach. With their swords drawn a horrendous fight broke out.

Finally they were separated and Don Pedro was placed under guard and an action brought against him. While it was pending Don Pedro took flight and placed himself in the Church of San Francisco. The governor went to take charge of the administration and confiscated a quantity of lead and other possessions that Don Pedro had there. This was carried out. After reaching Nuevo León, the governor demonstrated his rancor by showing very relentless diligence in inquiring of other possessions of Don Pedro. He put some of them up at public auction and sold them.

78

His government lasted but a very short time, however, because he ate too many watermelons and cantaloupes. He was struck with a three-day fever from which he died very shortly, after having governed no more than three months and nineteen days.

Excerpted directly from the book *La Historia del Nuevo Reino de León*, by Juan Bautista Chapa

CHAPTER 7

Francisco's Visitor

Journal Entry: 9 May, 1660

Today I learned that the hacienda *of Don Antonio de la Garza was attacked by another band of savage Indians. They killed the poor man in his bed and stole his livestock and horses. His wife and children were kidnapped and surely have already been subject to the most abject depravations. Even now, the Governor is assembling the militia to rescue these poor souls.*

What possesses these godless creatures to refuse the gifts of civilization and the salvation of our Church? They can no longer claim ignorance as their ancestors might have. They see how good it is to build towns and tend livestock, but they choose instead to raze and kill. They were born to destroy instead of to create.

I confess that at times I rue the day I left Ciudad de México for this pestilential frontier. Indeed, there are moments when I wonder why I ever left the beautiful shores of Albisola — that precious land I valued too lightly when I was there. Do young men ever see the true merit of the gifts their fathers give them? Does our poor little vineyard there still lie fallow?

Captain Alonso recently returned to Spain to represent our reino *before the Royal Council. I wonder, might I one day be sent on such a noble errand? If I did, could I steal away to visit Genoa for a month or two? If I went, would I be tempted to stay in those civilized lands forever? Of course I would never abandon my family, but I must leave these musings behind, lest these thoughts corrupt and poison my mind.*

Although I must be reconciled to my roots here in Nuevo León, I wish I could leave this hacienda, where I have worked now for almost 10 years. Joseph is an honorable and capable man, who relies on me greatly, but the mundane nature of the work I perform here wears on me. His father, the late General Alonso de León, ran a strict household and kept me busy, but at his heart he was a man of letters. I think often of his great Historia and wonder if it shall ever be published. Indeed, would any man but me care to read it?

The governor would, I know. Don Martín de Zavala is a great man, both courageous and learned. If I could labor in his service I know my anguish here would abate. Perhaps I should write to him and offer my pen.

I pray to God for aid and guidance in these dangerous times.

***

Chapa slept fitfully throughout the rest of the day and into the night. Each time he woke he saw Francisco near at hand, sometimes bringing him food and drink, other times changing his sweat-soaked bedclothes. At still others Chapa would open his eyes to see his servant hunched over the bundled manuscript of his *Historia*, deeply engrossed in the account of distant events.

After eating a small portion of soup, Chapa sat up for a short time, finding this brief interlude of wakefulness somehow more restful than his actual sleep. The sky was dark, though if it was closer to sunrise than sunset, he had no idea. After Francisco took his bowl of soup away and returned, Chapa decided to visit a topic that had troubled his mind throughout his feverish dreams.

"Francisco, I have a question to ask you," said Chapa.

Francisco sat on the stool he had brought up from the kitchen and inched it closer to Chapa's bed so as better to hear his master's weakened voice.

"Yes, Don Juan. I am here."

"Earlier this morning—or was it yesterday morning?" Chapa said, finding he was fighting through a daze to speak his thoughts.

"Yesterday," Francisco assured him, "I have just heard the bells for matins from the friary on the hill."

"When I awoke to find Doctor Alaniz at my side yesterday morning, I noticed that the key I keep around my neck was missing," said Chapa, "I can only assume you know of its whereabouts."

"I have it safely here," said Francisco, tapping the pocket of his tunic, "When I found you in a delirious state, I began to dress you in a fresh night gown and the chain around your neck became caught on the neck of the gown, so I removed it. I apologize if this was in error, Don Juan. You were not in a state to approve or deny such a request and in the interest of haste I acted."

"But you did not see the need to remove my crucifix or this ring which also hang around my neck?" asked Chapa.

"They were not caught," answered Francisco.

"It is curious," said Chapa, taking a breath before continuing, "that you should by chance remove the key from around my neck mere hours before my son Gaspar tried to open the trunk that contains my papers."

Francisco stood and busied himself with the tray, preparing to take it downstairs, his eyes avoiding Chapa's. "I did not know Don Gaspar was in need of it. As he is your son, I would have given it to him had he asked, of course," said Francisco.

Chapa observed him carefully, trying to assess Francisco's demeanor, wondering at his willingness to take such a bold action in light of his own history. Why take such a chance? Was his loyalty, his desire to protect his master's privacy, so great?

"Should I give you back the key now?" asked Francisco.

"No," said Chapa, trying to shake his head but quickly realizing such movements would bring him pain, "It would do me little good. Whether it was your intention or no, I think the key serves me better right now in your pocket. And while I suspect you do not require such instruction, let me be plain: you should decidedly not give the key to anyone besides me."

"Of course," said Francisco, "I make such a promise gladly, with only one limitation. If Padre Joseph should ask for it, I would have to comply, as I belong to the Church."

"Yes, I understand," said Chapa, "I'm tired now. Thank you for your constant attendance on me these many days, but try to find some time to rest when you can."

Francisco nodded and helped Chapa lay back on the bed. Within seconds, Chapa was drawn back into fitful sleep, and Francisco returned to his reading.

***

Historia del Nuevo Reino de León, Chapter 22

These rationales and arguments were touched on briefly by Father Instructor Francisco de Ribera in his opinion and verdict. Therefore, without verbosely giving more reasons than the ones previously advanced or wearying with infinite authorities on the two bodies of law and with masters in all faculties, one may judge and consider the war against the Indians as just and punishing them in conformity with the occasions in which they may give reason therefore.

There is only left to be feared—and in no small measure—the insolences, cruelties, and atrocious acts into which the soldiers, having the license of public authority against the enemies, thrust themselves. These acts are well proved and experienced in all the conquests of the Indies. Perhaps it is for these sins that all these provinces today suffer the calamities and punishments that God has sent us.

For although in public battles of opposed armies there appeared persons and saints—and the Saint among Saints, holiest Mary—to favor and assist them, nevertheless, this did not occur in the private actions of the soldiers, who did them without fear of God and without the aim and goal of Serving Him...

As to the rest, let there be noted the not-insubstantial distinction between the enemy's coming to look for me in my house and my going to kill him in his.

Letter from the Order of St. Francis, San Luis Potosí to Governor Martín de Zavala, 1632

Excerpted directly from the book *La Historia del Nuevo Reino de León*, by Juan Bautista Chapa

***

After three more days and nights had gone by, Chapa awoke, convinced that he was feeling better. At the very least, he didn't feel worse, which was no small victory for a man so gravely ill in this late stage of life.

Francisco helped prop him up in bed and even brought in a small table and inkwell. On even his worst days Chapa was compelled to write, even if hours went by between the start of a sentence and its completion. The old servant prepared his master a light breakfast and a bowl of *xocolatl*, though Chapa had very little appetite for either. With the breakfast cleared away and Chapa's chamber pot emptied, Francisco returned to announce that he had finished reading the *Historia*.

"That is welcome news," said Chapa, "I have been dreading the days ahead confined to this bed without being able to properly attend to my work. Our discussion of the *Historia* should keep us occupied for several days. It feels more important than ever now, given how close to death I have so recently stood."

"If you wish," said Francisco, "Thank you for the honor of reading your great work, one that I am sure someday will be read and treasured by many."

"Thank you, Francisco, but more than your praise, I'm seeking your earnest critique. The work has been a labor of love, written with the utmost care to be both accurate and complete. However, I worry whether the *Historia* will be deemed dangerous by the powerful here in Nuevo León. I am sure you heard my own son expressing similar concerns. I want to be thorough and truthful, so that future generations might learn from the founding years of this *reino*, but I must tread carefully with ideas or even choices of words, anything that could imperil my family's standing."

"I will do my best, *patrón*. Though a simple slave such as I can offer little as to the thoughts of great men like the Governor or the Inquisitor," said Francisco. "Should I begin by asking questions? There is so much I don't understand, and your answers might also help you think about how your *Historia* appears to the eyes of a new reader."

"That's very sound judgment, Francisco," said Chapa. "Begin."

"The first question that occurs to me, Don Juan, concerns the Indians of your *Historia*. Not a chapter goes by without violence or unrest. You almost always call them 'barbaric' or 'savage.'"

"And so they were. And are, I'm afraid," said Chapa, "You've lived in Nuevo León for many years; you know as well as anyone how little rest we have had between attacks by any one of dozens of tribes."

"I only ask because I sometimes found the voice of the man who wrote this *Historia* very different from the man who I attend each day. You are so courteous to the indigenous men and women of our *pueblo*; I know you do not despise every Indian from his birth," said Francisco.

"Of course not," said Chapa. "There are many gentle Indians who have accepted Christ and now live among us in peace and humility. Your own ancestors were such Indians, I have no doubt. In this *Historia,* however, I write of the lawless savages living in the mountains, deserts, and swamps. The beasts that defy God in spite of the tireless efforts of our friars. They have no laws or church of their own. They have wives in common and eat men's flesh. They think only of stealing and hunting and fighting. These Indians are a scourge on this land, and it will be a better place when we are finally rid of them."

"Your feelings are quite strong," said Francisco.

"They certainly are. I have given this an enormous amount of thought. As you rightly observed, it is a primary subject of my *Historia*. Think of the human sacrifices that your ancestors practiced, your very grandfather who was an Aztec priest."

"My great-grandfather," Francisco offered gently. His own face betrayed no emotion, even though Chapa's words betrayed the ignorance of the northern Indians that was so typical among Spaniards. While he himself had no affinity for their nomadic and warlike ways, he knew these tribes were now mere shells of their former societies, driven to desperation and lawlessness by hunger, disease and the loss of their lands.

"Your great-grandfather, yes," Chapa said dismissively. "Think of the thousands of souls we Spaniards saved by ending the barbaric rule of those Aztec cannibals. From that great city we now call México, they terrorized every tribe in this land, demanding fresh sacrifices and treating their subjects no better than beasts." Chapa sat up in bed, warming to his subject. "And yet, rather than hail the Spaniards as saviors, these northern tribes choose instead to rebel, harassing our way of life and threatening our very existence. It is barbaric and profoundly ungrateful."

Francisco just nodded, listening to Chapa's intensifying diatribe.

"Take the Guachichils. They binge on killing and are mad with violence. There is nothing a civilized man can do to pacify them. You cannot educate them, you cannot give them religion. There is nothing the Spaniard can do to change their ancient savagery. I can see no solution but to finally exterminate them once our own militia here has grown to sufficient strength and size. Until then we can only suffer their outrages. As for the Boboles, I have seen them commit acts so heinous that . . ." Chapa stopped, suddenly realizing what he was saying, ". . . that I should not speak of them."

"I thought the Boboles were our Christian allies, Don Juan. Were they not the tribe who fought bravely by your side against the Cacaxtles?"

Chapa paused and breathed deeply, seeking to calm himself before replying in a voice calculated to convey disinterest, "I may have misspoke. At times I can confuse these many tribes."

"Of course," said Francisco, noting the shift in tone with curiosity; clearly something had touched a nerve.

86

"I know, Francisco, that you have nothing in common with these savage Indians."

"Don't worry, Don Juan. I take no offense," said Francisco. "However, returning to our discussion, I wonder if you might help me understand a difficult portion of your *Historia*."

"Certainly," said Chapa.

"Difficult not because of a flaw in your writing, but because I understand too little of the laws and ideas of the Spaniard."

"Which chapter are you referring to?" asked Chapa.

"It is a passage concerning a request made by the Municipal Council of Monterrey to the governor of that time, Don Martín de Zavala," said Francisco.

"Ah, yes, the learned opinions by Friar Francisco de Ribera about the just nature of war against the Indian. Very astute of you. I was particularly pleased to be able to include that document, because these arguments make clear the legal and moral foundation for action against the Indian. Spaniards, you know, are fundamentally men of law—we must only act according to God's law, the King's law, and the timeless philosophical principles which govern the acts of great nations."

"But please help me understand," Francisco said, "The Council made a request to their governor, Don Martín, asking him to make war on the Guachichil, the Cayaguagua, and other Indian nations."

"Precisely."

"And the Governor—"

"Who was not bound by the advice of the Council but received it with great seriousness," interjected Chapa.

"The Governor sent the request to the friar, Fray Francisco de Ribera. But why this friar?"

"Fray Francisco was a great scholar and teacher at *Villa de San Gregorio de Cerralvo* and his opinion was greatly valued by Don Martín," answered Chapa, "There could not have been two or three other men in the *reino* at that time who were as learned and judicious as Fray Francisco."

"And he answered that this war was just and righteous?" asked Francisco, tentatively feeling his way through the events and gauging Chapa's reactions.

"Quite right," said Chapa. "He cited St. Augustine and other great men of the church to demonstrate beyond a doubt that Christian law permitted such a war."

"And then," said Francisco, "after several weeks, Governor Zavala sent the friar's opinion to the Order of St. Francis at San Luis Potosi."

"He did. And as you no doubt read, the good friars confirmed their Fray Francisco's opinion."

"I am curious," said Francisco, "why the Governor saw the need to seek the opinion of so many before acting."

"Don Martín was a very learned man; you must understand that he valued the opinion of scholars like these above all others."

"He did not trust his own opinion on the matter?"

"You misunderstand, Francisco. Don Martín was a man of boldness and courage, but this did not diminish his dedication to the knowledge of the law and other great matters."

"I see," said Francisco, "but if our own council today should send a similar request to Governor Juan Pérez de Merino, must he also seek the advice of the friars before making war?"

"No, there would be no need. The reason I included those noble opinions in my *Historia* was to show the abiding justification for war against the savage in this *reino.* Do you understand?"

"I am beginning to, Don Juan. These great matters of state are all unfamiliar to me, as you know quite well."

"Francisco, clearly you have something to say about the topic. Go on, man, and just say it."

"I merely . . ."

"Yes?"

"I merely try to imagine myself as the governor—though I could never aspire to such a lofty position. But if I were a governor and my aim was to delay this war, my actions would be hard to distinguish from Don Martín's."

"You suspect that Zavala was stalling by asking the friars for their opinions?"

"I do not suspect, Don Juan, only wonder. I was merely imagining myself in his place. I do not know this friar, but I do know the Order of St. Francis, which loves peace to a fault. I found their written opinion to be a strange one—it abhors every act of war while agreeing that it is legal and just. If I wanted a case against war, I myself would ask the Franciscans."

Chapa chuckled, "Well, that is a very reasonable hypothesis, Francisco. I enjoy very much your exercise of thought and imagination. But I knew Zavala quite well and can tell you he would not need to resort to such tricks. If he opposed war, he simply would have denied the request."

"Then there is no doubt."

"It is only a coincidence of course," said Chapa, "that a smallpox outbreak broke out at the same time the final opinions were rendered and the campaign was never undertaken."

Francisco nodded gravely, "The pox has killed many more Indians than all the Spaniards here ever could, even if it were their sole vocation. Perhaps it was God's will after all."

***

While Chapa napped in the afternoon—far longer and deeper than his typical *siesta*—Francisco received a visit from his daughter Luisa. It was the Sabbath, and Francisco ordinarily received permission to attend Mass with his only surviving child, but in light of Chapa's present condition Francisco could not risk leaving his master alone for more than a few minutes.

Luisa entered the front door nervously, then walked with her father to the cozy warmth of the little kitchen. She had never been in Chapa's house before and knew the important man's reputation. She wore the simple dress and rectangular collar of a serving woman. In spite of her plain attire, she exuded a certain quiet grace, and an intelligence ill-suited to her lowly station.

"Thank you for coming to visit me," said Francisco with a smile, taking his daughter's small hands in his.

"It is good to see you, Father," said Luisa warmly.

Francisco looked down at his daughter's hands. The palms were rough from years of manual labor, but his eyes were drawn instead to the backs of her hands, which he could see even from a distance were red, cracked, and scaly.

Luisa could feel his eyes on her raw flesh and pulled her hands back from his. "We were making soap yesterday," she said, defensively, "The lye burned my hands."

Francisco remained silent, his eyes probing her for the truth.

"Father, let's talk of other things."

"Everything about you is beautiful, Luisa. Your hair, your face, your skin. God made you perfectly."

She stepped to the other side of the small room. "That's easy for you to say. Half of your blood is Spanish. You could have had a *mestiza* for a wife but you chose an Indian. So here I am, brown as silt."

"If I had chosen a *mestiza* wife instead of your dear mother, it would not be you standing with me today."

"Perhaps that would be for the best."

"What is it you use to rub your skin, ash?"

She bit her lip and then relented, "Ash, ground corn, and water. Marta says it will lighten my skin."

Francisco despaired of his daughter's rejection of her beautiful Indian face and body, but he knew that a woman's status, her very worth as a human being, depended on how European her hair, skin and face appeared. His grandmother once told him that the conquest of Mexico was really the conquest of the *Indigena* woman; the imposition of Spanish blood on Indian bodies now set the standard for beauty and worth.

"It won't work," Francisco said. "Your mother and her sisters tried the same thing. And far too many Indian women before them. You only torture yourself. If a man doesn't want

90

you because of your brown face, then he is not a man worth having."

Unwilling to argue with her father — but equally unwilling to agree — Luisa stood silent, searching for a way to change the conversation. Francisco let the matter drop and they sat amiably next to the hearth, talking of more pleasant topics.

***

After a quiet afternoon in the little kitchen, Luisa left the don's house and walked towards the *traza*, a small but important package her father gave her tucked under her *rebozo*.

She bought some chiles and *yerbabuena* from the little woman who sat on the corner, counting out carefully each *real* that her mistress had given her for the shopping. Her next stop was the little dry goods store run by Doña Alicia, a middle-aged widow. Here Luisa purchased some thread and a packet of fine iron needles. Leaving the shop, she turned left and headed towards the rectory attached to the *Iglesia de San Francisco*. She walked around to the side and knocked on the kitchen door. She was greeted by one of the nuns who cared for Padre Joseph's quarters and cooked his meals.

"Hola, Sor Maria! May God bless and protect you."

"And you little one," said the old nun. Sor Maria had known Luisa since her childhood, and had grown up almost like a sister to Luisa's mother. She invited the girl to sit at the table in the center of the kitchen, poured the young woman a glass of fresh goat's milk and placed it on the table. "Drink, child, and tell me the news."

Luisa took off her *rebozo* and hung it on a peg near the door, placing her little parcel on the shelf next to the door to the rectory and her shopping bag on the floor beneath it. "I have just come from visiting my father. He is well, and seems content at Don Juan Chapa's house, although it must be a dull life with just those two *viejitos* alone in that house all day."

"How is the *don's* health these days?"

"He is sick right now," said Luisa, "but he has been ill before. That old goat is a strong one."

Sor Maria laughed in spite of herself, "Now, now. Luisa. He is an honorable man. And you say he treats your father fairly."

"Most of the time."

Sor Maria shook her head, "That Don Juan, he makes everyone nervous. He has been here so long, longer than the priest, longer than the Bishop at Guadalajara, longer than any governor or any of the great ranchers still living. He knows everyone's secrets."

"So what if he does?"

"If he stays quiet, then nothing. But when men come close to death, they sometimes decide to speak their mind. If he does . . ." Sor Maria made a vague but violent gesture to suggest some sort of tumult, ". . . no one is safe. Then look out. Besides that, my *tía*, who used to work in that house, says he was always writing, working in secret on his papers and hiding them like a squirrel in an old trunk that he kept locked at all times."

Luisa shrugged, "I'll be safe. He doesn't know my secrets . . . not that anyone would care."

"But enough of this," said Sor Maria, "Give me some happy news."

"Yesterday I saw my Tia Josefa on the street. My cousin Lydia is getting married to the blacksmith from Cerralvo."

"Oh, he is a *criollo*, isn't he? Or at least close. Such blue eyes. Quite a good match for her."

"I don't know about that, Sor Maria. He looks almost as old as my father, and has seven children besides. I feel sorry for Lyly."

"What about you Luisa, when will some lucky man ask your father for your hand?"

"I don't think that will ever happen, Sor Maria. With a father as a bonded criminal and a pure-blooded Indian mother, I will surely end up a spinster," Luisa said, with a nervous laugh, her eyes cast down on the table. "Or a nun."

Sor Maria looked at her with a serene smile, ignoring the unintended slight. "You have a beautiful face and a kind heart.

And I have seen you dance *la zambra*," said Sor Maria with a wink, "so I know any red-blooded man would covet you."

"Do you really think so?" asked Luisa with a blush.

The old nun nodded, "I know it. Shall I take you to Padre Joseph now?"

"Yes, sister."

CHAPTER 8

Albisola and Cadereyta

The water runs around my feet, past me and up the beach, and then draws back. It beckons me to return with it to the sea from whence it came.

The waves taste land and then reconsider. "Come with us." The waves talk to me. They each have a woman's voice, the same voice, but I don't recognize her. How can this be? "We have known both land and sea and can tell you truthfully where you will be most happy."

Each wave echoes the same call, some softly and some with a brash roar. I long to follow them . . .

This sea is sometimes blue like the sky, flecked with cloud-white caps. Sometimes it is gray and foreboding. At still others it is green and docile.

U Mediterànio. The sea between land. I love it here. I close my eyes and I float in the sea. Nothing matters. I feel good, happy. I smile with my eyes closed tightly against the salt water, the sun on my face. I am content.

A great ship pitches under. Far above the deck, I crouch in the crow's nest. The waves cap white far below me. Cristoforo Colombo is at the helm. He stares up at me with stern eyes and shouts, "They no longer respect me. The Spaniards used me. I should have stayed here and served La Serenissima, noble Genoa. Those Iberian rustics could not appreciate my genius."

I say nothing in reply. He is my hero, the greatest man of common blood to ever walk the earth. I stand mute as he continues, "You, boy, from Albisola. I am your neighbor, from Savona." Cristoforo Colombo? How can this be? Where am I?

As I see myself high on the rigging, I am but a boy. My feet are small and fair, the skin on my hand taut, my face smooth and hairless. Back on the shore, I crouch down — easy and effortless — and push my fingers into the course sand, but the retreating wave tugs at them, pulling me back towards the sea.

My Nonna, my sweet grandmother, calls me.

Torn a cà.

I walk up the stony path away from the beach and look for the turn to my grandfather's inn, counting each step. As I come off the bridge, though, I am no longer in Albisola. Around me instead is the rough plaza of Cadereyta. What is this road that lies beneath me? It is but a long empty stretch of dusty ground. I am alone. The wind gusts and blows the dust around. I shield my eyes, looking around to see who else might be caught out of doors in this dust storm.

There is a low whistle as the wind whips through the short bell tower of the church but I cannot see or hear a single soul. The hot, dry summer is fading into autumn. Everyone must be out at the haciendas *preparing for harvest. Few truly live here — indeed, the governor has been forced to fine many for neglecting their houses in the city. We must keep up the artifices of civilization, even when they serve no apparent use. It is a town of false promise. The whole place could crumble back into the earth and never be thought of again.*

The swirling wind finally makes up its mind. It blows strong and steady eastward. The dust blows around my feet — I am a solid beacon amidst the motion. My strong young legs can resist the gale no matter how fierce.

I look down at my shadow. I stand immovable but he begins to waiver. He takes one step forward, and then another. Shall I lose him to this wind?

And to where? To my homeland? A mi patria? *Back to the wide ocean sea? Where do you beckon me?*

***

The next morning Doctor Alaniz visited again and asked Francisco to bring a small pan. The experienced doctor set the pan under Chapa's elbow, rolled up the sleeve of his nightgown, and made a small, expert incision along the vein running up the old man's arm. The blood trickled down and collected in the pan. From his vantage point a few feet away Francisco could see nothing amiss about his master's blood. It was dark and red and coursed as one would expect. If there were humors out of balance they must be invisible to the eye.

After bandaging the incision, the doctor inquired as to Chapa's vigor and appetite and was heartened to learn that both were returning, albeit slowly. He examined Chapa's stool and urine carefully, both by sight and taking in their odors — though what he hoped to discern he did not share. He finally pronounced that Chapa was making great strides towards wellness but that he had entered a very critical stage. He urged Francisco to make sure the shutters remained unopened and encouraged him to increase the proportion of wine to water.

After Alaniz left to see to other patients, Francisco took the pan of blood downstairs. He set it down and then poured his master a cup of wine as the doctor had suggested. For a moment Francisco gazed at the two next to one another — the blood and the wine — and wondered at Christ's mystery. His Indian ancestors had drawn much blood. They drank it and ate flesh. The Christians too drink blood and eat flesh, through a miracle that required the sacrifice of but one man instead of thousands. The Aztec gods demanded sacrifice of many but the Christian one chose to sacrifice himself instead so that men might live eternal. If these gods could ever meet, what might they say to each other?

Putting such immaterial thoughts aside, Francisco returned to his master's bedchamber with bread and wine. Chapa was in a poor mood — he was never partial to being bled even in the best of times, and the experience exacerbated his discomfort.

"Would you like to discuss the *Historia* again today, Don Juan?" Francisco asked, setting down the tray by Chapa's bedside and sitting down on his stool.

96

"I don't know," said Chapa, a little petulantly. "I wonder if our experiences of the world are so different that it is of little use. Don't misunderstand, I quite enjoy our discussions and your active mind never fails to surprise me. But ultimately this book is written for Spaniards and perhaps only a Spaniard can render thorough judgment."

"Of course. I understand," said Francisco, his voice betraying a slight disappointment. He had enjoyed this exercise, both for its own sake and also for the unexpected pleasure of finding himself, however briefly, elevated to the level of an equal to a great scholar like his master. Francisco relaxed his shoulders and quickly accepted the situation. In a life full of tragic loss and countless disappointments, this was but a small matter. His mind searched for his most pressing chore, and he began to stand up.

But quite unexpectedly Chapa spoke again, though in such a strange tone it was hardly clear if he was speaking to Francisco and not himself. "I had a dream of my youth last night . . . I was a boy again, in my little town by the shore. And then I was a man, a young man, here in Nuevo León. In the first I was drawn by the sea. In the second the wind pulled me, but I do not know where it wanted to take me."

Francisco felt a sudden chill, perceiving the breeze that cut through this small house regardless of how tightly he shuttered the windows and sealed the doors. The small brazier behind him made no dent in the cold of that November day.

"Francisco, set my tray in the living room. I will eat later. In the meantime, can you please put my chair closer to the door," Chapa, asked, "I'd like to sit near the doorway so that I can feel the warmth of the sun."

"*Sí*, Don Juan."

Francisco brought the tray into the living room and then carried the chair towards the door as Chapa followed him, his hand clenched. He tried to restrain himself, but as Francisco set the chair down too far—any man could see it was too far—he had no choice but to comment.

"No, no, Francisco, not so close to the door. It's breezy outside and I'm a little chilled. I merely want to be near enough to see the sun go down and to have it warm my body."

"Of course, Don Juan. I will move it back a little."

Francisco moved the chair back to the spot Chapa had indicated and, after helping Chapa to the chair, Francisco sat down in the doorway, his back against the side of the doorframe. It was quite unlike him, but he felt unexpectedly tired after dragging the heavy chair, and couldn't resist the opportunity to warm himself as well in the dying sunlight.

The sun had already dropped enough so that they could see the full sun peeking under the top of the doorway and they sat in silence, both men enjoying the pleasant touch of the setting sun. Chapa closed his eyes and let himself relax, the rays of the sun bathed him in warmth, glowing red through the thin skin of his eyelids. Why did a sunset so often remind Chapa of his father?

"Don Juan, may I ask you a question?"

Chapa looked over at Francisco and could only see the outline of a man sitting on the floor. The sun behind him was now so bright that Francisco was simply a dark sillhouette.

"As long as I have been in this house, your sleep has been plagued by terrible dreams. When did these dreams begin, Don Juan?" asked Francisco.

"Like all men, I have always had nightmares on occasion, particularly in times of great peril or stress. But the dreams which trouble me now are different, darker and more intense. They first came to me when I started writing my *Historia*. I wrote incessantly from 1686 almost until 1691, determined to finish the work Don Alonso de León had started when he wrote his first history of Nuevo León. I discovered that after a long night of writing, especially if it concerned a matter of great personal significance, when I went to sleep I would relive the subject of my writing with an intensity and vividness that frightened me. At times, I could almost direct my dreams—in some cases even the nightmares."

Chapa paused, considering how to phrase his next thought. "But I wonder now whether my writing directed my dreams or were my dreams, somehow, dictating the course of my writing? I still don't know. I have often asked myself whether I was too fearful to write of some events because of the dreams that would follow? Other times, I wondered if there was some unseen power that was guiding me through my dreams? Regardless, Francisco, I will say that sometimes it felt almost magical, the way my writing became intertwined with my dreams. I became obsessed, even though some of the nightmares were terrifying. But I didn't care. It was like eating hot *chile*; I couldn't stop myself. I kept wanting more."

Chapa paused and took a sip of wine, lost in thought. Francisco sat quietly until Chapa once again began to speak.

"But since the completion of the *Historia*, my dreams wander without guidance, like a cart horse that serves quietly its entire life and then one day breaks free and runs wild. I continue to tinker and edit my work, but I no longer can direct the visions that haunt me each night. If they are trying instead to direct me, I don't understand what they ask of me."

Francisco began to say something, but Chapa interrupted him and said, "One second, Francisco, let me just finish," as he put up his hand, gesturing Francisco to hold off. "There is one nightmare I've been having on a regular basis that really confuses me. I have it at least once a week. In it, I'm walking in a *cañon* that has a slow moving stream. The *cañon* feels very familiar, but I don't know where it is. Regardless, in this dream, everything is mysteriously out of order. My shadow is out of step with my gait, the canyon's echoes sound like screaming children. I sense, but cannot see, people looking down at me, filled with malice. Honestly, Francisco, I can feel a hatred, but I see no one. I feel sick in this dream, or as if I've been poisoned. I can also hear a flute playing in the distance. It's an eerie, dark, vile tune, as if foretelling my death. I want to run, but I cannot. I feel condemned to the place. The dream always ends with me looking down into the stream, but I see only a distorted reflection—a head, but no face," Chapa finished, lost in deep thought, almost as if he were looking down into the stream in search of a reflection.

"I know little of dreams," said Francisco, "And less still of what the Church teaches on these matters. My ancestors spoke often of dreams, but these were only foolish superstitions."

"Share what you know with me, if you would," said Chapa, his interest piqued, "As a scholar of Indians for many years, I confess I know nothing of their views on dreams."

"As you wish, Don Juan. But let me be clear these are only tall tales. As a devout Christian I do not believe their heretical meanings."

"You are safe to speak further," said Chapa, impatiently.

Francisco thought for a moment and then began. "My Indian grandmother always said that dreams are as powerful as waking life. They reflect a person's true nature as clearly as a still, dark pool of water; deep truths that are more powerful than we care to admit," said Francisco. "My grandmother told me that dreams are like the slate-black pyrite mirrors found in the Aztec pyramids: they have the power to show us not just the truth visible on the surface, but the secret truth that lies buried within."

To Chapa it seemed that the shadowy light of the gathering evening made the orderly Spanish features of his servant recede a little, replaced by a more ancient symmetry--his eyes angled and creased, the planes of his cheekbones made sharper by the fading light behind him. Chapa leaned forward, intrigued.

"She told me that dreams are a sacred world, where we wander the plains, naked of pretense and free of illusion. Dreams follow the path of our waking lives, like a long, slender shadow in the late afternoon. But, she said that in those dream journeys we break free," Francisco continued. "When we dream we are no longer bound to the reality of our waking lives, no longer slaves to the logic of the temporal world. There are no laws in dreams, they are ruled only by feelings and deep emotions."

Chapa took this in, though if he found value in it he did not share. He thought of Beatriz' little mirror, the one he kept always near, and wondered what reality was reflected within it

– did it also tell a deeper truth about the man it reflected? "Have I spoken before of the town where I was born?" he asked.

"Only that it is in a land near Spain. A peninsula. *Italia*, is that correct?" asked Francisco.

"Yes, it is a peninsula. Not like Iberia—four kingdoms united by one crown. Italia is a dizzying patchwork of principalities and republics. The Holy See is in *Italia*, as well as much land owing fealty to Spain or other great powers. Italians are constantly at odds with one another and have not been united since Roman times. It seems unlikely they ever will be again."

"Much like the tribes of the *Tejas* region," Francisco offered.

"Decidedly not," said Chapa, a little annoyed at the comparison, "The states of Italy are fragmented in the modern era, but they form the very foundation of civilization. They exceed all others in the arts of warfare, music, painting, sculpture, engineering, architecture and literature. It is their vibrancy which makes them fractious, not their barbarism."

"I apologize," said Francisco, "I spoke before I thought."

"We can forget it," said Chapa, easing his tone. "You know so little of the old world that I can't fault you for such ignorance. My own hometown of Villa Albisola Superiore is as unlike Tejas, or even Nuevo León, as the bottom of the sea is unlike the mountaintop. The first stones of the oldest building were laid down even before the Romans came. If there is an older place in Christendom I have never heard of it, although there are those in Cádiz who claim their city is the most ancient. It is a small town of weavers, fisherman, and traders, although it is most famous for the fine ceramics made there. The salt breeze wafts far inland and gives the olives that grow nearby a distinctive flavor. It is a beautiful place and I confess that I long for it more and more in these late days."

Chapa continued on, lost in reminiscence. "I was the third Giovanni Battista, you know. My uncle was the first, the man I would later serve in Cádiz. The second was my older brother, who lived and died in the year before I was born. My parents, Bartolome and Battistina, chose to give me his name. I wonder sometimes if I am living his life as well as mine; if I strived so hard to achieve enough for two, so that he might not have died in vain.

"My father was a farmer, though we had little in the way of land. He also worked alongside my grandfather at his little store and at the modest inn that he ran. Our family had a vineyard they called "Cavo," half a *labor* of farmland that he received as a dowry from my mother's brothers, a little plot that sat on a cliff above the sea. On that plot he also planted wheat as well as some vegetables and fruit to keep our family fed in the months before the grape harvest. The land was poor and we struggled in dry years to produce any harvest at all. My father was a good farmer, and no one worked harder, but the powerful families had long ago claimed the best land. People like us struggled on land that the richer families would have considered almost worthless.

"My father was a sturdy man, with a strong body and a face brown and lined from long hours in the sun. His hearty laugh and ready smile were famous throughout Albisola, as were his wit and humor in the tavern. He told me in his youth he nearly became a monk, tempted by a life of solitude, service, and prayer. However, my grandfather had no money to sponsor his education, so my father instead dedicated himself to God through his work as a farmer, husband and father. I always remember him with a smile on his face, and although he was a man of faith, he still loved a good joke."

"Don Juan, I am surprised to hear how much your family struggled. And to hear you speak of it, there were some in your homeland who were worse off than you," said Francisco.

"Oh surely," said Chapa, "as I said, my father was a small farmer, but he owned his own land, and was his own master. There were many who were serfs, tied to the land and the whims of their lord almost like the Indians under the old *encomienda*. Others were so destitute that they were dependent on the charity of the Church just to survive the winter."

"You may find it strange," said Francisco, "but the *mestizos* and Indians in New Spain often imagine the lands across the ocean to be kingdoms of vast riches. *Peninsulares* here all act as lords, so we only assume that all men there live the same way, in wealth and leisure."

"No matter how rich the soil or how majestic the architecture, in any land there must be men who rule and men who serve," said Chapa.

Francisco nodded, "Then the whole world is not so different."

"On that single principle, I suppose," said Chapa. "In any event, my father was his own master, but he had no formal education. He could scarcely read or write, but he had a wisdom and knowledge of the world that came from observing, thinking, and reflecting on the teachings of the priests and friars he came to know. He sometimes took their counsel too much to heart, sharing food with a poor widow when his own family could hardly afford the loss, or giving shelter to a winter traveler when his children slept three to a bed. Some derided him, saying that he was more monk than merchant, but I think he took quiet pride in this insult.

"He died when I was ten, overtaken by cholera far from home. He died alone." Chapa could feel his eyes well with tears, struck by the loss as if it had happened yesterday. "My God, Francisco, here I am, an old man crying over a father who died fifty years ago. Forgive me a moment."

Francisco had seen this many times—how the loss of a parent, even fifty years later, created a cavern of sorrow that could never be filled. He had walked away from his father on his own accord, and now, witnessing Chapa's pain, he felt ashamed to have abandoned him. "I never learned when or how my father died. But still, his absence also fills me with sadness."

"Our little vineyard was not enough to sustain the family and so each fall he set out to work the olive harvest on larger estates in the hills surrounding Albisola. He left in early November, and we never saw him again–receiving word only that he was buried in a mass grave with the other victims felled in the epidemic. It was so hard for me, as a young boy, to accept that he was really gone. For a solid year afterward, I used to catch myself watching the path up to the house, half expecting him to return."

Chapa's voice trailed away and his gaze turned out towards the mountains looming silently over the horizon, his thoughts drifting elsewhere. Francisco, not wanting to intrude on Chapa's reflection, stood up quietly and went to fetch another blanket.

***

Walking up the hill, I see my father at work tending the vines. I turn the corner, counting each step as I walk up towards the vineyard. He is looking away from me, out towards the sea, his hair matted with sweat and his shirt drenched in the hot summer sun. What's he thinking about? Slowly, a smile builds upon his face. I know that smile so well; it is his alone, springing from some secret corner of his own charmed inner world. How can a man like him, with so many burdens and cares, find such joy in every corner of life? And why does such joy elude me?

Turning around, he sees me and waves me to him. We sit together and drink the cool water Mama sent with me, talking about everything and nothing the way only we could do. Mama always laughed at us, chattering like a couple of crows.

Sitting in the shade we watch the bees meander back and forth to our little hive. "We are born with both good and bad instincts," he tells me, "but God gives us the power to decide how we respond to those instincts. Animals don't get to choose, they just react. Our power to decide is what makes us human, Giovanni. You must choose wisely and make thoughtful decisions, being careful not to let your mind fool you, convincing you that what you want is the right path. Your conscience is what makes you a child of God."

Pápa, are you smiling at me? Have I followed the right path, or have I just fooled myself?

***

"My mother died when I was a boy," said Francisco, as he tucked the blanket around Chapa's knees.

"Then you understand how terrible that loss is at such a tender age. It is said that each year closer to manhood, the loss of a parent is easier to bear, so I thank God he didn't take my father when I was eight instead of ten. But it was a terrible blow. And my poor mother outlived him by only a few months."

"What was she like? Do you look more like her or did you take after your father's family?"

"She was tall but slender. She married my father at just fifteen. Her own father had died and her brothers were eager to marry off their dependent sisters. Like all women of her station, she worked long and hard each day, cooking, washing, tending the garden, and of course caring for her children. She was always ill, made weaker still by grief — of her nine children, only three of us survived infancy. Much of the meager income from our farm went to purchase costly medicines. While she was never strong, I believe the loss of my father in the end was just too great," Chapa wiped his eyes again with his sleeve, and continued on with his narrative.

"When my mother died, my brother had already left for Spain, leaving me the head of my family at a precariously young age. At ten I could not manage even a small farm and my grandfather rented it out. While he did his best, the poor man simply had too many mouths to feed and fell so deeply into debt that he was imprisoned several times. When I was thirteen, my uncle Giovanni came to visit the family, and when he saw the state into which we had fallen, he took me back with him to Cádiz. And so I said my last goodbye to my *Nonna*, my sister Battistina and my little town by the sea."

"And you sailed here to New Spain?" Francisco asked.

"No, not yet," said Chapa. "To Spain herself. To Andalucía. But let us save that part of the story for a different time. Now that the sun has set I am cold, and hungry — you forgot about my bread and wine, and now the bread has likely grown stale."

"Of course," said Francisco, struggling to his feet, his legs stiff after sitting so long on the ground. He nodded and withdrew, taking the tray with him into the kitchen to revive the bread with a little water and griddle it in a little olive oil on the *fogón*.

***

<u>*Journal Entry – November 1650*</u>

I write this on the eve of my last night in Ciudad de México. Tomorrow I travel to the northern frontier in the service of Don Alonso de León, as secretary to his household and to the city of Cadereyta.

The decision to leave for the Nuevo Reino de León was made in haste, and many friends shake their heads at such a rash move. But in my bones I sense the possibilities of this new life. This marks an unexpected but welcome change for me–leaving the crowded capital for the unsettled frontier, yes, but also leaving commerce for a more learned and honorable profession, that of a scribe and jurist helping to bring order to an unsettled country.

I long for a place to truly call home, having lived a turbulent and unsettled life since I was a child of thirteen. When I traveled from Albisola to Cádiz with my uncle Giovanni, I left the settled warmth of my home and joined the ranks of the Genovese diaspora, a tribe of restless traders whose intricate network of colonies and family relationships make them the envy of all Christendom.

Cádiz then was bustling with the trade of the Indies, and I loved the energy and excitement of the port. Although burnt to the ground in 1596 by the Earls of Essex and Nottingham, the city had come back to life even stronger, and by then was the home port for the flota, crowded with merchants and bankers from all over the world.

The Genovese merchants, though, are the smartest and most powerful traders in the city and have been in Cádiz for centuries. Most have become almost completely assimilated, marrying Spanish or Portuguese women and adopting Spanish customs and language. Even so, they maintain strong family connections back to Genoa and to the other trading colonies scattered in distant lands, allowing us to trade goods and arrange credit with an ease that no other people could match.

During my six years in Cádiz, I grew to manhood and learned how the Genovese trade was conducted. After my disagreement – I shall not write of it here or elsewhere – with my uncle's partner, I approached the Giustiniani family and begged for an opening in their house in New Spain. Finally agreeing to take me on, they arranged passage for me on the flota leaving for Veracruz within the month—even paying the requisite bribe needed to get past the prohibitions against the emigration of foreigners, requiring only that I commit 18 months of service to their consulado.

After a miserable few months in Veracruz, I finally arrived in Ciudad de México in the summer of 1647, finding a city that was in many ways grander even than Seville—busier and wealthier and with a variety of people and goods that was truly dizzying.

In these last two and one half years, I've served the Giustiniani with loyalty and diligence, and my skills as a merchant have grown apace with my effort. However, I long ago realized that a merchant's life was not for me, and resumed my clandestine studies in law, believing it to be an honorable profession that would better suit my nature.

Last month, as I was leaving our house to attend to my studies, I stumbled across the corpse of a slave that worked for another consulado, and who had been abandoned to the streets when he fell too ill to work. The sight of that old black slave filled me with such sorrow and disgust that I vowed then and there that I would find a post, any post, that would allow me to escape a life founded in such greed and cruelty.

Tomorrow I take my final and decisive step into a life that I hope will bring me both honor and peace. May God protect me on this journey.

CHAPTER 9

Good Masters

One morning Francisco received an emissary at Chapa's door, a young messenger who brought word that the Governor of Nuevo Reino de León, Juan Pérez de Merino, would pay a visit to the esteemed Don Juan Bautista Chapa that afternoon— provided of course the old man was in sufficient health to receive the visit.

In truth, Chapa's health had substantially improved with each passing day. Whether it was his naturally strong constitution, the attentive care provided by Francisco, or the favor of the good Lord, he found himself climbing step-by-step out of a valley from which, in his heart of hearts, he suspected only a few days prior he might never escape.

But the old man was vain and jealous of his prestige in this *reino* and so became greatly agitated at the notion of a visit from the governor, even if it was a governor three decades his junior with whose administration Don Juan found many faults. Even in this sparsely populated town—which in Spain or Italy would be the merest village, undocumented on all but the most thorough map—this was a royal governor, appointed personally by a king who ruled an empire greater than any the world had ever known. There was no overstating the visit's importance.

So Francisco went to work making the already tidy house even more orderly. He then helped Chapa out of bed for the first time in over a week and into his finest attire. Francisco combed his master's hair, but Chapa kept running his fingers through it agitatedly.

Francisco hastily walked to the merchant, breathing unusually heavily, and purchased several types of wine. He returned and, under mild protest, set three different species of fowl to roast over the hearth, and prepared three different *salsas* to serve with the fresh tortillas that had been delivered that morning. Francisco reminded Chapa that the messenger had said nothing about supper, but his master was not to be dissuaded.

At long last the young governor and his even younger secretary, Rodrigo Ulías, arrived at the door. Francisco gave them entry, and they joined Chapa in his sitting room. The governor was adorned in the latest fashion (although the unavoidable delay in transmission from Madrid meant he was almost certainly dressed in last year's style). He carried a sabre at his side but was otherwise unarmed and unarmored. His secretary was much more simply dressed, in keeping with the tradition established by Chapa in his long years holding that post.

"I thank you for your hospitality, Don Juan," said the governor. "I hope this hastily announced visit is not too great an inconvenience."

"Far from it, your Excellency," said Chapa, "You do me too much honor. This humble house has not been graced by a governor of this *reino* in years."

Chapa of course held the office of the governorship in far greater esteem than the man himself. In truth, most of the governors he had known were incompetents, and few held their post more than a few years (there were six different governors in 1681 alone.) But the great ones shaped the office and the land around it. And none was greater than Martín de Zavala, who led for forty years and whom Chapa esteemed above all others.

They sat for nearly an hour and discussed many topics relating to the administration of Nuevo León. On some matters, times had passed the old man by, and Francisco could plainly see the governor was merely humoring him. But on other issues, more fundamental to the unique and persistent challenges of this unforgiving frontier, Francisco could see that the words of his learned master found their target, even at times when the governor did not expect them — or welcome them. Chapa lit up at these moments; he was valuable again if only for a few fleeting minutes.

After the men washed their hands in a porcelain bowl filled with cool, clean water, Francisco carried in the elaborate meal he had spent the bulk of the day preparing. The governor picked at a few dishes idly, and the secretary consumed a quite substantial portion of the capon, but Chapa ate almost nothing, sipping his wine mixed with water and nibbling on a rolled up tortilla sprinkled with salt.

At the end of the hour, the secretary reminded the governor of an imminent appointment, and the governor made a prolonged apology at the brevity of his stay. Chapa of course expressed his pain at their parting, but in truth he was tiring quickly and would soon find it almost impossible to maintain the façade of a man in good health.

As he stood, the governor said, "Oh, Don Juan, I almost forgot to mention — in two weeks' time our *reino* will be honored by an official visit from the Most Reverend Bishop Juan de Santiago y León Garabito. He travels here at great effort from Guadalajara, so I dearly hope you will be sufficiently recovered in joining us to receive him."

Chapa was taken aback, "What brings His Excellency to our town?"

"A pastoral visit, of course. Nuevo León is small but it is growing. And it has been nearly ten years since he last traveled here. Because he is visiting only Monterrey, and has no time for similar visits to Saltillo or Cerralvo, he has asked that the visit be kept quiet, with no official record of the visit in either our records or those of the Diocese."

Chapa nodded distractedly, his mind racing. A secret visit? With Francisco's subtle help, Chapa stood to see his guests to the door.

"I know the Bishop is very keen to meet you at long last, Don Juan," said the governor. "He has heard a great deal about your service to my predecessors as well as your tireless scholarship. Good day, *señor*."

"Good day."

Chapa watched them leave and quickly became too weak to stand.

***

After the governor's departure, Francisco returned Chapa to his bed. The old man was shaking and Francisco wrapped him in all the remaining blankets in the house. Concerned that his illness would reverse course, Francisco decided it was best to sit by his master's side and let the pots and dishes lie dirty for the moment.

Chapa was quiet, lost in thought. Francisco knew better than to make undesired conversation with his master, so he too sat silently. He wondered if his master would forgive him if he took another book from the shelf, but Chapa broke the silence before he worked up the courage to ask.

"Francisco," Chapa said.

"Yes, Don Juan," replied Francisco.

"How did you come to Nuevo León?" Chapa asked.

"By what means?" Francisco said, unsure what his master was driving at.

"You said your parents met in Jalisco, no? I assume you were also born there?" asked Chapa.

Francisco was honestly quite surprised that his master recalled the details of their little game. Chapa had been so eager to guess Francisco's *casta* identity and seemingly so little interested in the events that brought him there. But here the question was.

"You are correct, Don Juan," said Francisco, "I was indeed born in Jalisco."

This seemed to please Chapa a little. "I have never been there. It is a mining region, is it not?"

"Principally, yes. Though there are small farms through the region. None so vast as the holdings of the great men of Nuevo León, of course," said Francisco.

"Well, it is not a simple comparison," said Chapa, "Cattle require much more land than wheat or grapes. And a wise farmer would rather have a single *labor* of good rich soil, with ample rain and sun, than tenfold that acreage of dry and windswept earth."

"You know much more than I about the matter," said Francisco.

"Did you not work a farm in your youth, Francisco?" asked Chapa.

"I did not," said Francisco, "so I can offer little in the knowledge of farming. My father was educated in the local Jesuit school for young *mestizos*. He could not enter the regional administration or the Church, but he could receive training as a journeyman carpenter. In those lands, the great mines require wooden beams and frames to keep the mine from collapsing on the mineworkers within. So a skilled carpenter is highly valued. A badly made joint can mean the death of a dozen miners, a great expense and delay to the mine owner," said Francisco.

"And a great loss for their families, it should be added," said Chapa.

"Yes, of course," answered Francisco. "By the time I grew to be a man, my father was a master carpenter, one of the most respected in all Jalisco. I apprenticed under him and slowly learned the trade."

"Why then did you not stay in Jalisco and continue what your father had built?" Chapa asked. "Many a craftsman has built an even greater reputation on the foundation laid by his father."

"A young man does not often see so far ahead," said Francisco, "or at least, the young man that I once was did not."

"You continue to surprise me, Francisco," said Chapa. "Did you continue to enrich your skills after leaving your father's side?"

112

"Like him I tried to be a better carpenter each day than I was the last. I have not seen him since I left home those many years ago. He was a great craftsman when I left, and I expect his skill only increased since that day," said Francisco.

"Could you, for instance, construct a table as fine as this?" asked Chapa, pointing at the table at his bedside, "Or a bookshelf as elegant, balanced, and strong as the one in my study?"

Francisco chuckled, "I did make that bookshelf. When I was a much younger man, and you were still in the service of Don Martín Zavala."

"What?" asked Chapa, with genuine surprise. "That very one? Such a remarkable coincidence, that you built my bookshelf, so long ago." Chapa marveled. "Don't you think so? There's much that I wouldn't have guessed about you, Francisco."

Francisco shrugged, "I spent many years building furniture for the great landholders and merchants of this *reino*. There are very few fine homes that don't have at least one piece of my work. I rarely think of it."

"That bookcase was a treasured gift from Governor Zavala, you know. Until then—I was nearly thirty, if I recall—I still kept my books in the trunk with which I crossed the ocean, the same one that now holds my papers. When Don Martín one day gave me a book as a gift, he saw the manner in which I stored them. He laughed at the jumble of books in the trunk and ordered the construction of the case for me. Little did I know that you were the one given the commission. It is a beautiful piece of work."

"Thank you, Don Juan," said Francisco humbly, glad that his work was appreciated for the artistry and not merely its function. "Because I built it for the governor, I gave it special care and attention. I still consider it one of my best."

"Don Martín was a remarkable man, was he not?" asked Chapa wistfully. "I am not sure Nuevo León will ever see his equal. When he first spoke Tuscan to me, I believed for a moment that I had finally encountered a native of my homeland. But he is no more Tuscan than you are Polish, Francisco. I am told his mastery of Flemish, a language of which I know next to nothing, was superb, and his French and Latin were without equal. Such a rare thing to find such an educated man in such a remote region, more unusual still given the circumstances of his birth." Chapa paused, a smile on his face as he remembered those better times. Francisco considered interjecting but decided to let Chapa continue to muse.

"When Don Martín enlisted me in his service I had grown very unhappy in Cadereyta. I dearly loved my wife and children but felt my talents were being wasted and the ambitions of my youth slowly dying on the vine. I was keeping the most mundane and simple accounts for frontier *haciendas*, knowing that I might have been an attorney at the court in Ciudad de México. I wondered why I had forsaken the chance to build a real career to take my chances out here in the frontier of Nuevo León.

"I don't know why the climb up the hill is always more interesting than actually seeing the view from the top, but for me, it's just the trying that beckons me. The rest does not concern me. All my life I had chosen the riskier, harder but more exciting path. But at that time I was disillusioned with where the road had taken me and secretly regretted the boldness of my earlier years, although I was too ashamed to confide this to anyone, not even Beatriz, especially not Beatriz.

"Don Martín was even older then than I am now, but he had an energy and curiosity about the world that made him seem a much younger man. He was fascinated with all of the latest experiments and theorems of the natural philosophers. He knew so much more than I did—I was always interested in matters of science and mathematics, but compared to him I was just a poor student. If a philosopher tells me light is composed of fire, I think it composed of fire. If he tells me instead that light is composed of air, I will adjust and believe it to be composed of air. But Don Martín considered and challenged each idea on its own merits. He would marvel at the work of one great philosopher and angrily challenge the work of another, or even a different work by the same philosopher he once praised! As my son hinted in his visit, he was particularly fond of Cartesius, though access to his works was very difficult in those days—and of course, they are now forbidden."

Chapa found himself sitting up and feeling somewhat recovered from the governor's painful visit. Francisco knew from experience that there were few subjects that animated him as much as talking about Zavala. Francisco often thought it strange that such an accomplished and learned man could still be so enamored, almost worshipful, of those he considered his superiors.

"Even in matters of administration and law, he was without equal. He had never studied the law, but still knew the most practical way to write a deed or draft an administrative order, so that they reflected the true intent and nature of the law itself. In these things he taught me so much. But alas, my time with Don Martín was all too brief. Though he governed this territory for forty years, I was in his service but two. I learned more in those two years than I did in sixty others, but they still went by far too quickly."

Chapa drifted into quiet reflection. Francisco spoke only because he sensed—how, he could not say—his master's thoughts were drifting again to more painful memories.

"We servants often wonder, Don Juan, what makes a good master different from a bad one. An angry or violent master is naturally worse than a kind and generous one. That is a simple thing. But many servants find themselves admiring a master who is dour over another who is genial. I wonder if there is some hidden quality that makes some men easier to serve. I know you did not serve these governors with your pen in the same way I did with my hammer and saw, but the question still comes to me: you served so many governors, what was it that separated Don Martín from the others?"

"No, no. You are right Francisco. More than almost any *peninsular* here in Nuevo León, I know what it is like to live as a servant, albeit in a more elevated fashion. With respect to Zavala, in truth it wasn't his learning or his great stature as a leader which made Don Martín a man of such rare quality. It was the simple way he behaved toward his fellow man that made him so admirable to me. In the morning he might confer over the gravest of military matters, planning a campaign or discussing the murderous intent of the savage enemy, and yet that same afternoon mediate a squabble between two petty merchants over an agreed upon price for grain. He showed the same grace and patience with his servants that he did with a visiting royal messenger. Looking back, I wish I had taken the example of his conduct more to heart."

"All the servants and laborers that I knew in those days were in agreement," said Francisco, "He was a great master."

Chapa nodded and said, "I pray that Nuevo León will see his like again, Francisco. I should soon go to sleep. Please bring me Beatriz's mirror before you return to your duties."

Francisco lit a candle, placing it on the table next to the bed and then brought the mirror to his master. Chapa thanked him, excused him for the evening and asked him to close the door. After Francisco departed, Chapa sat in quiet thought for a few moments, then crossed to the study, opened his trunk, and pulled out one of his battered old journals. Returning to his bed, he opened an old book and once again stepped into the past.

***

Journal Entry: 28 September, 1662

Today was a day of such importance that I must record for all time the details and their significance.

This afternoon I was working at the Governor's office, attending to my ordinary administrative duties, when Governor Zavala stood over me at my writing table and announced that we would end the day early. He then extended to me an invitation to join him for supper at his home. Never before had I, a humble secretary, been invited to the home of such a great man. I sent word to Beatriz that she need not tell the servants to prepare a tray for me, as they typically did when I worked late in the evening.

We traveled by carriage to his hacienda, *which was over two* leguas *away but reached quickly over the new road the governor had ordered constructed. The* hacienda *is grand, a graceful collection of buildings in the new* Plateresco *style, with beautiful arcades surrounding a large, cool patio, and a little chapel off to one side. On*

116

the grounds were a large garden, orchards, and corrals for his many fine horses, which did not resemble in the least the small, surefooted mounts of the common Spaniard here in New Spain. The Governor had the finest Andalucían horses in all of Nuevo León and took great pride in their exalted pedigrees – their parentage recorded in large books, with bloodlines stretching back to the time of the Moorish invasion of Andalucía.

We sat together – as if equals! – in the cool magnificence of his dining room and shared a late afternoon meal. Colorful tiles from Talavera lined the walls, and we sat on heavy oak furniture in the style from the reign of Emperor Carlos V. Massive doors opened onto the patio, shaded by lemon and orange trees, and lively with the sound of birds hanging in pretty brass cages from their branches. Throughout, we were serenaded by the low, sweet murmur of a small fountain.

Don Martín pointed out the little sirena, carved from cantera stone. "Her pitcher is fed from a little spring up on the hill," he said, "I spent months working out the calculations and engineering the clay pipes that carry the water to the center of the patio, opening up the floor of the kitchen to lay them down. We always have fresh clean water and the whole house is healthy because of it."

We were served silently by two young Indians, who demonstrated such perfect manner and service that they might have been at the court in Madrid. As Don Martín and I ate, he recounted how he had come to reside in this far corner of the Empire. He told me, without shame or hesitation, that he was the illegitimate son of one Don Augustín de Zavala, one of the original miners in Zacatecas, and one of the wealthiest men in New Spain. Don Martín said that his father had taught him never to apologize or be ashamed of his parentage, telling him, "Never give others the chance to look down on you or question your worth before God. Stand tall, and they will be forced to treat you as an equal."

After we finished dining on delicate little antojitos, roasted codornices with salsa rojo, and a fluffy arroz flavored with tomato and carrot, Don Martín pushed himself away from the table and motioned to the smaller of the two indios to fetch a bottle of a curious new brandy made from agave in a small town near Jalisco called Tequila. He bade me join in him in his library and led the way along the shaded patio and through the doors of his magnificent library, our steps echoing in the cool arcades of the patio, our reflections following us in the panes of glass, a rare luxury in Nuevo León. The smell of leather, paper, tobacco, and dust brought forth a rush of memories – of my days in the library at the university, the great Casa de las Indias I once visited in Sevilla, and even the small library my uncle kept in his house in Cádiz. In taste, if not in volume, Don Martín's exceeded them all.

He invited me to inspect his collection of books arranged on his shelves. There must have been at least three hundred books in Tuscan and other Italian dialects, with hundreds more in Castilian, Latin, French, and Flemish. He even possessed a few books in German, Polish, and English, which he did not speak but aspired to translate someday. They were organized not by language but by subject, from the great works of classical Greece (in Latin, of course) to translations of Arabic texts on algebra, medicine, and astronomy. As I perused the stacks, I couldn't help but to line up the spines perfectly against the edge of the shelves. Don Martín noticed the intense absorption in my face and laughingly suggested that if the Inquisitor knew he had some of these books he could be prosecuted – as if they would dare challenge his status and authority.

As we sat in the cool dim library, his servants served us a sweet wine made in the style of Oporto. I peppered him with questions about his library and we talked for hours about some of his favorite texts. It has been years since my mind has been so stimulated.

***

Journal Entry – 19 October, 1662

I write this entry on page 57 of this book (Seneca's Epistles) and in my native language. I need to write down my swirling thoughts so that I can bring some order to my mind, but I must keep them from the sight of others.

Last week, Don Martín told me about a new book that Alonso de León brought back from Spain. It had to be carried at the very bottom of Don Alonso's trunk, because it was the work of a notorious Frenchman who was writing and working recklessly in the Protestant city of Leiden, in the rebellious province of Holland. Although the man, René Descartes, was a confirmed and practicing Catholic, his thoughts are considered quite disruptive. He believed fervently in God but

118

argued that man could reach such a belief through reason alone – that moral virtue could be reached through the calculations of the mortal mind alone. Don Martín admitted only to finding these dangerous ideas amusing, but clearly he also considered them serious enough to share with me.

Before I left, he gave me his own copy of The Ingenious Gentleman Don Quixote of La Mancha, the most treasured book of my youth. He knew I had lost my copy in México, and so he wanted me to have this one. He asked that I read it over the next few weeks and invited me to come to his house every Thursday to discuss it. On these visits, he would also have me continue to read his copy of Descartes's treatise, Meditations of First Philosophy. While Don Martín felt safe from suspicion, he could not risk lending me his copy of Meditations, in case someone accessed my library. He invited me to treat his library as my own so that I may continue to educate myself.

Don Martín had enjoyed more than a few glasses of wine when he made this request, but it was clear to me his intentions were sincere and that he, like me, longs for an opportunity to engage in a more intellectual discourse than commonly found in this crude, rustic land. While he loves his homeland, it is clear that this kind of intellectual stimulation cannot easily be found here in Nuevo León.

Don Martín is quite enamored with Descartes – or, should I say, his ideas. For Don Martín holds no idols but the truth, and believes Descartes's concepts around methodic doubt will have a profound impact on philosophical thought. He also told me that Descartes was so arrogant that he initially wrote this manuscript anonymously, in order to see what his contemporaries would say about it. Who would write such a book and not take credit for it?

Before I left, Don Martín grabbed my arm and said abruptly, "The next time we meet, I want your thoughts on Don Quixote's visit to the Cave of Montesinos and what it says about the confrontation of two worlds in Quixote's mind–the chivalric and the real. More to the point, ponder this one question as you read: how do you know at any moment in time that you are awake and not dreaming? And do not give me a tautology. How can you truly know?"

His intellect is like none I have known and his challenge to my own is both exciting and humbling. I have spent these last two weeks pondering the nature of truth and imagination, trying to tease out a *position on the line between illusion and reality. I want to be ready to acquit myself well in my next conversation with Don Martín.*

***

Chapa lay down the journal entries, lost in thought about those long ago discussions and how they had changed him, made him a man beset with questions and doubts about all sorts of things. It had obsessed him for a while, that ceaseless questioning and scribbling. As a result, his thinking became both clearer and more obfuscated. He was both more open to the world, and more secretive in his habits, hiding his writing between the lines of books, guarding his tongue even more carefully, especially when it came to conversations about the Church or the practices of the Crown. At the end of the day, it was that metamorphosis that led him to defy Governor de Vidagaray, placing himself and his family at great peril. A curious mind is clearly a dangerous thing in this *reino* or any other under the Spanish crown, and because of it, he feared that the development of Nuevo León, like the rest of New Spain, would continue to be stunted and slow.

He set his papers down and picked up the mirror. Instead of his own reflection, a young man's face looked back at him. The young man seemed so familiar, but he couldn't quite place his face.

***

What's wrong with you tonight, Giovanni? Are you afraid that you won't be able to sleep? Does your conscience bother you? Of course you are very tired. You've been awake for sixty-six years. Have you finally earned your rest? No. Not yet. You haven't finished reckoning with the past. In truth you've barely started. You love thinking back to the elevated conversations with Zavala, your impassioned pursuit of truth. You think it sets you apart, don't you, makes you stand above the common clay of lust and greed on which this land was built. But you weren't really above it, were you? Did you put those baser thoughts down in your journals? Did you record them for posterity? Are they all written down next to your fevered search for answers?

I pretend to be better, but in my heart I am as full of sin as any man. I know how I lusted after the *negrita*, in particular one black slave, the one I saw on the pier in Veracruz amongst the other miserable chattel. Although I write about loathing slavery, I stared without shame, as if she were a statue on the boulevard or a fine horse owned by a friend.

I saw her living flesh in the bright morning sun, ripe young flesh, but I didn't see the woman. Not the whole woman at least. A collection of parts that might, upon later reflection, make a woman, but not then. Her breasts drew me first, of course, round and taut, her dark nipples so like another's. The sunlight revealed every contour. How I longed to touch them.

Her lips pouted forth from her mouth. Plump and soft, I knew exactly what they would feel like. Taste like. Her lip was bloodied. Did she bite it in her nervousness, waiting to find out which leering man would own her? Or had she been struck? Did I even care? I remember her round ass and long legs, those soft thighs between which I longed to lie.

You wondered, didn't you, what it would it be like to lie on top of her? To own her. To do whatever you wished to her. If you met their price, her flesh would be yours. She herself would not own a piece of it. You would be its sole master. You wondered what would it be like to be inside of her. Would she have given herself willingly? Or would she have resisted? Fought you with clenched muscles and screams?

But you did lie with her, didn't you? You could not of course afford her that day, a man of just 19 years of age, with not a peso to your name. But you possessed her anyway from that day forward — long after she was taken away from that pier in chains. You were with her, weren't you, when you lay with Beatriz. You slept with your beautiful Beatriz but you still thought of her, that black flesh you gazed upon for scarcely ten minutes.

Beatriz never knew, I could never tell her, but I did it all the same. The sins in my thoughts are the same as if I had taken her that day; God doesn't care that I couldn't afford her. He knows the crimes of my heart and cares little for the accounting. If I enjoyed the pleasure of lying with her in my thoughts, don't I have to pay the price as well?

Think of her face, can you? Is it a stranger's, or one that you held dear long ago? It is easy to focus on that casual lust, but those fantasies hide a much darker sin.

***

Though the night was still young, Chapa put down the mirror, flushed with shame in remembering that long ago lust, but reminded once again that it was not even close to the greatest of his sins. He went to his bed and knelt to pray.

CHAPTER 10

Journeys and Expeditions

Chapa woke early the next morning and declared to Francisco that he would finally leave his bed and return to his neglected work. Francisco suggested caution but Chapa was insistent. And so Francisco helped his master dress in his typical daily clothes and shoes. He prepared a small morning meal of eggs scrambled with onions and fresh cactus served with a few tortillas. And for the first time in many days, Francisco set out a vial of black ink and sharpened anew the nibs of three quill pens. Chapa was back in his study at long last. The return to the exacting rhythm of his daily routine soothed Chapa, who had grown increasingly uneasy with the shapelessness of his days. He began by reading the section of the *Historia* that he had been revising and editing before he fell ill.

***

La Historia del Nuevo Reino de León, Chapter 33

They made camp in a good location and, with only fourteen men, De León approached the Frenchman's habitation, which was a room of buffalo hides. Arranging for ten of the soldiers to remain on horseback, General Alonso de León with Fray Buonaventura Bonal (a friar, who was going along as chaplain) and General Martín de Mendiondo dismounted and entered this habitation — although there were more than six hundred Indians in this encampment, and forty-two standing guard with their weapons in their hands.

In the most spacious part of this habitation, the Frenchman was seated on buffalo hides, as if they were a throne. Two Indians were fanning him and others were cleaning his face. When the priest approached, the Frenchman did no more than — without leaving his seat — bend his knees, kiss the sleeve of his habit, and show great courtesy to the governor and to General Martín de Mendiondo by giving them his hand and saying, "I, Frenchman." The Frenchman asked the governor carefully how many soldiers had come, to which (heeding the malice with which he must be asking him) the governor answered, "Many." Then to ingratiate himself to the Indians, the governor called for valuables he had brought for them, including blouses, skirts, knives, earrings, tobacco, etc. He turned them over to the Frenchman so that he could distribute them to the Indians with his own hand. The Frenchman was decorated on the face in the Indian manner and knew their language very well.

The governor told the Frenchman, through an interpreter, that he was to go with him. The Frenchman resisted — and the Indians did the same — but by diligence they captured him from his encampment.

Excerpted directly from the book *"La Historia del Nuevo Reino de León"* by Juan Bautista Chapa

***

Chapa then went to his trunk, opened it again, and this time, perhaps because of the way that Francisco had earlier questioned the accuracy of the accounts recorded by the *Historia*, sorted through the different bundles of documents until he came across a tattered journal from those same years. Pulling it out, he sat on the lid of the trunk, rifling through the pages until finally settling on a passage from one of his expeditions.

***

Journal Entry: Expedition in Search of the French, 12 April, 1689

The heat today was sweltering. De León had us afoot at least nine hours, and would have made us walk for another three unless we found a stream or at least some shade where we might break for the night. Rodrigo was behind me, bitching and complaining as usual; that day, however, he was just saying what everyone was thinking. 'What the hell are we doing here?'

The air is so hot and humid, and water so scarce, that we had to walk the horses to spare them. I have spent years wondering why on God's earth people chose to settle in Monterrey, but the country we crossed today makes it look like Paradise. Nothing but miles of low brush, alkaline swamps, skittering lizards – worthless for anything – no springs, no rivers, nothing but flat scrubby plain. De León kept checking his map; in truth, I don't think he even knew where we were going – there wasn't a landmark anywhere that could tell us where we were. Not even the damn Indians had use for this place; we kept looking for trails but all we saw were the natural gaps and deer paths that made us think we were actually going somewhere. My feet were so blistered that the flies buzzed around my boots, attracted by the blood.

We are now ten days into the expedition and have found not a single human soul. If de León's information is correct, we should have seen a sign of the worthless French by now. The Tejas Indian who sold that map to him is laughing somewhere, I'm sure. I know that de León has pursued this folly to prove himself an heir to his father's reputation, but we could walk until next year and he would still not be a quarter of the man his father was. So old now, I don't belong on these expeditions; I can barely ride for six hours, much less walk. Why must I still play at being a conquistador? *Is it my loyalty to de León's father that keeps me here? Or to our* reino? *Or is it something else entirely?*

Later in the day, as we searched for water, I heard a cruel snap, and the heavy fall of a man's body. My stomach heaved and my hair stood on end–in some way your gut knows the sound of a breaking bone even before it registers in your ear. Rodriguez was on the ground, his hands wrapped around his shin, trying to push his bone back under the skin. I tried to whistle at de León, but choked on my own

125

bile. Rodriguez finally caught his breath and started screaming. We will camp here tonight, and if Rodriguez survives I will drag him back to Monterrey. If he dies I am to bury him and ride to regain the group. Honestly, I am praying for his survival as much for my own sake as for his–I have no stomach for this journey and long to return to my Beatriz, who I left ill and in bed.

15 April, 1689

By the grace of God, Rodriguez has now survived three days and I am managing with difficulty the journey back to Monterrey. If all goes well we should reach home within three days. This star-crossed expedition is so miserable that I have suffered the most intense regret I have ever felt for leaving Liguria.

Oh, to lay just once more in the warmth of the setting sun, the breeze off the sea with its saline tang, carrying with it the scents of lavender and lemon and rose from my mother's garden; the colors of the house matching the evening glow of the hills, a color like nothing else in the world. If I close my eyes, I can almost taste the olive oil, fresh and peppery, just pressed from the olive trees ringing the house. The flowers, leaning out of the balconies like pretty girls, like the pretty girls swinging as they walked past our house, laughing because they knew their whole lives stretched ahead like a smooth, well-tended path. Life there was like one of the old Roman roads, worn smooth with tradition, warm and predictable and as solid as a thousand years of history, culture and custom.

But in the end, my mind turns always towards Beatriz, my Beatriz with the laughing face. Don't laugh at me, sweet wife, just remind me that I have a good life. My choices brought me to you after all, warmer than any sunset in Liguria.

***

126

Though he had counseled against it, Francisco found himself relieved to see his master once again behind the old desk. Chapa's recovery had been slow but steady, with few serious setbacks. Francisco had found himself increasingly fatigued over the days of Chapa's convalescence. His days were always taxing, but the effort to both maintain the house and attend to the sick man's constant needs was proving too much for a single servant. Now perhaps he could rest, even steal a short nap after he returned from the market. He'd wait for the steady, pulsing scratch of Chapa's pen to lull him to sleep . . .

"Francisco," Chapa called out, "Shall we continue our discussion of the *Historia?*"

His nap would have to wait. Francisco turned around and returned to the study. "Of course, Don Juan, but don't you need some time to work first?" Francisco said, hovering in the doorway, leaning heavily against the frame.

"Not at all. This is the foremost work in front of me. I must review this *Historia*, and whether you know it or not, the thought your questions provoke has been quite useful."

"Thank you, Don Juan." Francisco sat down at the stool across from Don Juan's desk and waited for Chapa's inquiry to commence.

"So" said Chapa, "where shall we begin?"

"Wherever it suits you, Don Juan," answered Francisco.

"What is another chapter that stimulated your inquisitive nature?" asked Chapa.

Francisco thought for a moment before answering. Chapa was in a feisty mood, almost combative, though if he was merely playful from the vigor of his recovery or driven by darker impulses, Francisco could not tell. He chose to answer warily.

"The entire *Historia* fulfills my inquisitive nature, Don Juan. I have learned so much about the history of our land. More than any man with Indian blood, I imagine. It is a great privilege."

"It is a privilege I am happy to bestow. Now that you have puffed up your master with the requisite flattery, fire your first arrow, Francisco."

Francisco ruffled a little at the mention of an arrow even as a metaphor—he was no pagan Indian, nor had any man in his family been for generations—but of course said nothing of it.

"I suppose one passage that greatly interested me, Don Juan, was the daring expedition to find the Frenchman across the Rio Bravo del Norte. This expedition was only a few years ago, was it not?"

The mention of this event seemed to brighten Chapa's spirits further. "Only four years ago," he nodded. "Though already an old man, I was not so weak then. I was not actually present when they met the Frenchman, but Don de León took excellent notes. What is it about the expedition that interests you, Francisco?"

"The feat itself fascinates me greatly, taking scarcely a dozen men across the great river into the most dangerous of savage Indian lands. But also, I wonder why such a venture was necessary to retrieve a single man," said Francisco.

"You question why we would travel at such great risk and expense for a lone Frenchman?" asked Chapa.

Francisco nodded. "Yes. He was not a kidnapped *ranchero* or a *peninsular* woman. In fact, if I understand your *Historia* correctly, the governor had only a rumor of this French gentleman. I could never of course question the wisdom of great men such as Governor Don Francisco Cuervo and General Alonso de León, but I do not understand why you took such a risk for such a small prize."

"You err, Francisco, in thinking the Frenchman was to us like a kidnapped Spaniard, a civilized man whom we wished to rescue from death or indignity. In fact, he was quite the opposite. His presence only a few dozen leagues from our frontier was a mortal threat. You see, the savage Indian is a great danger to we Christians here in this land, a threat with which we must contend year after year--like the bear or the mountain lion. He is vicious but instinctive in his wrath. He is a force of nature—a test from God for the Spaniard to overcome and, eventually, to civilize. The Frenchman, however, is more than just a danger, he is an *enemy*. On the continent in which I was born, the kings of Spain and the kings of France have fought so many wars over the centuries that few can recall their origin. Even as I left Spain, the two great kingdoms were still embroiled in the bloodiest war known since ancient times, a series of unending battles in the Germanies that drew in every great king and lord in Christendom for thirty years. The two great leagues, Catholic and Protestant, fought until not a single village in the German lands was unmarred by devastation and death. And of course treacherous France, Catholic—or so she claims—fought on the side of the heretical Protestants. Now and always she is our implacable enemy."

"The King of France seems fearsome indeed," said Francisco, "and were his armies marching on Nuevo León I understand why the governor would take every measure to fight him. But can a single Frenchman truly be so terrible?"

Chapa smiled. He often suspected Francisco feigned ignorance at times, a defensive tactic among slaves and servants he had observed throughout his life, but on this subject the old *mestizo* was clearly out of his depth. "You're right, of course, that Frenchman alone was no great threat to us," Chapa said, "Nor would he be, even if he were at the head of the fierce Indian tribe which protected him. The menace he posed was not in physical violence to the settlers of our *reino* but in the skulking and spying he no doubt intended. His intention was almost certainly to provide intimate knowledge of Nuevo León to the French crown—its rivers and roads, our militia's strengths and vulnerabilities.'

"But why would France covet these lands, Don Juan? There is so much land north of the Rio Bravo still unsettled by Christians. Surely there is more than enough for each great king to possess his heart's fill."

Chapa chuckled. "You think of a king as if he were a man such as I, or Don Lazaro de Avila, a man whose desire for earthly pleasures can be sated by an estate rich and vast enough to satisfy any material need. A man who might rest when he has accumulated sufficient wealth and prestige to ensure the comfort of his children and his children's children. But we are taught to believe that a king is more than a man, Francisco. He reaches his lofty position not by his labor and ingenuity, nor even, solely, by the fortune of his regal birth. According to our customs and traditions, he is appointed by God himself to rule. A great lord's estate may fall into ruin, and his title may wither away into obscurity, but a king's rule is believed to be divine and eternal. As his title is absolute so is his obligation to increase the power and wealth of his kingdom.

"The king of Castile, for instance, was once merely first amongst equals in Iberia, nothing more than an elder brother to his fellow kings of León, Navarra, Portugal, Valencia, Catalonia, and Aragon. But God desired that all these lands be united under one king who would rule a great Empire that spans the earth. His only rivals now are the *musulmán* Turkish Sultan and the treacherous King of France, and so to serve God's will, the King must contest these great rivals on every sea and continent on this earth, until at last His Most Catholic Majesty is triumphant."

Chapa was somewhat surprised to hear himself expounding on these points, as privately he had his own doubts about how invested God was in the fortunes of one King over another, equally Christian King. Still, in the face of Francisco's questioning, he felt he had to explain the way the Spanish Kings justify their dominion.

Francisco reflected on all of this. He never ceased to marvel at these tales of the clash of empires, so unlike the small and messy skirmishes and raids he had witnessed in this frontier. Fighting in his eyes was deadly but often comical — the foibles and acts of cowardice he had seen in battles far outweighed the noble acts of courage. But surely across the ocean things were different. "I wonder then," Francisco said, "if the men of France are so fearsome, why do so many men in Spanish lands, such as I, bear their name?"

"Bear their name?" asked Chapa, mystified.

"The Franciscan brothers who spread the word of Christ. Does not their name, like mine, mean 'French'?"

"The workings of your mind never fail to surprise me, Francisco, but in this matter you are mistaken. Your name does of course derive from the word "France," as does the common name we use for the most pious Order of the Friars Minor. But both words honor not men of France but that most humble of saints, St. Francis."

"Was San Francisco not a Frenchman, Don Juan?"

"In fact he was not. He was a man of Italian birth, from a town called Assisi in the province of Perugia, not too distant from my own hometown. At the time he lived, nearly 500 years ago, France was a great center of learning and beautiful things, and the young man, before his revelation, was wealthy and loved all things French. His own father chided him by nicknaming him 'Francisco.' He kept this name to always remind himself of the vanity and folly of his boyhood, though now we give the name reverence in honor of so great a saint."

"What was his actual name?"

"St. Francis's real Christian name was Giovanni, like my own."

"So he was both Francisco and Giovanni. It seems we both are named after the same saint," said Francisco.

Chapa smiled, "In a way we are. I have never thought of it. Did you know I lived with the Capuchin brothers when I first arrived in Ciudad de México?"

Francisco shook his head. "I did not, Don Juan. I assumed a man of your learning and status would not need to seek shelter with the friars."

"I was hardly either," said Chapa, "when my feet first touched soil in Veracruz. I had no property, no money and as an *extranjero* my legal status was inferior to even your own."

Francisco didn't believe that claim but chose to let it pass without comment. "What was that voyage like? I have only crossed rivers in an open boat and have never even seen the ocean. I have often wondered what it must be like to cross the ocean without seeing land in any direction, riding for days confined to what seems like just a floating wooden house."

"In truth it was misery itself," Chapa said. "The *flota* was a majestic sight from afar—twenty proud galleons in one powerful formation. But once I was on board and the ship began to heave on the open sea, it became a watery kind of hell. The vessel was so crowded we had to take turns sleeping and resting in the center bow. The living quarters for the crew and passengers were cramped, airless, and full of a stench far fouler than I had ever experienced--a putrid mix of vomit, urine, excrement, and something like spoiled milk. There were insects and rats everywhere—the more we threw overboard the more seemed to spring from the bowels of the vessel—as if summoned by some witch's incantation. Worse than anything, though, was the boredom; the days crept by so slowly that it drove many passengers a little mad.

"Thankfully, I had my books—and, although I shouldn't really mention it, the memory of a woman, the only one I had known before leaving Cádiz. It's embarrassing to admit, but truthfully I made love to her in my own fevered mind more times than I could count during that voyage." Chapa laughed, partly out of embarrassment, but also with a certain fondness for the young man he had been. Then he fell quiet, ashamed at the way he had held that image so tenderly on that journey, without thinking of another voyage that must have been much, much worse than his own.

"I was on that ship for exactly 70 days and nights in such conditions," Chapa continued. "Our daily ration was no more than a pound of hard bread, which was invariably moldy after the first few days afloat, and some salted pork. We also were given two pints of stale water—unless it had recently rained—and a pint of rather poor wine. The wealthier passengers brought along chickens and young pigs to slaughter and cook, and we were tormented by the smell of fresh meat roasting on the ship's deck. These wealthy travelers also carried lentils, peas, olive oil, vinegar, and cheese, and so their diets were far more varied. I confess at times I might have killed a man for a wedge of good cheese."

"I cannot quite believe that, *patrón*," said Francisco.

"Thankfully I managed to resist that temptation," said Chapa, with a bitter smile. "There was too much death on board as it was. My own vessel saw at least five deaths that I can remember. Like any man, I have seen plenty of death in my time. But in the close confines of the ship, there were two deaths which struck me especially hard, so much so that I can still picture them if I close my eyes. The first was a young child, maybe five years old, with whom I had developed a playful friendship. Halfway into the voyage he fell ill, laying sick and feverish for days. His poor mother begged the sailors for clean water, some fresh broth, anything that might have eased his suffering. I shared a little with them. I could have shared much more, but I was hungry and ill myself and so hoarded my meager supplies.

It still haunts me to remember that, and I have prayed many times for forgiveness for my selfishness. In the end, he slipped away, his mother holding him, staring vacantly out over the water. Once her son died, the grief-stricken woman refused to eat or drink and died just two nights later. After a short prayer, the other women wrapped her in linen and the sailors threw her overboard. I can still see her lifeless body floating upon the waves, drifting and then finally sinking. Did she find peace? Did she meet her son again in the presence of God? I hope so."

"Was life in Spain so terrible?" Francisco asked gently. "Why did so many suffer these dangers, just to reach this hard and unforgiving land?"

"Not terrible, Francisco, at least not for most, but bound, limited," mused Chapa. "Without possibility. Most traveling with me were poor men, young like myself. However, there were also a few women, determined to leave their families and follow their husbands or fathers to New Spain. They were mostly people from Andalucía who, by dint of their birth, would never be anything but poor no matter how hard they worked. They heard that in New Spain poor men could become wealthy, a man who was landless from birth might one day leave his sons a vast *hacienda*. Because of this hope, they braved the hell that was the crossing.

"Most came in search of a dream, a better life. You have to know, Francisco, the wild exaggerated stories that were told about the boundless wealth of New Spain. People came with this hope, but, I won't lie to you, Francisco, there was often a darker impulse as well. In Spain a peasant is the lowest of the low, but here, no matter how poor, he is the superior of even the

133

richest *mestizo* or *mulato*. And women, countless women of Indian blood could be had easily, too easily I'm afraid — the devil places that desire in all men's hearts. In some ways it is shameful that the roots of New Spain rest so deeply in the greed and lust of those who came to settle her.

"And you, Don Juan? What was your own reason for coming?"

"I did not come for the riches or the women. Although I was then a poor man, had I continued to work in one of the Genovese trading houses of Cádiz I might have become a rich one. Richer, to be sure, than I am today. No, I journeyed because I felt a calling. God gave me intellect and ambition and I dreamed of becoming something greater than a trader. I really don't know what I was searching for. I just knew that there had to be something better and I strove to apply those gifts fully that God bestowed. I only hope, with this *Historia*, at last I have achieved that goal of a larger purpose."

"You have served the Crown more faithfully than almost any man in this *reino, patron*," said Francisco, quite honestly.

"I don't expect an answer until I leave this earth," said Chapa, "As Ovid reminds us, *Scilicet ultima semper: expectanda dies homini est, dicique beatus ante obitum nemo, supremaque funera debet.*"

Francisco attempted to translate, his Latin rusty from years of disuse. "You must always await a man's last day: before his last rites and death, no one should be called unhappy. Is that the gist of it?"

"Close enough," said Don Juan, "Simply put, a man cannot truly know if his life has been happy or unhappy until the day it ends."

***

Journal Entry -- Arrival in Veracruz May 1647

I waited out the night, surrounded by my fellow travelers, watching as the torches and lamps were extinguished one by one

134

around the rim of the harbor, then turning my eyes starboard as the first glow of pale yellow light appeared on the eastern horizon. I had seen land earlier when the flota made stops in Guadalupe, Jamaica, Santo Domingo and Caiman, but this was different. This was no island, but New Spain herself. As dawn gained force, our boat again became a hive of activity. The first shore boats appeared before us. My wakefulness served me well, and I was among the first to disembark. My belongings were hoisted off the deck and down into the boat, and I clumsily descended the rope ladder and settled myself in the stern.

At this moment, I caught my first sight of an Indian – in the form of two brown oarsmen who sat silently on their bench – their faces blank masks in the morning heat. In Cádiz, I had often seen those called Indianos, but now I know they had been mere mestizos. Their features and coloring were nothing like the squat, walnut-colored creatures now sitting across from me in the little dory. To my eyes, they looked scarcely human. As the boat settled low in the water under the weight of the trunks and bodies piling off the barco, they muttered a few words to each other in a strange tongue, all clicking consonants and strange throaty sounds.

Even though it was barely dawn, the heat was already overpowering. I welcomed the slight breeze as the Indianos rowed us steadily towards the wharf. As we pulled alongside, a young boy, clad only in rough cotton trousers, reached out for the lines tossed by the oarsman, laughing when he had to reach low over the edge to catch the second one.

Finally I stood on dry land in Veracruz, my battered old trunk and bedroll beside me. I took a step towards one of the porters standing nearby and staggered, almost falling, the ground pitching underneath me as if it were a deck rolling in a storm. My stomach heaved and I threw up, missing my blanket by only a few inches, making the young boy who secured the lines laugh once again. I sat down on the trunk and waited for the world to settle, taking a moment to absorb my first look at this new continent.

Fronting the wharf, across from the great fortress San Juan de Ulúa, was a broad, crescent-shaped plaza, paved in cobblestones carried from Spain as ballast. The aduana stood directly in front of the wharf, flanked on both sides by the warehouses of the trading companies, their names, helpfully, written in ochre paint above the large vaulted doorways facing the plaza. On the left side of the plaza stood a rough corral for animals loaded off the ships; on the right another, larger corral, holding a much more valuable kind of beast: black African slaves, recently unloaded from the great slave ships that dotted the harbor, drinking deeply and washing themselves from a stone tanque filled with water.

Judging by their speech – which I could do with some confidence after so long in Cádiz – they hailed from Sierra Leone, the colony where many of my uncle's slaves were obtained. I scanned the group for that one familiar face, even though it made no sense to do so. She could not be here. One of them, a skinny young man about my age, glanced over at me. Our eyes met. So fresh from his barbaric but free existence, he had not yet been taught to avoid the gaze of his betters. He would soon learn that harsh lesson, I knew. For an instant we stared at one another – what thoughts were in his head, if any, I will never know. I finally forced myself to look away.

Despite the early hour, the plaza was already crowded, full of colors, smells and sounds so completely foreign that my head was once again swimming. More than anything, it was the smell of the place that was so confounding, a mixture of the sour, salty water of the bay, the blossoms of the orange and lime trees ringing the plaza, and strange spices that burned my nose and caught in my throat. Underneath it all was a note that I could not recognize, both sweet and earthy, with a mineral edge that smelled of fresh plaster or whitewash. Looking around, I traced that scent to a group of old women in colorful embroidered blouses, sitting over small braziers, shaping and filling little cakes of various sizes out of wet yellow dough and cooking them on some kind of clay platter resting over the coals. My now-empty stomach lurched urgently back to life.

I was stirred from my reverie by one of my companions, a dull young man from Jerez named Antonio, who was pledged to the same trading house as I. "It's over there," he pointed, "the yellow one with the red bugambilia on the balcony." He had already summoned a porter, who was loading our trunks onto an old wagon. While the porter struggled to pile on as much as he could, I walked over to the old women. I asked one of them how much for some of the pastelitos. In response she held up two fingers. I fished into the little pouch around my neck, took out two reale and handed it to her.

After pocketing the coin, she pulled out a piece of broad green leaf, heaped six of the little cakes onto it, doused them all with a bright red sauce, and added a strange green paste to one side. Starved, I shoved a whole cake into my mouth at once, burning my fingers as I grabbed it off the leaf. The sweet earthy dough hit my tongue, but a moment later my mouth was consumed by a fire so intense that I choked on the food, spitting most of it out before casting about wildly for some water. Dropping the leaf on the rim, I plunged my hands into the well in the center of the plaza, I drank deeply, my face sweating, tears coming from my eyes.

The same little imp who had tied up the boat was watching every step, laughing harder than ever when I lifted my head away from the well. "La salsa!" he said, making a motion for me to scrape it off the cakes. "Aguacate" he pointed, at the green paste. I stuck my finger in it and lifted it to my mouth – the smooth creaminess cooling my lips and tongue. Starved, I did my best to wipe away as much of the angry red sauce as I could before wolfing down the rest of the cakes – this time the burn was less intense, and the flavors of the food were intoxicating, so vivid and fresh after months with nothing but hard bread, sour stews, and stale water. I sighed with pleasure and nodded my thanks to the old lady, who acknowledged me with a quick smile before returning to her cooking.

When we reached the trading house, we announced our arrival by knocking on the open door of the warehouse. Stepping into the cool darkness, we saw a man, a Spaniard, his face flushed and sweaty with heat and fever, suspended off the floor in a hammock woven out of some kind of rough fibers. Waking on our knock, he struggled out of the hammock and approached us with a sleepy but friendly grin, extending his hand and saying, "Welcome to Veracruz."

And so my life begins here in New Spain.

***

Chapa and Francisco spoke an hour longer, at which point Chapa announced he would like to be alone in order to write a letter. Francisco had still hoped to take a short nap on account of his fatigue, but he saw how far the sun had risen in the sky and knew it was time for him to begin preparing his master's midday meal.

When Francisco returned with the plate of bread, cheese, *membrillo* and some boiled eggs, Chapa was adding his signature to a long letter. The letter was so long—at least four pages—that it seemed he could not have written it all in the brief interval in which Francisco prepared the food. In such a mass of papers, the letter could easily have been written weeks earlier without Francisco knowing for sure. Chapa folded the letter, then refolded it twice because the lines were not precise enough. He melted the wax and marked the back with three seals in a perfect line across the back before writing the name and address of its recipient on the other side.

"Francisco, I would like you to carry this letter for me," Chapa said, folding more paper around it and sealing that sheet also with his wax stamp. "I want you to go to the market and find the merchant Manuel Astorga, who sells birds and jewelry and other fine items brought from the capital. Please give him this letter to take back to Ciudad de México on his next journey there. He will know where to take it so that it reaches its final destination."

"Of course, Don Juan," said Francisco, placing the food on the bare left side of the writing desk, "After I fetch your wine I will deliver it immediately

***

Francisco stepped out into the street in his rough cap and course woolen coat. The weather was cold; he was fortunate that the wind had finally died down overnight. He usually warmed quickly when he reached a good pace, but on this day his fatigue somehow held his inner warmth in check—a chill remained near his heart that he was unable to shake no matter how quickly he strove to move his legs.

He walked along the rutted dirt street, up the slight incline towards Monterrey's *traza*, gripping the letter tightly. Chapa's last letter had been lost in the mud in that furious storm—was this letter a replacement, or something else entirely?

The letter was addressed to *NICOLÒ CHAPA, MONASTARY OF THE VICTORY, CÁDIZ, ANDALUCÍA.* This could not be the uncle in Cádiz of whom Chapa often spoke. Surely that man must be dead by now. Could it be Chapa's brother? A cousin? He had a son named Nicolas, but it seemed unlikely the old man would Italicize the name for delivery to Spain. Francisco could only wonder.

When he reached the small covered market he began to search for Señor Astorga. Francisco rarely found himself speaking to this seller, as Chapa's household had little need of his wares, but the market was small enough he knew he would know the man by sight.

As Francisco walked past the wine seller, the portly middle-aged man looked a little mystified as one of his most frequent customers passed him by. Over his left shoulder, he heard a familiar voice call out to him.

"Eh, Francisco!"

Francisco turned around to see Padre Joseph behind him, a basket on his arm full of bread and cured meats.

"Francisco, it is good to see you out of doors. How is your master?"

"He is well, Father," answered Francisco. "Against my advice he has returned to his study, but he is stronger and stronger each day. His appetite was hearty at his midday meal."

"That is a blessing," said Padre Joseph, "I have prayed daily for his recovery, and his daughter Maria purchased several prayer candles to beseech the Virgin for her father's good health. It seems these efforts have not been in vain."

"They have not," said Francisco.

"You have no basket," said the priest, "What brings you to the market?"

"I only have this letter," said Francisco, a little reluctantly. "Don Juan bid me to deliver it to Señor Astorga, who might carry it to the capital for him."

The priest reached his hand out, "I would be more than happy to make sure the letter is delivered. Please give it to me."

Francisco shuffled his feet a little and hesitated. "Don Juan gave me strict instructions to hand it only to the merchant, Padre."

Padre Joseph smiled broadly, concealing his irritation at the servant's reluctance. "Do not worry, my son. You are not endangering your soul or your good standing with Don Juan by giving it to me. Remember, as a slave under loan, you are but a possession of the parish. You may call him '*patrón*,' but your true master is and always will be the Church, and I am its representative. He could not fault you for acquiescing."

Francisco knew he had no choice but to hand the letter over.

"Thank you, Francisco. Your service has done much to erase your grave sin in the eyes of the Lord. You have but one year left on your sentence."

"I look forward to that day, and hope the Lord will see fit to forgive my sins once I have completed my penance."

They soon parted and Francisco returned to Chapa's home, sweating heavily under his clothes.

CHAPTER 11

Bad Masters

After Francisco left to deliver the letter to Nicoló, Chapa returned to the trunk, this time pulling out all of the correspondence that dated between 1660 and 1670. Although he had planned merely to review them quickly in order to confirm dates and other details for the *Historia* section that he was currently revising, inevitably he found himself drawn into the old letters, reliving once again the events recorded in their pages.

TO THE HONORABLE DON FLORENTINO AQUINO – CIUDAD DE MÉXICO

My dear Don Florentino,

I pray this letter finds you and your family in good health. I write to you with very sad news: our great Governor of four decades and my personal mentor Don Martín de Zavala has passed from the land of the living. All of Nuevo León mourns the grievous loss.

He succumbed to an illness that began with a persistent cancerous growth in his leg. The infirmity had been with him for years, and it was almost amputated several times. Perhaps it should have been. But the cancer spread rapidly in these last months, wasting Don Martín's once strong body. He was a great and wise leader, but what set him apart from other men was his strength, his pride, and the fact that no man on this earth — Spaniard, Indian, or other — could strike fear or shame into him.

Although Don Martín was ill for a long time, he never let his affliction affect his work. Indeed, he hid it from all but his closest confidantes. He labored selflessly to the very end. Wise Ovid prayed, Cum moriar, medium solvare inter opus. *Truly Don Martín shared this prayer and had it fulfilled by almighty God. There are richer provinces in New Spain — indeed, there are few poorer — but there is not a one that better exemplifies the principles and promise of our Christian civilization in this heathen land. And for that we can only thank Don Martín de Zavala.*

The Municipal Council has appointed León de Alza y de Garbiso as acting Governor while we await the official royal appointment. I regret to say that Don León is a hopeless administrator. He is a good man and no doubt will learn in his post, but for the moment, the business of administering this reino *falls hard on my own shoulders.*

Pray for our new Governor and for Nuevo León, dear friend. And do not let your most recent visit to Monterrey be your last.

May God preserve your health and safety.

Your devoted friend,
Juan Bautista Chapa
8 August, MDCLXIV
Monterrey, Nuevo León, México - Nueva España

COPY – 10 August, 1663 - JBC

***

The news of the letter's interception, delivered with great reluctance by Francisco, was a terrible blow to Chapa. Had he not been sitting when Francisco delivered it, the old man might have staggered and fallen. As it was, he grew immediately weakened and asked Francisco to help him to his bed.

"Why would Padre Joseph take my letter? Do you think he would open it?" Chapa asked. He had always considered the priest harmless — self-serving perhaps, but not dangerous. Francisco was unsure if the question was really meant for him, and so chose to remain quiet.

"Would his piety and his conscience allow such a thing?"

Francisco didn't answer that question either, silently pulling Chapa's boots and collar off and then placing the blankets over him. Better to let Don Juan rest now and then help him undress from his workday clothing later, after he recovered a little.

"I will bring you some brandy, Don Juan, to help you sleep," Francisco said. "Is there anything else that might aid you?"

Ashen-faced, Chapa said, "Bring the *Historia* to me. Retrieve it and bring it to me now."

Francisco nodded and walked through the patio and into the kitchen. He opened the cupboard and removed the large manuscript, now bound with two strands of rough twine. He poured his master a deep draught of the brandy that the winemaker at Parras de la Fuente made with the pressings left over from his winemaking and returned upstairs to his master's bedroom.

"Here Don Juan, drink this. It will do you good."

Chapa held the cup with both hands and took a large gulp. It did not restore his strength but did temporarily ease the shaking of his hands. He handed the cup back to Francisco, who set it down on the small table adjacent to his master's bed. Chapa sat silently for at least a full minute before speaking. Francisco, as usual, stood attentive but silent.

"I wonder if I should destroy everything," Chapa said at last.

"Destroy what exactly, *patrón*?" asked Francisco.

"The *Historia*, my papers. Perhaps even my books. All might damn me. With the bishop and the *comisario* coming to investigate me I cannot be too careful."

"I did not hear anyone say a *comisario* traveled to Monterrey on your account, Don Juan."

"You do not understand these things, Francisco. You are a clever *mestizo* but you are naïve in the ways of powerful men. The governor came to give me a warning. On my son's behalf no doubt. In the Bishop's shadow shall certainly be the Inquisition's eyes and ears, the *comisario* of this diocese. There is no other reason why he would make a secret, undocumented trip to Monterrey. These papers, these writings, everything I have labored over for years, I know that they endanger my status, my family, and perhaps even my soul," said Chapa. "Beyond *La Historia* I have written many things about life, philosophy and nature itself. But I fear now that these ruminations and confessions could cause grave harm. I am an old man, and no longer fear what they may do to me. My family, though, my family must be protected."

Francisco knew better than to attempt an argument. At this stage he wished most of all simply to calm his master down. "I am no priest, Don Juan, but I can't imagine you endanger your soul merely by writing what you know to be the truth. Surely God himself would approve of your *Historia*."

Chapa shook his head but did not respond.

"I will do as you wish," said Francisco, "but I only urge you to sleep on the matter before proceeding. Even if your worst fears were realized, the Bishop is still days away from arriving in our *reino*."

"I have sinned so much, Francisco. Far beyond the lies and obfuscations in these papers."

"As have all men," Francisco said.

Chapa calmed down a little and took another gulp of brandy. He set it down without Francisco's aid, and turned to him, looking to him for support, as he did so often these days. "Why is it you show me such loyalty? You who were born free and now are a bonded servant. A master carpenter, it seems, and now but a humble domestic, cooking my meals and cleaning my floors. Why is it that you do not despise me?"

Francisco smiled gently, "It is no fault of yours that I became a slave, Don Juan. Indeed, it was your intercession that saved me from a worse fate, or so Padre Luis told me."

"Padre Luis was too generous in his estimation, I suspect," said Chapa. "The fate you received was neither more nor less than what you deserved."

"There was never a magistrate in Nuevo León fairer than you, Don Juan," said Francisco.

"We have never spoken of that time, have we?" asked Chapa.

Francisco shook his head.

"Sit then. This might calm me to speak of it. I wonder about the circumstances, now that I know you better, because the crime does not seem like you. What could have possessed you to do such a thing?"

"I wish I could claim possession, that some sort of devil took hold of me. But it was only the sin of a foolish and desperate man," said Francisco. "My wife had died in childbirth with our third child. The eldest is my daughter, Luisa. The second died as an infant. The third did not survive the day of his birth. After my wife was taken from me, in God's infinite wisdom, and with no sisters or other relatives in this land, I was left to raise my daughter alone."

"She is now a ladies' maid, is she not?" asked Chapa.

"She is a serving woman," replied Francisco flatly. "Her mother being an Indian, and her father a dark-complexioned *coyote*, she looks too much the *indigena* to serve in a fine lady's chamber. I confess I struggled greatly to raise her alone. There is so much different about a girl that a man never learns from his mother or sisters. There were many times she dearly wished she had a mother."

"Why then did you not remarry?"

"In the grief after my wife's death I drank pulque in excess, Don Juan, and my carpentry lost its subtlety. I was a lost man for several years, grounded only by the need to provide for my surviving child. You can imagine it was but a short road from there to my shameful theft."

Chapa nodded slowly, drawing up the dim memories. The incident had mattered little to him at the time, acquiring only minor significance when the parish loaned him this taciturn but

145

dependable servant upon the death of Father Luis and the appointment of the spry young Padre Joseph.

"From whose house did you steal, Francisco? I cannot recall."

"From the house of Don Alferez Jose de Tremiño. To my great and everlasting shame."

"And what was it you stole? Something of great value, no?"

"It was a necklace belonging to his wife, Consuela. I stole into her chamber during the work day and took a necklace of great value, acquired by their ancestors during the *Reconquista*."

"And where did your daughter work at that time?"

"The same house, Don Juan."

"It is odd," said Chapa, "that you should choose to steal from the house of your daughter's service. It was almost inevitable that she should be charged with the theft."

"As she was, yes."

"You had not the foresight to see that danger?"

"In my depraved state, no, *patrón*. I acted so rashly and foolishly. When my daughter was accused I had no choice of course but to confess to the crime."

"And you produced the necklace, didn't you?"

"I did, unmarred, I am happy to say."

Chapa nodded. "It was a very curious incident. Very curious, indeed."

"I will forever be grateful you took interest. And persuaded the governor — or so Padre Luís told me, and I have no reason to doubt him — to stay my sentence of death and commute it to one of indenture," said Francisco.

"No, Francisco, you were not going to be put to death. However, you would have been physically punished. Regardless, I thought little of it, other than that we had hanged too many men and made many more suffer severely, even more than this servitude, for such petty crimes. A man can better repay our community with his hands at work than with his body in the earth. Now that I reflect upon it more, I wonder if we still did not act too harshly."

"You were more than fair," said Francisco.

"Have you made a table or cabinet since? Or any expression of the art you learned from your father?"

"Besides a simple repair to a roof or replacement of a cupboard door, no."

"That is a pity and a waste of a rare talent."

"If so it is one I brought upon myself," said Francisco.

"Is it strange to live as an indentured slave? Especially because in this land Indians may no longer be taken as slaves, apart from punishment for crimes such as yours. Does it wound your pride each time you think of it?" asked Chapa.

"I have had an easy time of it," answered Francisco. "While there are not as many African slaves in this ranching country as in mining regions, my understanding is that they live a far harsher life than the one I have been given. The Padre treated me well and you, of course, are a master who is more than fair. I cannot complain."

"Yes, I suppose you could have been sent down a mine; your experience then would have been much different."

"And I thank God for it."

"While the law of our *reino* permits it, and as an official I have been forced to do much to further its use, in my own heart I believe slavery is a terrible thing," said Chapa, knotting his hands. "In truth, Francisco, I'm talking about what we do when we enslave *negros* and *mulatos*. I wonder sometimes if I chose this *reino* knowing that these slaves would be unlikely to stain these lands in great number. I saw it so intimately in Cádiz and Veracruz, in my heart I never again wanted to live with it so closely," Chapa said as he stared down at the floor. He thought for a moment of the countless slave transactions he had authorized over the years, how much human chattel he had taxed and documented over the years in this *reino*, justifying these acts to himself because he wasn't the one actually taking on slaves. How we fool ourselves, he thought, considering how even now he reaped the benefits of Francisco's bondage.

"Is that why you left Cádiz? Left the employ of your uncle?"

"It is hard to say why a man chooses to set sail over the ocean. My uncle had left Cádiz by then, and I was working for his partner, Captain Ocelo. I thought it was one thing when I left, another thing when I touched land, and still another these many years later. Who is to say what the true cause was?' said Chapa, deftly turning the conversation away from that long ago decision. "Which reminds me: why did you really leave Jalisco, Francisco? Surely you did not travel so many leagues simply to avoid competing with your father. A shorter journey would have reached the same end, no?"

Francisco shrugged, "Like you, Don Juan, that is a question I cannot answer."

"I wonder," Chapa said, sighing a little. "There is much more to you that you let on, Francisco."

Francisco could find no reply to this observation, or perhaps simply chose not to answer, and just stared back blankly, the two men sitting in awkward silence until Chapa ventured on with his story.

"In any event," continued Chapa, "I came to Cádiz in the care of my uncle, and with the idea of joining my brother Nicoló in the monastery at Sevilla. The same brother whose letter now sits in the hands of Padre Joseph, I'm afraid. He was the hero of my youth, and upon the death of my father, I sought to join the Franciscan Order. Yes, as a boy I yearned to become a friar, and like my father I was never to fulfill that desire. My uncle Giovanni knew early on that my temperament was ill suited to a life of quiet prayer and instead took me into his house, where he trained me in the skills needed to carry on in the world of trade.

"When the Genovese caravel docked in Cádiz and my feet touched Spanish soil for the first time, I had almost no education and knew nothing beyond our little village of Albisola. Though I hadn't a single coin in my purse, on the waterfront I was surrounded by riches: spices from the Orient, fine silken and woolen fabrics from Calais and Antwerp, glass from Venice, pearls from Goa, brightly colored dyes from the

Levant, furs from Bergen and Riga, and surely even greater riches that were hidden in the bottoms of the great trunks that were carried all around me. My eyes were open to a world wider than I had ever imagined."

"It sounds like a wondrous place," interjected Francisco, almost without intending to.

"It was wondrous, yet, but ugly as well. Because the most valuable commerce of all was not held in trunks or bags, but instead was brought forth in chains, eyes blinking in the sun after their long journey from the banks of the Gambia or Congo. I did not know then how closely my own fate was to be entwined with these poor miserable devils."

"Did you regret that you never become a friar? Was it not truly your wish?"

"At times yes. A lifetime vocation of study and translation would have been a very sweet one, or at least I felt so at fourteen. But my path to investiture was obstructed from the start. To become a novitiate, I would have had to abandon all worldly property, and as a minor, I could not renounce the title to my father's vineyard without a guardian's consent. My uncle, already disappointed that Nicoló had chosen the cloth, would not allow me to renounce my lands, and as an obedient nephew grateful for his care, I apprenticed in his trading business."

"He sought your best interests, no doubt," said Francisco.

"Perhaps," replied Chapa, "Now, I must rest and think. Please let me sleep until morning unless you hear me cry out."

"Good night, Don Juan."

***

Walking along the long stone passageway, each step of my boots echoes loudly down the hall – cold and metallic. Try as I might, I cannot walk more softly.

Other than my footsteps, this monastery is eerily silent. They could only spare a single ofiçieu *to light my path. Sunlight streams in the room far behind me and perhaps ahead, but this hallway is so dark.*

I reach the end, the small, dim room where I was told I would at last find my frǽ Nicolò. Inside, kneeling in prayer by the narrow window is a solitary friar, barefoot, with a rough and ragged hood drawn over his face. In that moment I wished that I, too had embraced a life of such austerity.

Is this he? The brother I have been seeking? He looks smaller, frailer than the robust boy who wrestled with me so many summers ago. Is he smaller? Or have I grown? Perhaps it is just an illusion, since he kneels at the far end of the room while I stand in the doorway.

"Nicolò, it is I, your brother, Giovanni," Salty tears roll down my face. My legs are heavy after my long journey, and I sink to sit, knowing that a far greater one awaits me.

The friar does not look up but turns his shoulders to me, just a little. To listen better? To judge if it is really me?

Why doesn't he answer? Has he sworn a vow of silence, like a Cistercian? I shake his shoulders, begging him to speak.

"Talk to me, Nicolò. Father wanted me to join you here in devotion. He wanted me to be with you and Uncle Giovanni, but most of all he wanted me to join the order with you and seek God through quiet study. That is why I am here."

Still the friar says nothing, but he turns away again, and his bony shoulders begin to shake very gently. Is he crying? His face is hidden by the shadow of his heavy hood.

"Nicolò, answer me! I've been looking for you. Our parents are dead and you are the only one left to me on this earth. Please. If you have taken a vow of silence at least show me your face."

Still nothing.

"Stàmme a sentî! Answer me, brother!"

Turning towards me at last, the figure finally draws back his hood. As he pulls it back, I rush forward to embrace my brother Nicolò, my heart full of joy until I stop, stunned and frightened, eye to eye with Padre Joseph, his fat face lit by the torch in my hand, grinning at me over the folds of his rough brown robe.

CHAPTER 12

The Muleteer

Even back in Albisola, I always knew uncle Giovanni was a trader, and a successful one. I have no apprehensions about the justness of slavery – these Africans are not men, not like us. But I must confess that at times I find the trade distasteful. I wonder if this is typical of young apprentices? Or is there something wrong with me?

I was working today with my uncle's partner, a Genovese who goes by name of Captain Juan Vicencia Ocelo here in Spain. I was loading several barrels of wax onto a ship bound for Veracruz when Captain Ocelo told me of an imminent sale of slaves, some 200 recently arrived from Angola, and said that I must attend him at the auction. He hoped to find a few good specimens to purchase and re-sell to West Indies planters.

He led me down to the pier where the sale was to take place. The poor animals were restless and agitated, causing the Portuguese man in charge of the auction to order several of them to be whipped, causing them to scream in agony. Ocelo reminded me that these creatures were not truly human and that I should be careful not to get too close. I had never been within arm's length of a Negro before – I wonder, do they all smell so terribly or is that just the result of the cramped and filthy ships that transport them?

I asked if any man with sufficient wealth could buy a slave for transport across the ocean. He told me that only those granted an Asiento by the Royal Court were licensed to transport chattel to New Spain. Ocelo said that granting such rights to an Italian like my uncle was a rare privilege – especially in light of the recent Neapolitan revolt against the crown.

Captain Ocelo also explained how the price of slaves in New Spain had dropped in recent years as the hardier breeds died off less quickly, and some planters and miners were finding success breeding their own. Perhaps one day the great oceanic trade might become unnecessary if the numbers born to the plantation owners of New Spain continue to multiply.

He explained that we were to identify only grown males between the ages of eighteen and twenty-fiveAny older and their value would be diminished. Any younger and they are less likely to survive the deadly passage across the Atlantic. I speculated that younger slaves might die at a higher rate but could work many more years if they arrived safely, so that they might be consequently of sufficient value, but the skill with numbers needed to calculate these relative values is beyond my abilities. Beyond their maximum value, Captain Ocelo explained why these ages were deemed the best for trading.

"A lot of times you have to beat the shit out of the young males because they are so rebellious," Ocelo said. "They are fucking animals and the younger ones are the worst. A good lashing is the only way to kill their spirit, but the younger slaves are also more likely to be harmed by such taming."

I wondered if beating might be best for the recalcitrant ones but that those more docile by nature, like some animals, might be better handled through less violent means.

"The slaves have no soul," he reminded me, "but unlike livestock they have brain enough to scheme. A docile horse is what he seems, but a docile slave can simply be a killer biding his time. Trust no such creature you own, even if he seems to show you loyalty, for it is in his nature to deceive and betray you."

This world is no easy place for a heart such as mine.

152

***

The next morning Chapa was again unable to leave his bed. Francisco had hoped the shock of the previous afternoon was just a brief setback but it was not to be. Chapa was weaker than he had been in all but the worst days of his illness. Before preparing his master a breakfast of mild broth—made mostly from chicken, garlic, and carrots—Francisco asked, Don Juan, I heard you moaning again last night. You sounded quite disturbed. Were you once again lost in that *cañon*?"

"No, no," responded Chapa, I had that nightmare two days ago. And, yes, I'm still lost in that damn dream . . . a faceless, confused man under the spell of that old Indian woman. God spared me from that specter. Nothing in that dream is logical. The more I try to suppress her from my thoughts, the stronger and more peculiar her invasion becomes."

While Francisco was gone, Chapa napped intermittently and pondered the best course of action. A serious decision was so taxing—in his youth he would draw up a long list of pros and cons and weigh them impartially, organizing the lists, writing and rewriting the order, until he ran out of paper. But now he hoped somehow a decision might creep up on him, like a dream, and slowly wrest its way toward inevitability without having to exert any effort for or against its behalf.

He found sometimes even before he had made a decision, before in fact he wrestled with the facts that would inform his choice, something inside of him had already settled on a path. That his deliberate method of reaching a decision was in fact merely the elucidation of a choice his heart had already made but kept secret, like a sculptor liberating an existent statue from the imprisoning block of marble. He could never be sure how, but almost invariably his rational mind found a way—a perfectly logical, defensible way, of course—to arrive at the decision that deep down seemed somehow inevitable. He wondered if somehow he never even made a conscious choice at all, that his heart—or some other force—had pre-determined his action before his mind ever considered it.

He hoped that this matter of his *Historia* and papers would be such a choice. All his adult life he had dedicated himself to truth, to an exact reckoning of the breadth of a parcel of land — or the measure of a man. He had never led this *reino*, but he had served as its memory. He had hoped his *Historia* would serve as a more permanent memory, laying out for generations to come how their lives on this frontier were fought and won, and at what cost.

But was his dedication to that ideal, and to the abstract good it might one day bring, worth the very real danger to his family? How incendiary were his writings, really? He only observed and wrote what had happened — he offered almost no moral commentary and certainly no theology. Could a *comisario*, even one looking to find error, really fault him? With such stakes, though, was that a gamble he could take?

***

When Francisco returned, Chapa was surprised to hear a second set of feet walk through the door with him, footsteps that moved with an energy rarely heard in this house. Chapa's voice was too weak to call out for the guest's identity, but the mystery was soon to be solved, as he heard the two bodies make their way across the patio and towards his bedroom, the steps echoing each other in a pleasant staccato rhythm.

Francisco peeked through the open door to see if Chapa was sleeping. "Don Juan, I hope I am not disturbing you."

"You're not," Chapa said sharply. "But why have you brought someone into the house on your own initiative?"

"I apologize. I did not leave with the intention of bringing anyone back with me, but a chance encounter in the market was something I could not pass up. I ran into an *arriero*, a driver of mules, who I have known some twenty years. He is a man quick with a story and song, and I thought he might cheer you up."

"Is he the *mulato*, this muleteer you have spoken of? The one who takes supplies to and from Saltillo?"

"The very same, Don Juan. I know you will enjoy him if you are not too fatigued. In the past, you've spoken about how much you enjoy it when he plays in the plaza."

"It was impetuous of you, Francisco, to make that kind of call when I have been so ill. But now that the poor man stands in our patio, listening to all this folly, I suppose you should let him in."

Francisco nodded and gestured to the still-unseen muleteer outside the door. Burgundy-colored boots turned the corner first, followed by the man as a whole. He was stocky and middle-aged, perhaps 40, with a cape thrown over one shoulder and earrings in both ears. His Negro features were striking, but he looked for all the world like a man unburdened by caste or class. In his arms was a five-stringed guitar of pear wood, a beautiful instrument that had nonetheless seen years of wear, particularly just beneath the sound hole where the man's strumming fingers had slowly worn away at the polished wood.

Smiling, the muleteer bowed gracefully to Chapa. "Don Juan Chapa, it is a great honor to be a guest in your home."

Chapa offered a weak gesture of greeting in return and struggle to sit up in his bed, pulling the covers higher around his chest.

"I thought that the *arriero* might play you a song, Don Juan?" Francisco asked.

"Yes, please," said Chapa, "but spare me any mournful ballads. Or anything that one would dance to — they sound too strange without the rhythm of stomping feet. Give me something lively, something with humor. Can you manage that?"

"I will do my utmost, *señor*," answered the muleteer with a wink, "Would you mind a song that was a little, how best to say it . . . bawdy? I am a poor crude man and apart from songs of devotion, these are all I know."

"Not in the least," said Chapa, "I have been visited by far too many priests and dignitaries in recent days. Don't worry, I have lived a full life and nothing you sing of will shock me."

Francisco stepped to one side and rested his hands in front of him. The muleteer slowly strummed a chord on his guitar, note by note, and then thought better of it and strummed a different one. He smiled — the song had leapt into his mind — and then began to play.

He sang in a bright, cheerful voice that varied from comically serious baritone to playful falsetto as he acted out the farce of the lyrics.

¡Dale, si le das,
moçuela de Carasa!
¡Dale, si le das
que me llaman en casa!

Do it so its done,
Carasa girl,
Do it so its done!
Like they say at home.

Una moçuela de Logroño
mostrado me avía su co. . .
po de lana negro que hilava.

The girl from Logroño, she
showed me the wooly black f-f-
fleece she was spinning.

Dale, si le das . . .

Do it so its done . . .

Otra moçuela de buen rrejo
mostrado me á su pende . . .
con qu'ella se pendava.

Another girl of good breeding
she gave me an eyeful
of her h-h-h-h... head,
which she was combing.

Dale, si le das . . .

Do it so its done . . .

Otra moçuela, Teresica,
mostrado me á su cri . . .
atura que llevava bien criada.

Another girl Teresita
Showed me her c-c-creature
Which was very well bred

Dale, si le das . . .

Do it so its done . . .

Por virgen era tenida,
mas çierto ella estava bien ho
. . .yosa de viruelas la su
cara.

She was taken for a virgin
But for sure she was full of
Pox on her f-f-f-face

Dale, si le das . . .

Do it so its done . . . :

Pidiérame de comer;
yo primero la quisiera ho . . .
rrar un sayuelo que llevava.

She asked me to eat
First I wanted her to s-s-s-ave
a long skirt she had

Dale, si le das . . .	*Do it so its done . . .*
Yo subiérala en un mulo: *mostrado me avía su ojo de* *cu . . .chlillo que llevaba en* *su jaula.*	*I mounted her on a mule;* *She showed me the b-b-blade* *That she kept in her cage*
Dale, si le das . . .	*Do it so its done . . .*
Ella por subir muy quedo, *soltósele un gran pe . . .* *daço de pan que llevava en su* *halda.*	*As she mounted it so gracefully* *she let drop a big p-p-piece* *of bread from her basket.*
Dale, si le das . . .	*Do it so its done . . .*
Y ella me mostró un *rrendajo;* *yo atestélle mi cara . . .* *peruça colorada para la* *bailla.*	*And she showed me a crack* *into which I put my colored* *c-c-c-cape so she would dance*
Dale, si le das . . .	*Do it so its done . . .*

Though he had begun the encounter in quite a sour mood, Chapa found himself amused at this raunchy tale, so energetically sung. Francisco himself blushed at some of the more explicit moments, but otherwise showed no reaction.

As he drew to the final chorus, the muleteer built to a grand finish and ended with a boisterous comic pirouette. Chapa laughed and clapped weakly.

"Bravo!" Chapa shouted, hoarsely, as the muleteer strummed the last chord. He clapped vigorously, but quickly set his arms down and found himself perspiring from the brief exertion. "Please play another before you go. It has been too long since I have had the pleasure of good music. You know,

157

when I first landed in Vera Cruz, I heard the magical music of your people. I will never forget the impact that it had on me."

The muleteer smiled at the praise, nodded and sat down on his stool, and leaned forward, furrowing his brow and marking time with his feet as he embarked on a wordless song that seemed to Chapa as if it spoke to his whole life. It danced with a propulsive energy but its melody felt sad and haunting. Moments of joy gave way to stirring anger, then turned sweet and plaintive. The muleteer's fingers danced lightly on the strings one moment and then strummed fiercely the next. The chords had a depth of tone as the strings reverberated, echoing each other with complex layers of sound.

Chapa lost himself in the music and his mind drifted to memories joyful and sad. For Chapa it ended all too soon. If the song had a name, the musician did not say.

"Thank you, my good man. I dare not ask you to play any more for fear that I would be overcome from the pleasure of it."

"Then I shall rest my strings," said the muleteer.

"Francisco, fetch this man some wine. And some for myself—this time don't cut it with water." Chapa said, thoughtless as to the fact that Francisco would stand aside while the other two men enjoyed themselves.

"Of course, Don Juan."

Francisco slipped out and left Chapa alone with the muleteer momentarily.

"Tell me, young man, were you born in Nuevo León?"

"It is kind of you to call me a young man," the muleteer smiled, "but I confess to you, Señor, only last month I became a grandfather."

"You are a lucky man indeed."

"I have always considered myself so. And to answer your question: no, I was not born here in Nuevo León but in the great port of Veracruz, where my mother, God rest her weary soul, was a slave."

"Was your father then a Spaniard, who purchased your mother and freed her?" .

The muleteer smiled grimly and shook his head. "No, my father, bastard whoever he is, raped my poor mother on the very pier by which they unloaded her. To hear my mother tell of it—and why would the poor woman lie—she was raped by not one man but four, one after the other until each were sated. In such a case, Don Juan Chapa, would you consider me the product of four men at once, or are each of those men just one quarter of my father, with none of them wholly so? Would that make it any easier to bear?"

The muleteer spit on the ground at the ugly memory and continued, "I take a certain pride in it, though."

Chapa now looked at him anew, sharply. "You take pride that your mother was raped?"

"In a way, yes," he said, "Because it tells me the Spaniards are full of shit when they say the *negro* is not truly a man. Would you mount a cow, Don Juan, or a sheep? Some men do, of course," he chuckled "and I have more than one song about them, but those are a strange sort. Whereas all Spanish men, whether they admit it or not, lust after the *negrita*. Would you not agree?"

"I . . . I'm not sure . . ."

"You cannot answer because you know it's true!" he said with a boisterous laugh. "You look at a black woman and you lust—as you should! She is beautiful and you are a man. She is a woman, and you are a man. It is that simple. The head and mouth, they can lie, but the loins always tell the truth. I could sing you a song, more fact than fiction, about the Spanish ladies this *mulato* has known, but Francisco would never forgive me."

"How then did you become a free man?" asked Chapa, trying to steer the subject away from these incendiary ideas, ideas that struck just a little too close to the bone. It was true, he knew. Once a slave was part of the household, they became so familiar that it was impossible to see them as they had to be seen in order to justify their enslavement. The idea that they were somehow less than fully human was put to the lie each time a master reached for a slave, or a *peninsular* baby cried for her *ama*. Chapa shook his head suddenly, as if to free himself from his own thoughts.

"That is my secret, Don Juan. But suffice it to say I have been a free man for many years. Any man who tries to make me a slave will die for it, or if not, then I will die at his hand. No chain shall ever bind me again."

Chapa, sat silent, unnerved by the mulato's boldness. After a moment, he decided to probe the man again. "You really won't tell me?"

"I will not, *señor*. I owe you my deference, but I do not owe you my secrets. And I would offer that if any man claims to tell you his, that man is a liar. For what does a man own that his more precious than his secrets? And who would give them up for such little reward? Nobody I know."

Chapa looked at the man, opened his mouth to speak, then closed it and looked away, towards the door, waiting for Francisco and suddenly unsure how to deal with the comical but impudent mule driver standing in his bedroom.

***

"You once worked in Veracruz," asked Francisco as he entered the room, sensing a tension and looking to diffuse it with a change of topic, "did you not, Don Juan?"

Francisco, and stretched out his arm to offer the muleteer one of the two glasses of wine on the little tray. The *mulatto* took it and drank it greedily, sighing with satisfaction, oblivious to Chapa's discomfort.

"When I first came to New Spain, yes," Chapa said distractedly, taking his wine from the tray and drinking it with the same intensity of the muleteer, nearly draining the glass in one long drink.

"What were those times like?" asked the muleteer. "I judge by your age, Don Juan, that you might have been a young man when my mother was first brought there. She rarely spoke of those days, so I know little of what the port was like then or now."

"It was the third great port I knew—and the last," said Chapa. "After the ancient port of Genoa and the majestic port of Cádiz, Veracruz was the strangest and most dangerous of all.

160

The stones of Genoa go back before the Romans, and the people from Cádiz claim a lineage stretching back even further, to the Phoenicians, but Veracruz at that time was a city only half-built and raw, surrounded by swamps and scrubby jungle. Many merchant houses and warehouses operated without roofs or with second stories still under construction, but there were also houses of great elegance and beauty. It is as if the city escaped from its mother's womb and refused to finish its gestation. And yet vast wealth coursed through her, more than in either of those great ports. In Veracruz, though, wealth did not linger and age with the city, but flowed through it in a constant and unseemly rush."

Francisco and the muleteer listened intently.

"I could not pay my passage across the ocean in money, so I bound myself to a *consulado* owned by the Giustiniani family. Just as in Cádiz, many of the great trading houses in Veracruz were controlled by the Genovese, although they were ostensibly owned by *peninsulares*. The foul air of that land made yellow fever a dangerous plague, particularly for those newly arrived from Spain like myself. For some reason slaves are less susceptible to it, perhaps on account of the hot, muggy air of the lands of their breeding. In any event, I was obliged to spend my first six months in Veracruz—indeed, it is the only way the *consulados* could keep the port staffed--and also suffered the weakness and fever of that terrible disease. Even though I was ill I was still required to work, but at least my skills as a scribe and accountant kept me behind a desk rather than under the hot sun.

"From behind that desk I saw all of the goods coming in and out of New Spain. Olives, wine, glass, paper, fine fabrics, and livestock all arrived from Spain. We sent back silver from Zacatecas and San Luis Potosí, as well as cacao, sugar, dyes, spices, and pearls. All would be loaded in the ships until at last the flota was ready to depart and brave the storms and English pirates that haunted the passage. There was some minor trade with other parts of New Spain, such as the shipment of tobacco from Habana, but the laws were such that almost all trade was restricted to that between New Spain and the mother country."

"Speaking of the noble weed, Don Juan, would you mind if I smoked?" asked the muleteer.

Francisco frowned and shook his head, "I think, old friend, it is time to let Don Juan rest. Let me fetch you fire and see you to the door."

"Francisco is right," said Chapa, sagging back onto his pillows. "I'm afraid I have over-exerted myself with your visit. But thank you for the cheer you brought this house."

"The pleasure was entirely mine, *señor*," said the muleteer with a gallant bow. "Don Juan, I know you will find your health again soon. You have the face of a good and honest man. Good day, *señor*."

Chapa gestured farewell, and Francisco led the man out. Had Chapa the strength to look out his window, he would have seen the muleteer leave with a parcel subtly tied to the back of his guitar. Instead, he turned on his side and closed his eyes, hoping that sleep would come to him peacefully. The moments before sleep were now fraught and uncomfortable. He had never gotten used to sleeping alone, and his thoughts turned to the empty place by his side where Beatriz had slept, curled up against him on cold nights like a cat. The guilt over how he had neglected her now washed over him once again. He reached out and picked up the mirror once more.

***

You miss her still, don't you, Giovanni? Funny how much more thought you give her now than while she still lived. You were always so driven, always determined to serve the reino *better this year than the last. Did it ever occur to you to show that same devotion to your own wife?*

She loved me without limit. She adored me. She bore me six children, and she loved them all deeply. But she adored only me.

Life to Beatriz was full of beauty. She always sought out the beauty of the world around her, and cherished the same beauty she saw inside all of us. Did she ever speak ill of anyone? From the highest royal messenger to the lowest slave, all were beautiful and good in Beatriz's eyes.

You found it quaint, didn't you? Endearing in a woman, for sure, but not an attitude to take seriously. You were cynical. You knew the terrible things men were capable of and had seen so much evil in your own life—and how much more there was that you didn't witness. Your world was based on fealty, order, duty. But not trust. Without hierarchy and the fear of punishment, you could not really trust any man, could you?

I remember the night we stayed up together, one of the few nights I indulged her. I gazed up at the stars and read them with my astrolabe. She was rapt, looking at me as if I myself had invented planispheric navigation.

"Are the stars not beautiful, Juan?" I recalled her saying.

I agreed, and told her how from the time I was a boy I lost myself in the stars. We talked about the way they gave me permission to dream—knowing that the stars I stared up at were the very same as those guiding a sea captain on his way to Rome, Athens, India, and beyond. Why did I so rarely share such private thoughts with her?

She told me that she didn't think of faraway places when she saw them, but she could stare at them all night, just the same - in her eyes there were people dancing, animals, faces. Not the boring constellations her father taught her, but the shapes and patterns as she saw them. I lectured her about how the constellations were named because it allowed people to talk about the same stars, that without them there would be chaos. She just laughed and told me that I could use a little chaos.

Was this the last good night? Can you remember the last? You can't, can you?

When you returned from your last expedition she was ill, already dying. You wasted those last few good months chasing rabbits through the mesquite, a journey that made you feel daring and proud and young again but in the end it accomplished nothing.

Why did you go? For what? For whom?

For de León? For Zavala? For Carlos el Hechizado?

She gave you everything. Her love. Confidence. Support. Honor. She never asked for anything in return. You could have given her half as much as you took.

But you didn't. We didn't.

CHAPTER 14

Omens and Mysteries

TO THE RIGHT AND PIOUS FATHER NICOLÒ CHAPA, CÁDIZ, ANDALUCÍA

My dearest Nicolò,

I pray this letter finds you in good health. I have not received any return correspondence in almost two years, but I know how difficult it is for letters to make their way to this desolate frontier. Still I write each time in full faith that these words somehow reach you.

Today I met the woman who is to be my bride: Beatriz Treviño de Olivares, on the invitation of her father and in preparation for our upcoming marriage. She is eighteen years of age, and according to all reports, has a sweet and forthright nature. She is taller than I expected, and the good Lord has graced her with pretty features and a lively, intelligent gaze.

I have anticipated our introduction for some time but stammered and stuttered upon meeting her, scarcely able to say more than, "At your service señorita. I am honored to make your acquaintance." She laughed at me a little, not unkindly, undoubtedly used to the awkward attention of hopeful suitors.

Don Alonso has been promoting the match with the girl's father, General Juan de Olivares for months, impressing on me the opportunity presented by the marriage, and praising my qualities as an administrator and confidante to the General. Don Alonso has come to rely on me greatly over the past three years; indeed our relationship has grown to be rather friendly of late; it seems that he looks at me almost as a son, especially since his own is now so far away.

Don Juan de Olivares is descended from one of the earliest settlers in this reino and has accumulated both great wealth and esteem here. He has nearly 2,000 head of cattle and almost 5,000 sheep and goats. His hacienda of San Antonio de Pesqueria Chica has its own flour mill, over 100 breeding mares, twelve fine warhorses, and eight Negro slaves. He has a house in Monterrey and one in Cadereyta, both of which he maintains at considerable expense. For a landless man to marry into such a wealthy and influential family is unusual. I can hardly believe my good fortune.

You must wonder, dear brother, why such a man would consider marrying his daughter to me, a landless foreigner without wealth or title of his own? I am an able administrator here in a land where they are scarce, but quite honestly Don Juan could hire me for a price far less dear than that of his daughter--not to mention the dowry he will include on our wedding day.

To answer that query, I must confess to you (and you alone, dear brother) that there are persistent rumors – baseless, I am sure – that the Treviños are one of several prominent families here in Nuevo León (along with the Garzas and the Benavides) who are whispered to be Judaizers. There are some, not many, who spread malicious stories, troublemakers who claim these families attend Mass only to divert attention from their secret Jewish rituals, that they chose to live in this remote frontier reino so as to be further away from the scrutiny of the Inquisition.

I give these whispers no credence, of course, but in a moment or two of weakness they gave me pause. Would I want to live under a cloud of unfair suspicion, even if it is based only on jealous gossip? Would I want my sons – should God bless me with any – to grow and live under such a poisonous atmosphere?

I must also admit to you I have noticed strange behavior at times at the house of Don Juan de Olivares. Last spring, during what I calculated to be one of the eight days of Jewish Passover, I was served corn tortilla but no flour ones, nor any bread. And this on a hacienda with a flourmill? Was this a coincidence? Is my suspicious nature getting the better of me?

166

Troubled by these questions, I probed my beautiful Beatriz on this matter--making no reference to Jews, of course--but only inquiring as to her devotion to Christ, Mary, and the Church. She spoke of her rapture at prayer and her fervent love for the Virgin. So sincere was she that I saw her eyes shine in passionate reverence. How could I have doubted this beautiful girl? Nicolò, I tell you, I do not deserve her.

My wedding to this sweet creature will take place in three weeks. I regret deeply that neither you nor any of our beloved family will be able to attend. Know that all are in my mind and in my heart during this time, you not least of all.

May God preserve your health and safety.

Your devoted brother,
Giovanni
3 July, MDCLIII
Marin, Nuevo León, México - Nueva España

COPY – 4 July, 1653 – GBS

***

"I know what section of the *Historia* I would next like to discuss," said Francisco early the next afternoon, taking the unusual liberty of sitting on the stool ahead of Chapa's invitation. Chapa could see even from his place at the head of the bed how weary the old *mestizo* looked, and did not begrudge him his forwardness.

"You presume, Francisco, that I have decided not to destroy the work entirely," said Chapa.

"I apologize, Don Juan. I serve at your pleasure and when given a task, such as the task of reading and discussing this *Historia*, I will work until told otherwise."

Chapa smiled, "Your words may be simple, but you use them as well as any lawyer I have known. So, yes, while I am making up my mind let's continue our work on the *Historia*."

That morning Chapa had awoken to again find himself recovering and hoped to be out of bed by tomorrow. He was certainly much stronger than the day the Governor visited, just a week ago, that day he had so rashly dragged himself out of bed, trying to present an image of strength and vigor.

"Which section would you like to discuss?" asked Chapa, "Should we bring in the manuscript to aide us?"

"No need, Don Juan. I read the chapters very carefully and remember them well. And, if you will forgive me, I believe I am temporarily overtaken with a mild fever, so a short rest on this stool would be of great value to me."

"Be sure to tell Doctor Alaniz about this next time he visits me," said Chapa. "So what are the chapters you speak of?"

"Yesterday you said that your *Historia*, without your intending it, might express some heresy. Most of it seems to be a straightforward recording of facts and events, but there are some instances that touch on less corporal subjects. So I thought we might discuss the chapter most concerned with the unseen hand of God, or other strange forces beyond mortal man."

"You mean the chapters concerning the strange occurrences, such as that of the fish?"

"Yes. These are very unusual events, are they not, Don Juan?"

"Of course they were, or I would not have written on them in such detail."

Francisco paused a moment before continuing, as if needing to catch his breath. "I wonder, *patrón*, if you witnessed these events. You write on many occasions in the *Historia* as if you were present, such as at several battles and the great expeditions —"

"As I was," interrupted Chapa, "at many of them. Though I tried to diminish the importance of a meek and irrelevant scribe in the presence of greater men than I."

"Were you present when the cooked fish returned to life on the plate of Captain Joseph de León?"

"I was not, alas."

"But you trusted the word of the captain."

"I did. And at least five other men witnessed it. The fish was caught, set out for hours, cooked, and then came back to life. Too many honest men swore what they had seen for me to doubt it."

"And the sword which caught fire in the hands of the lowly *mestizo*."

"Don Martín de Zavala's sword, yes."

"Did you witness this miracle?"

"Miracle may be too strong a word, Francisco. We do not know if it is the work of the good Lord or merely the acts of ghosts, devils, or other strange spirits. With God's knowledge and permission of course: *nihilfecit natura frustra*. But no, I again was not present for this remarkable occurrence."

"But there were many honest witnesses, were there not?"

"Fourteen if I recall," said Chapa, curious what Francisco was working his way towards—for he knew by now the winding path of questions would ultimately lead towards the servant's true intention.

"So with so many witnesses you felt sure there was no danger to including their testimony in the *Historia*?"

"I suppose," said Chapa. He was more than a little uncomfortable with this line of questioning. He had his own reasons for including those incidents, but he knew as well as Francisco that it cut against the grain of his natural skepticism.

"Then help me understand an earlier chapter, Don Juan. One that speaks of an event that you do not hesitate to describe as a miracle from God. How on Saint James's Day, God saved the life of Santiago de Treviño during a battle in the Pilón Valley."

"Yes . . ." Chapa blinked. He had not thought upon this chapter in several years.

"There were no witnesses to the miracle besides Don Santiago himself? The remarkable way he survived the avalanche the Indians started, and how he then escaped notice of the large company of Indians who passed by his place of hiding?"

"There were witnesses to his safe arrival in camp after the battle."

"The next day."

"Yes, the next day."

"But no one saw God stay the boulders from killing this man unlike those poor souls that were with him."

"No," said Chapa.

"Nor any explanation of what occupied him those hours between the attack the evening before and his safe emergence at 8 o'clock the next morning."

"I do not believe so."

"Forgive any impiety, but it seems odd to a simple reader like me that you should be satisfied to have no witnesses to this miracle, especially since you emphasized them in the other mysteries. I am sorry to waste your time with my confusion."

Chapa hesitated. He honestly had not thought about the contrast of these chapters, so far apart in the book. Nor had he really considered them as sources of potential danger.

"I am not sure, Francisco. I suppose it was because I knew so well of Santiago's subsequent piety and his lifelong devotion to St. James that convinced me. What man would put on such a show in jest?"

"That is what I missed," said Francisco. "I did not think of his acts after the battle."

"Yes, it has been some time since I wrote that chapter, but I imagine that must be it."

"By the way," said Francisco, "Is this Santiago de Treviño, a relative of your late wife's?"

"He was," said Chapa. "Her brother."

***

Journal Entry: 23 October 1663

    My conversations with Don Martín have ranged over many topics, but of late they have returned again and again to this Meditations book by Descartes. I must confess that they have created great turbulence in my mind. Can one, as this Cartesius urges, truly doubt everything? Is there nothing we can take as self-evident truth? My mind has never been placid and at ease like my Beatriz, but it is now truly disturbed, almost feverish with doubt and questioning. Can we not at least take for granted the existence of God himself? I cannot tell Don Martín, but I have gone to Padre Hugo for confession on this matter. I pray that our Divine Majesty will forgive me for this sin.

    Over these last few months, these questions have burned in my mind, compelling me to fill page after page with my questions and doubts, my attempt to reason out and prove even the simplest of truths. Such a strange compulsion; I question and I write. I doubt something else, and I am compelled to write again. I have filled the margins of Seneca's Epistles as I wrestle with the infuriating ideas of this Cartesius. Dangerous ideas, I know, and I should destroy these writings before they endanger me and my family. However, while I have prayed – and shall continue to pray – for peace, this writing is the only thing that can begin to soothe what feels like a kind of madness.

***

    Chapa sat quietly after Francisco left the room. He knew Francisco was correct in questioning the miracles in *La Historia*. Their inclusion fit awkwardly in the historical narrative, and in truth, he had held the miracles and portents in great doubt ever since his mind had been infected by his discussions with Don Martín.

    He chose to include them because they had become an accepted part of the local history – to leave them out would be conspicuous and, in a real way, unfaithful to the experience of those who lived through those events. But they also served as a kind of diversion to future scrutiny. Some of these happenings might very well have occurred, but if he was completely honest, Chapa was almost sure that the power of suggestion had taken hold amongst those who claimed to witness them. He had seen it time and again with magicians and other tricksters – watching as they convinced onlookers that they were witnessing a miracle. Over the years since reading Descartes, his natural skepticism had been reinforced with a more disciplined and critical approach to observation.

What drives men to seek portents and signs? Wasn't the natural world God created miraculous enough? Did men use miracles and visions to bridge the gaps in their understanding, to fill the spaces between the naked observations of life and the beliefs they held in their hearts? Were these superstitious visions necessary to stay sane in such a harsh and confusing world?

These questions weighed on him more and more of late, in a way they had not since those distant afternoons with Don Martín. Chapa had always felt superior to those who saw the devil in every sick cow, or the act of an angel in every misplaced key or unexpected meeting with an old friend. He knew it was because they couldn't live with the ambiguity of this vast and complex world, couldn't just accept that it was well beyond the comprehension of any human mind.

And yet now, here he was at the end of his life, entranced with the mysteries of Beatriz's little mirror, watching as its voice finally stripped bare the fabrications of a lifetime. It was nonsense of course, he knew that. The mirror could not actually speak to him, he realized; it was nothing more than his unforgiving conscience, throwing into sharp relief the compromised old man reflected in his gaze. But still, peering even deeper, it had taken on some kind of life of its own, revealing to him the lies and rationalizations that he had sown and nurtured. The mirror had taken on some otherworldly power to finally force the truth into daylight.

Here, at the end of life, his cheap delusions were unraveling, the truth laid bare before his eyes. Francisco's persistent questioning, polite though he was, were serving as a different kind of mirror, a darker glass that forced him to reexamine all the justifications of Church and Crown, the partnership that had conquered an ancient land and built this new empire across the waves, this New Spain.

The Spaniards needed labor to build their empire, the Church created the *encomienda* system of force labor and justified it in the name of bringing the Indians to God. When reformers inside the Church finally forced her to recognize the brutal *encomienda* as the slavery it was, the Spaniards developed the more refined *repartimiento*, a different kind of forced labor, this time managed directly by the Crown. This 'enlightened' system, which he had spent his career enforcing and protecting, was supposed to ensure more Christian treatment of the *indigenas*, but in his heart he knew it was just a new coat on the same fat, corrupt *hidalgo*.

We all knew it, but never dared speak it aloud: all knew that maintaining this empire required the free labor of the Indians. Without that foundation, the whole edifice would collapse. So-called reforms shifted the names and conventions just enough to appease those few moralizing factions within the Church, just enough to help the priests keep their hold on hearts of the Indians.

Here in New Spain, the Crown had enslaved Indians and Africans under the guise of bringing them to God, but all that really mattered was Spain's power and wealth. Truthfully, though, the heathens were no better in this regard, selling and enslaving each other over the entire course of their history, even eating the flesh of those they conquered. In that dark moment, Chapa despaired that the whole of humanity rested on exploitation, hidden under a threadbare blanket of fabricated morality. Chapa knew in his heart that he was as guilty as any man, since he was the one person in Nuevo León who made sure every policy (whether great or terrible) was executed faithfully and efficiently.

He stood up and crossed the room to open the shutters, inviting some light into the darkening pools of his thoughts. As always when he felt this darkness, he turned to his talismans of love and beauty—his father, his Nonna, above all, his Beatriz. Letting his thoughts run like cool water over their memory, he reminded himself that God also gave his children compassion; that they are just as capable of kindness as cruelty; that truth could be beautiful as well as ugly.

Chapa remembered, as clear as if it were yesterday, a conversation he had with his father as they walked home from the vineyard, shortly before his father left them forever. 'Giovanni, remember that God in his wisdom allows us to make our own choices—he created us so that we have both good and bad instincts. But he also gave us a conscience, and it is that conscience that gives us the power to respond, and to choose, the good instinct over the bad one. That power creates its own responsibility. We are not bound to follow his path, but instead must come to his grace willingly. That is what makes us human.'

Chapa now wondered at the simple wisdom of his father, who knew of the works of philosophers and theologians only through homilies given by their parish priest. Did the Church foster that moral wisdom, or did it simply give him the words to express what was already inside him? Did Christianity make men good, or just give them a moral cloak to disguise their selfish aims? Certainly, the Church gladly exploited its flock to build great cathedrals—for the good of their souls, of course— and was careful not to upset the ambitions of the great Christian kings. In truth, the Spanish empire was a close bargain between Crown and Church, one that materially benefited both almost beyond measure.

How deep was that bargain? Was the promise of a Christian world merely muddied by petty greed that could be cleansed, or were the very beams of the house rotted from the inside? Kings naturally serve themselves and the glory of their nation. But the Church, supposedly, served the greatest, yet most elusive power of all. Who did the Church in New Spain really see as its true master? Were it shown its own true reflection, its own dark mirror, would the Church choose to serve Power, or would it choose Truth? Chapa was reminded of Seneca's pithy statement, which he had once read but could never repeat out loud, "Religion is regarded by the common people as true, by the wise as false and by the rulers as useful."

***

Early that evening—far later in the day than he typically received visitors—Chapa heard a knock at the door. The sun had set, but the sky still glowed with a faded blend of pastels: green-blue, pink, and orange. Even the stoic Francisco could not hide his surprise and moved to open the door warily, and only after receiving a nod from Chapa.

Francisco left his master's bedroom, crossed the patio, and unlatched the door. The open doorway revealed a figure with a low hat of medium brim and a simple woolen cape, silhouetted against the dying light. It was Padre Joseph.

Francisco bowed his head and stepped aside for the priest to enter.

"Francisco, my son. How are you?"

"I am well, Padre. Tired but well."

"You do look tired, poor man. I hope Don Juan's illness hasn't run you ragged."

"May I take your coat?" asked Francisco.

"No, thank you, it is not too warm in this old house and I don't expect to stay long. I wish to speak to your master, after which I will talk to you alone, in the kitchen. Is that all clear?"

"Very clear, Padre."

Padre Joseph walked across the patio to Chapa's bedchamber and entered slowly. Chapa had finished his evening meal and set aside the plate and bowl from which he ate. He sat in bed with a studied casualness and nursing a small cup of wine and reading by candlelight, spectacles perched low on his nose. He was disappointed, but not surprised to see the priest cross into the room, but composed his face into a conventional smile and said, "Welcome Father. I did not expect you."

"I did not announce my coming. I apologize for the suddenness. I won't stay long. You are still an ill man, and need rest. Francisco looks to be taking ill as well. If he continues this way I may have to send another servant for you. Perhaps one of the sisters."

"Please don't. He is a good man and once I'm back on my feet, I can manage without his constant care."

Chapa certainly didn't want to see Francisco taken away. But any worries about losing his faithful servant and companion paled against the creeping fear that the priest had come to discuss the letter he had written to his brother. Would the Padre have dared to unseal it? Does a priest's lawful authority extend to the private correspondence between brothers?

"I have come again to offer you the Rite of Reconciliation, my son," said Padre Joseph.

"Confession? I do not have that much to confess since our last session," said Chapa, keeping his tone light, although he found the idea bizarre. Padre Joseph's visit was strange enough, but that it was made to solicit a late night confession was inexplicable. "A man can only get into so much mischief when he is bedridden."

"That may be. I never took you for a great sinner, Don Juan. But nevertheless, I implore you to confess whatever sins you have, so that you are as pure as possible when the Bishop arrives."

"If you ask me to confess, Father, I cannot say no."

"It cannot be coercion, you understand. You must come to confession willingly. There is no sword of Damocles hanging above you if you do not."

The threat of a hanging sword was now meaningless. This time if he confessed, he must confess the truth. All that was left for him was truth. But this patronizing young cleric made it so hard.

"Yes, Father, I will confess."

"How long has it been since your last confession?"

"Approximately three weeks. Maybe four. If I am wrong, I do not intend to deceive—this is merely the faulty memory of an old man."

"That is fine, Don Juan. Now, how have you sinned since your last confession?"

"Well, I have missed Mass. I am old and leaving my home is difficult. But a more pious man might have weathered the elements and the distance. Surely a saint would. In this I am sure I sin."

"It is a small sin, Don Juan, but yes, you should attend Mass whenever possible. It is a great aide to the fate of your soul that you have taken communion here while infirm."

"I have also been short with Francisco. I become tired and petty and am ungracious with him, though he is a servant. I ask too much of him sometimes, and chastise him too quickly."

"What else, my son?"

"I am inconsistent in prayer. I pray when in need but become lax when I need God less. I treat prayer selfishly and not as the act of regular devotion that it should be."

"Try to pray every day, and your soul will benefit. What else?"

"I, I take the Lord's name in vain at times. When I strike my toe against a floorboard or spill ink. It is a reflex but I should know better."

"That should be corrected, my son, but is no great sin. Surely, Don Juan, there is something greater weighing on your conscience. Not just in the last six months since you last confessed, but in your entire life," said the priest, "Is there any sin, however distant, that for some reason you did not confess. The greater it's magnitude and the longer you have delayed confession, the more urgent the need for reconciliation. It may be convenient to forget old sins and unpleasant memories, but I assure you the Lord does not."

There was a sin, Chapa thought, a great sin that he had never confessed. He had prayed weeks and months and years over the error. But true repentance required confession. And perhaps God found it appropriate that he should finally confess it now, not to a wise, elder priest that he admired, but before this fresh-faced schemer. Confession must not be too easy.

"There was a woman," Chapa said, "that I knew in Cádiz."

"A woman? A tryst before marriage?"

"In a way, yes. Her name was Josefina. I was but eighteen, and she was twenty-two. I was the ward of my uncle, a prominent trader in Lisboa and Cádiz, whose Castilian name I took."

"An older woman who led you astray. The sin is still great, I cannot pretend otherwise, my son, but she should receive the lion's share of the blame."

"If only that were so, Father. But she was not just a woman several years older than me, she was an African slave, the property of my uncle."

"Did you take her by force, my son?" asked Padre Joseph.

"I swear to you, Father, I did not. So many men will rape their slaves, concluding that if you own a body it is yours to do with as you please. But I am not such a man. And yet, it was still a great sin I know."

"Fornication is a grave sin, my son. You are most fortunate that at such a young age it did not corrupt you."

"Perhaps it did," said Chapa, "Who knows what sort of man I might have become."

The priest remained silent.

"She had no family name," Chapa continued, "And Josefina was but the name my uncle gave her, but her birth name was something like "Jetta." She tried to teach me many times but I could never pronounce it. She was from the Kongo River, taken as a young girl. She was pretty and quick to learn, so my uncle chose to keep her in his own household instead of selling her on to New Spain. Did my uncle ever have his way with her? I honestly do not know. I never asked her and I certainly would never have asked him.

"In truth, Father, she came to me. I worked at my figures and accounts and she lingered when her duties brought her near me. She flirted and teased. She knew nothing of letters and found my constant scratching away with a feather to be something ridiculous. One night after my uncle and the other servants were in bed, we sat by the fire under the pretense of me teaching her basic figures. She asked me if I had ever been with a woman and giggled to see me blush at the question. I will not belabor the details, Father, but suffice it to say that very night we crept back to my small bed and she initiated me in the ways of carnal passion."

"Was it on that one night, my son?"

"No. I confess to you that I became hopelessly infatuated with this creature. It was an impossible romance, of course. She a slave from Africa, the property of my uncle's company, and I, an ambitious young trader from Genoa. It was the folly of youth in full flower—which is not at all to diminish my culpability. My work grew sloppy and I found excuses to spend more and more time with Josefina. I had wild, impossible fantasies of purchasing her from my uncle and sailing off together to Cabo Verde or some such place, some place, a place that does not exist, where we might live together in peace."

"In the end, when my uncle returned to Albisola, he sold Josefina to his partner, Captain Ocelo, in settlement of a debt. That act alone drove me to offer my services to his house, and for two years I worked in Ocelo's trading house, sneaking off to visit Josefina at night. One day, however, he discovered us embracing in the courtyard one evening. He was furious with me for so openly violating the rules of his house, but took out his anger on poor Josefina. He started to beat her and I grabbed his arm to stop him. She told me to stop, that I couldn't understand—she would rather have it now than later. But I struck Ocelo violently, and we fought until his servants pulled me off him and held me back as he beat her. What will never leave me is not the violence of the blows, but the way she took them in complete silence, her eyes fixed on me, impassive."

"It was the man's right to enforce order in his own household, particularly with a slave. You were wrong to strike him, Don Juan."

"I know," said Chapa, "The greatest punishment of all came two days later when Ocelo informed me that Josefina had been sold. He told me she was bound for the sugar fields of Cuba, where I knew her days would be long and hard, and her life short and ugly. I cursed him, swore every black oath I ever heard, swearing to leave his house and find a way out of Cádiz somehow."

"And this is why you came to New Spain?"

"That very night I packed up my trunk with my meager belongings, sleeping that night on the street down by the wharf. As an apprentice, I had no money of my own, so I sought out a *consulado*, one of the Genovese merchant houses that had somehow gained trading privileges in New Spain, and pledged them my labor in exchange for the passage. I promised them far too much, but I was young and desperate and would have worked twice that long to see Cádiz at my back. I blame no one but myself, Father. Through my lust and arrogance I sent Josefina from a safe position in a good house to a death sentence under the cruel Caribbean sun. I ask God's forgiveness, but I could never ask hers."

The priest nodded, "God's grace will have to be enough. Let us pray for his forgiveness."

Chapa closed his eyes, his heart full, seeking peace and absolution. He wondered, as he often did, especially in these days of loneliness and regret, was she still alive? And if so, did she ever think of him? He swallowed hard, and joined his hands in prayer, remembering the last day he spent with her; wondering if by some miracle she was still alive. Even though it had been almost fifty years since he had last seen her, in his mind she would always be twenty-two. His eyes filled with tears, and the young priest, embarrassed, stood up and took his leave.

***

Journal Entry: 23 April, 1647

I am now officially Juan Bautista Chapa. The Captain warned me that foreign names create great suspicion in New Spain – there is a royal edict against emigration of any who are not peninsulares – and I would be wise to take a Spanish name. It is with sadness and shame that I borrow my uncle's name without first seeking his blessing, but there it was, on the manifest as I boarded the ship: "Juan Bautista Chapa, scribe, destination Veracruz."

I have written to my grandmother to tell her of my departure. It is almost certain that I will never return to Albisola – I hope they sell my father's vineyard and make an easier life for themselves. My own future, whatever it will be, now lies to the West.

I brought my trunk on board this morning, the one given to me by my uncle before he returned home to Liguria. In it are all my belongings in this world:

> *Three pairs of breeches*
>
> *Three pairs of underclothes and stockings*
>
> *Five white shirts, two of fine Cambrai linen*
>
> *A simple black waistcoat*
>
> *A black hat of the latest fashion from Madrid*
>
> *An* espada ropera *I purchased at the market last year*
>
> *A bronze pistol (I hope I shall never see need to use it)*
>
> *An astrolabe*
>
> *14 Italian, 5 Latin books and one Castilian,* Don Quijote de la Mancha
>
> *A sheaf of paper, a jar of ink, and three quill pens*

The Captain, when he heard my accent, warned me against carrying any foreign books because they might identify me as an extranjero. *But I can't bear to leave them, and surely there are learned men in New Spain that can read Tuscan or Venetian. Cádiz was full of them. I vow to lead a life where I am never afraid of what I read, or what I write. If I dedicate myself to truth, what man can accuse me of doing wrong?*

CHAPTER 14

Family

I see her, helpless, crows pecking at her eyes.

A mæ mogê.

She scarcely moves. One crow tries to rip off her flesh. Her body hangs against the iron gate. Does she hold on, clinging to life, or is she pinned somehow?

The black cage hangs from the gallows, twenty feet above the traza. It is constructed in the shape of a fat woman, her skirt wide and bust swelling. An awful woman of death. The Virgin's antithesis.

It dangles off the end of the cathedral's finial – anchored to a great stone cross. I don't recognize this place, the cathedral in Monterrey was never this grand. Have they finished it finally? Must they baptize it with the cruel death of my wife?

The scorching sun makes the sight of the suspended coffin even more awful. A crowd of onlookers are staring, their hands shielding their eyes from the penetrating rays of the sun, laughing and pointing as if it were sport.

Beatriz looks down at me in silent sorrow. I step towards her, but I am powerless and can't move. O mæ Dê, why am I such a coward?

Something flies past her. Is it a rock? Then another. And another. The crowd is now flinging stones at her. What evil is this? Lean away from the front of the cage, my darling. Don't let the rocks strike you!

But it is too late. A rock strikes her head. Blood courses from her temple. The stream of red sàngoe excites the vicious birds even more. They tear tiny chunks of skin from her face and hair from her scalp.

I cry out in helplessness and disbelief. Why am I so weak? She gazes down at me with a kind and forgiving sadness.I say and do nothing: I am frozen with fear. In that moment I know: I did this to her. My doubts and prying put her here. "She is not a Jew," I think to myself, "but what difference would it make if she were? I don't care!" These people are so cruel, so ignorant. She suffers for my sins, not hers. Why is she tortured instead of me?

Lying in the plaza, only a few feet from me is the desiccated corpse of another woman. Her body encased in its own iron cage. The sun rots her body – she has ceased to be human and become something else, something strange and terrible. An old man next to me – is he a priest? – tells me this woman was put to death for not confessing her husband's heresy.

I stand in silence, I have no words. Such a coward--I might as well have thrown that first stone myself.

Sto l'é inferno.

***

The following morning Francisco staggered and collapsed on his way across the patio, sending the breakfast tray crashing down onto the stones. Chapa leapt out of his bed with a start and rushed to see what had caused the commotion.

Francisco managed to avoid serious injury from the fall— he sprained his left wrist and would certainly carry bruises for several days—but it was clear he was now very ill. Chapa chided himself for missing the signs of Francisco's descent into sickness and helped Francisco make a bed on the ground next to the fireplace. He fetched Francisco bread and water and wine, a mirror to the servant's own actions for him just days earlier, and assured the old *mestizo* that he could ignore his chores this day.

Francisco feebly thanked his master and curled up to sleep. Chapa stoked the fire and added another log. The December air was quite cold, and Francisco wore only a long linen shirt. Chapa fetched a fine woolen blanket from his own bed—one

183

that had been woven by his own Beatriz—and wrapped it around the shivering man.

How much had Francisco sacrificed so that Chapa might now be well? A few months ago, Chapa wouldn't have felt so responsible for the old servant, but now pledged to himself that he would not let the sacrifice be too great. He brought down another treasured book he had received from Don Martín de Zavala—a book of pastoral poetry by Garcilaso de la Vega—and sat reading by Francisco's side.

***

Later that morning there was a polite knock at the door, a woman, judging by the light force of the rapping. Chapa rose and answered it himself, surprising his guests: in the doorway stood his son Gaspar and his daughter Maria.

Chapa smiled widely at the unexpected visit. It was good to see his children, especially now that he was back on his feet. "Welcome, my children. It is so good of you to visit me. Please come in."

"Thank you, Father," said Gaspar.

Chapa embraced them—Maria first, then Gaspar—kissing each of them warmly on both cheeks. His daughter, an elegant woman now in her late 30s, had inherited her mother's kind eyes and her father's strong jaw. She wore a modest long-sleeved dress under a cloak and hood. Gaspar wore rougher riding clothes and boots.

"Come, sit with your father," said Chapa, gesturing to chairs in the sitting room. They entered and their eyes were soon drawn to the old man curled up on the floor.

"Father," said Maria, "Why does your servant sleep during the day?"

"Francisco is very ill, I'm afraid."

"It makes for an awkward visit to have him lying here in the *sala*," she said. "Can he not move to sleep by the hearth in your kitchen? He would doubtless feel more comfortable there."

184

"He is sleeping soundly, and I shall not wake him," said Chapa. "Besides, even if he were awake, he is the model of discretion, so you may speak freely. What news can you give me of your families?"

Gaspar interjected, blunt as ever, "He is a confessed and convicted thief. You cannot trust a man like that, father. I'm sure he flatters you skillfully, as servants learn to do, but you should be careful. People are not as simple as they were in your day. Nuevo León is now a complex and devious place."

"Please don't talk down to me, Gaspar. The world has been a treacherous place since Cain slew Abel. I have seen far more of this world than you have," said Chapa, in a measured tone, but annoyed just the same. He loved his son dearly, but Gaspar in recent years had developed the habit of treating him like a child.

Maria touched her father's shoulder and spoke before Gaspar could respond to the provocation, "Father, Gaspar, please! We did not come to quarrel with you."

"In any event, I won't move him," said Chapa firmly. "If you don't wish to speak in his presence, we can speak in the study. This is my house, after all."

Gaspar looked at Maria and sighed. She picked at her fingernails, irritated at Gaspar's tone, and tried again to bridge the gap.

"We won't be long," said Maria. "We can just talk here. I doubt there is much of a risk talking in front of this *viejito* anyway."

"Are you staying in town, Maria?" asked Chapa. "It is such a long way back to your husband's *hacienda*, and you shouldn't travel it so late in the day."

"Don't worry, I am staying in Monterrey," she answered. "We do too little to maintain our house by the *traza* and so I am spending several days here to attend to certain repairs. I have a couple servants with me, and my girls, who always look forward to the trip into town."

"I just arrived this morning," said Gaspar, cutting Chapa off as he started to inquire after his young granddaughters.

"What coincidence brings you both to Monterrey at the same time?" asked Chapa, trying to move the conversation back to a more convivial footing.

Gaspar took a heavy breath and answered gravely, "The Bishop from Guadalajara arrived in Monterrey yesterday. I am told he will soon send word that he wishes to meet you."

"Will the Bishop come here?" Chapa asked, looking at the sleeping Francisco and wondering how he would prepare for such a visit. Maybe Maria could send over one of her servants to help him.

"That would be very unusual, so I suspect not. You seem recovered enough to make the short journey to the church. I know you pretend that you cannot make the climb uphill to the *traza* so that you don't have to attend mass, but you will have to submit to the discomfort this time. I will have my carriage brought round for you."

"I can get there under my own power. When did he ask for me? Tomorrow? Sunday?"

"Padre Joseph told me that he will send word tomorrow and request your presence the following day."

"Will you be at this meeting, Gaspar?"

"I will. As will Nicolas, Jose Maria, and our uncle Santiago."

"Thankfully I will be on my way back home," said Maria.

"Since you seem so well-informed," said Chapa, "you must know why the Bishop wants to see me?"

"Padre Joseph has given only cryptic clues," said Gaspar. "But surely you remember my last visit here, father, and like me you can guess at his purpose. You promised me that you would not put your stubborn pride ahead of your family. Now is the time to fulfill that promise. Padre Joseph tells me the bishop isn't coming here to persecute you but only to assure himself that you and your writings have no possibility of infecting this *reino* with heresy or disloyalty. Please, for the good of the Chapas as well as the Treviños, think carefully before you answer him. If there is even the suggestion of disloyalty to Crown or Church, the repercussions could be very serious."

186

"I've always acted for your benefit, and I always will," said Chapa. "Please be at peace, my children."

"No, you haven't," replied Gaspar, his long-held resentment finally boiling over. "You may believe you have but it's long past time you realize that you have chosen your own vanity many times over the welfare of your family. Just as on that day just ten years ago, when you almost ruined us because you wouldn't enforce a simple order. Too often you have been stubborn, selfish, and high-minded when it comes to your career. You hold yourself to some esoteric standard of righteousness, and think nothing of the harm you do to those around you."

"Gaspar, please!" said Maria, stepping in between Gaspar and Chapa. "We love and respect you, father, and your position in Nuevo León is one which makes us all proud. Gaspar had no right to chastise you like that. We are here just to remind you that soon you will not be here to fight your own battles, and left alone we may not be able to wage them as cleverly as you once did."

Gaspar sat down heavily in one of the old chairs, ashamed at his outburst. In truth, while he was still angry about what his father had put them through, he was mostly afraid for the frail old man. He looked at his father, and cleared his throat, wiping his eyes roughly with the back of his hand. "Forgive me, father. I shouldn't have spoken like that."

"No, you're right. It is you, my dears, who should forgive me," said Chapa, once again overcome with guilt for the risks he had placed on his family. "I'm sorry to have been such a burden for you children. I always believed that if I did good work in service of our king and this *reino,* that honor would ultimately cascade down to each of you. Perhaps I was wrong; but you have my word that now, in these last years, my decisions will be guided only by what is best for you and your children."

"Thank you, father," said Maria, "I know our mother smiles down from heaven to hear this."

"I hope so," said Chapa, his eyes welling with tears. These days he could not hear Beatriz mentioned without being overcome with emotion. He surreptitiously wiped his eyes on his sleeve and stood up, glancing over at Francisco, happy to change the subject. "Maria, can one of you do me one small favor today?"

"Of course, father. What is it?" asked Maria.

"Can you ask one of your servants to locate Francisco's daughter, Luisa, and bid him permit her to visit her poor father. I believe she works in the house that sits directly behind the Benavides house."

"I know the house and will send someone today," said Maria.

***

"Francisco, wake up a moment. I have prepared a hot drink of *xocolatl*, although I'm sure I don't make it as well as you."

Francisco opened his eyes, his throat burning and his body aching. He rolled over and blinked in the dim firelight.

"Come, take a few sips. It will be good for you."

Francisco nodded and reached out for the cup that Chapa was guiding towards his mouth. He took a cautious sip of the hot liquid—Chapa had made it with grounds far too coarse and some stuck on his teeth as he drank it. But the warmth reaching down into his stomach felt good, so he took another sip, then another.

Seeing Francisco drink capably with his own hands, Chapa sat back and watched, ready to assist if the old *mestizo* wavered. Chapa had not played nursemaid to anyone since his own wife was dying some four years ago. Like Francisco, Beatriz had long served the daily needs of Chapa, doting on him in tasks that most wives of her stature would delegate to a servant, so the reversal of care had been striking and touching to both of them. Pleased at the good the beverage seemed to be doing, Chapa smiled and leaned back in his chair.

"Would you like to hear some poetry, Francisco? Perhaps you have already read this book. Now that I know how often you stole into my study to read, you may know these verses better than I do."

"I would like to hear you read, Don Juan Chapa," said Francisco slowly. He started to form another thought but gave up on it, the cost of breath not worth whatever thought had congealed in his mind.

"Good," said Chapa, "Garcilaso de la Vega is one of my favorites. He was a great soldier and also a great scholar. Unlike your poor *patrón*, Garcilaso mastered Greek, which I hold to be the sign of a true man of letters. Here he writes of two poor shepherds, Salicio and Nemoroso, who lament loves they have lost:

> *Saliendo de las ondas encendido,*
> *rayaba de los montes al altura*
> *el sol, cuando Salicio, recostado*
> *al pie de un alta haya en la verdura,*
> *por donde un agua clara con sonido*
> *atravesaba el fresco y verde prado,*
> *él, con canto acordado*
> *al rumor que sonaba,*
> *del agua que pasaba,*
> *se quejaba tan dulce y blandamente*
> *como si no estuviera de allí ausente*
> *la que de su dolor culpa tenía;*
> *y así, como presente,*
> *razonando con ella, le decía:*

> The sun emerged from behind the waves,
> already ablaze, flooding the mountain tops
> with golden light, when Salicio, stretched
> at the foot of a tall beech in a lush, green spot,
> where a stream of crystal water

ran laughing through the green meadow.

He began to sing, in harmony

with the delicate sound

of the running water

a plaintive song, so sweet, so soft and gentle

it seemed she was not absent from that place,

she who was responsible for all his pain

and, just as if she stood there,

he laid his thoughts before her, sadly saying:

Chapa paused, marking his place with a narrow slip of scrap paper and closed the book.

"That was very beautiful, Don Juan. What did the shepherd say then, about the woman who left him?" asked Francisco quietly.

"I am afraid I do not remember. I'll continue this poem later if you like. But right now I have sent for your daughter, Luisa. I hope you do not mind my taking that liberty"

"I would like that very much, *patrón*. But in the meantime it will be good to rest my eyes upon my little daughter."

"You've told me that she is your only child, haven't you?"

"That is correct, I am sad to say."

"Don't be sad," Chapa smiled and sighed a little. "You have one child who comforts you, and only one child to worry about. I have six, and while they bring me great joy, I have to admit they can also vex me at times."

"Why is that?"

"Each in their own way, I suppose." Chapa chuckled, "but most of all because they remind me so much of myself and so little of my lovely wife. I have been cursed with children who are as headstrong as their father."

"You judge them too harshly, Don Juan. And yourself."

"I know I do. Mostly I struggle with my own failings as a father."

190

Francisco considered the fire for a moment, musing. "It must have been very difficult for them to have a man like you for a father."

Chapa laughed, "At long last you take advantage of this illness and my sympathy to insult me."

Francisco smiled and shook his head, "What I mean, rather, is that you are not a typical man. You are an exceptional man, in fact. You are not a rancher, happy to gain land and cattle and a place to lie out in the sun in your old age. You are not a soldier, hungry for rank, eager to become immortalized in the name of some conquered valley or discovered river. You are not a merchant, counting the coins in your purse and hoping to die fat and happy with a young mistress at your side. No, you are different, and harder to understand."

"Governors came and went, but always you were there, influencing, creating order, recording events for posterity. If the Church was the heart of this *reino* you were its brain. For four decades, more than any single man, you were Nuevo León. No one talks about it but everyone knows it implicitly. What you have achieved cannot be inherited. You cast a shadow over this entire land, shaping its history in a way that your children struggle to grasp, yet have no hope of escaping from," said Francisco. He trailed off with a weak cough. He had spoken too much in too short a time and laid back to rest.

"I have never thought about it like that," said Chapa, "But there's truth in what you say. I judge my poor children too readily, without thinking about the burdens I've placed on their shoulders, the suspicion and controversy that they must labor under."

"Don't judge them too harshly, but also spare yourself, if you can," said Francisco.

Chapa leaned in and spoke in a low voice, "Francisco, tell me the truth. Was it really you who stole that necklace from Don Alferez? Or did you confess to save your daughter?"

Francisco thought a moment before answering. "False testimony is a mortal sin, just as theft is. Isn't that right?"

"It may be," said Chapa, "It is a sin, certainly."

"Then in either case there is a dark blot upon my soul," said Francisco, avoiding the question. He looked darkly into the fire, "I am a worse sinner than you can even imagine, Don Juan. I must somehow try to repent and find favor with the Lord in the time I have left."

There was then a knock at the door and Francisco rose to his feet slowly, walking unsteadily to the door. He found, as he expected, Luisa, a look of deep worry on her face.

Chapa looked at the two of them, then quietly left the room and crossed to his study. What father and daughter chose to say to one another was no business of his.

***

Journal Entry: 10 June, 1690

Today I buried Beatriz. It is the lowest day of my long life. All she touched felt her warmth. In all the years we spent together, she knew only kindness and beauty, and blessed me and our children with her love and tenderness.

Standing today at her graveside, I was overcome with remorse and sadness, knowing that I never gave her the life her kind soul deserved. I was always too self-absorbed, prideful and ambitious, my mind too focused on honors, titles and accolades, things that did not matter to her in the slightest.

These clumsy words express nothing. My heart is torn apart. I don't even know why I write. Instead I should kneel and pray that the Lord takes me soon, and hope that my life was good enough to let me stand once again by her side.

Life has lost its savor. I will cast this pen aside and never pick it up again.

CHAPTER 15

The Bishop

As predicted, the following day brought a messenger to Chapa's door. He carried an invitation from His Excellency, Bishop Juan de Santiago y León Garabito. The Bishop wished to meet the venerable old administrator and hoped he would join him for a glass of wine the following afternoon in the garden behind the rectory. There was no possible reply but "yes," and Chapa sent the messenger off with a polite smile.

The remainder of that day Chapa occupied himself with caring for Francisco and tidying his house. How long had it been since he scrubbed a pot or dusted a shelf? As Francisco had slowly succumbed to illness, his care of the house had clearly suffered and it was now in rather poor shape. There were all sorts of things out of place, Chapa noted with irritation. He found one of his own cups behind a chair, sticky with dried red wine. He also was surprised to find a spent quill and a small jar of ink in the kitchen. The old *mestizo* was losing his faculties as he fell into sickness, it was clear.

As he worked at tidying the kitchen, Chapa found himself enjoying the work, lost in the steady rhythms of physical labor, an unfamiliar feeling for someone who had spent his life bent over a writing table. While he swept the kitchen with the little willow broom, he thought ahead of the tricky conversation that was to take place the next day. Surely the *comisario* would be there as well. What would he want to know? How would

Chapa answer? Would he be forced to choose, as Gaspar insinuated, between his life's work and his family's security?

He rehearsed imaginary questions and answers over and over again in his mind, speaking them half-aloud, sometimes in strange fragments that must have convinced the resting Francisco he was hallucinating. Throughout his long life he had seen many go before the Inquisition, some to prison and others to the stake. When he first arrived in Ciudad de México, a *Gran Auto De Fe* was held in which dozens of Judaizers were arrested and twelve were publicly strangled and then burned. A thirteenth, Tomás Treviño de Sobremontes, refused to renounce his Judaism like the rest and he suffered the horrific fate of being burned alive—friends from the university had implored Chapa to attend the public burning but he refused.

There were others besides Jews who were charged. There were a great number of alleged sodomites, many of whom managed to surreptitiously flee New Spain before their trial. There was also the strange case of that Irish adventurer William Lamport—he styled himself Don Guillén de Lombardo y Guzmán—who spoke passionately against Negro slavery and tried to raise a rebellion of *negros, indianos,* and *mestizo* merchants against the Viceroy. This "Lombardo" was given every opportunity to leave México but chose to stay and publicly harangue the Inquisition. Naturally this final affront couldn't be ignored, and the curious Irishman was sentenced to burn. On the way to the stake he flaunted a final act of defiance by strangling himself to death with his iron collar.

Perhaps most relevant to Chapa now was the example of Fray Diego Rodríguez, a mendicant friar who was also the foremost astronomer and mathematician in the New World, perhaps in all the empire. He advocated the new theories of Copernicus and other natural philosophers banned in Catholic lands. The reckless friar escaped with his life, but his writings were destroyed and his effort to spread the new mathematics was permanently suppressed.

Chapa was of course no deranged insurrectionary like Lamport nor a genius with dangerous new ideas like Rodríguez. He read much but advocated no dangerous theories. His writing mostly recorded the events as they occurred in his lifetime — simply and without implication. Until the death of his wife he was a regular at Mass and publicly supportive of every governor, those who employed him as well as those who chose not to. His personal life was entirely ordinary and most people would find his sins to be quite banal. In short, all reason suggested that he had no need to fear this conversation with the Bishop and his *comisario*. And, yet, here he was, trimming the wick of a candle, his hands trembling.

***

Gaspar met Chapa at his door the following day around eleven o'clock and together they walked slowly up towards the *traza*. The last time Chapa had been this far from his door he had been overcome with fever and collapsed in the driving rain. He noted the point as they walked by — it was only a few dozen *varas* from his house. What a fool he had been to attempt such a thing that day; he was lucky he was still alive. Was Francisco now paying for his folly?

The day was mild and the sun shone brightly on the dusty ground; fat white clouds dotted the sky. Their destination was the little church built a generation before by the brothers of St. Francis. When they moved their friary to the mountains near Saltillo, the stone church became the seat of Monterrey's little parish, under the supervision of the diocese of Guadalajara. Chapa often wondered if the brothers preferred the cooler climate of the mountains, or if they instead desired some distance between themselves and the seat of governance here in Monterrey. In any event, the church was now Padre Joseph's and the honor of the bishop's visit was his as well.

As they neared the church, Chapa gazed over at the partially constructed cathedral. It was strange to see the foundation of such a monument in a town as sparsely populated as Monterrey, but by the time the work is completed, in another hundred-and-fifty years, there would undoubtedly be many more souls here. Would any of his descendants be here to see it? Would they remember their old ancestor, who saw its first stone laid?

They reached the church and walked around to the rectory. Padre Joseph was outside waiting for them and smiled as he reached out to Chapa. The priest embraced him warmly and ushered him inside as the two younger men exchanged polite nods. "It is so good of you to join us, Don Juan. The Bishop has so many duties during his brief sojourn that it would no doubt have been impossible to visit you in your home. And he has so looked forward to meeting you."

They walked through the spare but spacious sanctuary—originally intended to house the numerous friars—and through a set of doors into the cloister, a broad open space surrounded by vaulted arcades designed to shelter the friars as they walked and prayed the rosary. Chapa, like most in the parish, had never been invited beyond the sanctuary and so had never seen how beautiful this cloister was. The garden was verdant and lush, and the simple architecture surrounding it was beautiful. Chapa wondered why the friars had abandoned such a tranquil place.

And yet, there in the center under a low-hanging tree, sitting in a wicker chair with a patterned blanket on his lap, was the Bishop. He was a genial looking older man, maybe five or ten years younger than Chapa. He wore a fine black cassock with red piping, and over his shoulders was a simple but elegant cape, the outside black and the inner lining a vivid scarlet.

As he approached, Chapa spied a few familiar faces sitting around the Bishop. His daughter Maria sat in her finest dress, an idle fan in her hand. He was surprised to see her, since she had planned to return to her ranch today. To her right were two of Chapa's younger sons, Jose Maria and Nícolas, and across from his children, flanking the bishop were Governor Don Juan Pérez de Merino, Beatriz's brother Santiago, Lieutenant Governor General Don Antonio Fernandez Vallejo, and the governor's Secretary, Rodrigo Ulias. Hovering behind the bishop was a young priest, standing quietly with hands folded. Surely this man—younger than Chapa had expected—was the *comisario*, the source of the intense fear that had long gripped Chapa and his children.

Three empty chairs awaited Don Juan, Gaspar, and Padre Joseph. Resting in the middle of the rough circle was a low, rectangular table upon which sat a plate of pan dulce and a jug of goat's milk. A glass of wine sat on the table near the bishop — apparently he was the only man there who would be drinking wine today.

Chapa knelt down on his left knee before the Bishop (the right knee was for God, the left for His servants), who then patted him on the shoulder gently in greeting and gestured toward the open chair. Chapa stood again, stiffly and with some pain and then took a seat as gracefully as his poor joints allowed him.

"So, this is the Don Juan Bautista Chapa of which I have heard so much," said the bishop with a slight smile. He seemed in good health but a bit tired, no doubt from the long journey from Guadalajara.

"It is a great honor to be your guest, Your Excellency," said Chapa, "I never thought I should live so long as to again see Nuevo León visited by so great a prince of the Church."

"The journey is not an easy one," said the Bishop, "but I know life on this frontier must be just as hard. I only regret it has been so long since my last pastoral visit."

The Bishop turned to Chapa, "You know everyone here, I trust."

"Yes, Your Excellency. Though I have not seen them all in one place in many years. And I doubt I will again, at least until my funeral."

The Bishop smiled at Chapa's sarcasm, "You of course cannot know the young man behind me. This is Father Mateo, my personal secretary."

The dark-eyed Father Mateo nodded politely to Chapa without much interest. Chapa returned the nod with a bolt of energy running through him — had he truly escaped the scrutiny of the *comisario*? Had he been a child scared of shadows all along?

"It is a beautiful valley you are blessed with here," said the Bishop, "I have no doubt that one day, when that cathedral of yours is complete, you will be granted a bishop of your own. Until then, know that, however great the distance, the Church watches over you."

Chapa was unsure if that was a message of reassurance or warning. "No man here will live to see its final stone set in place," said Chapa, "But it is a hope that nourishes all of us, I am sure."

"Now, Don Juan . . . excuse me, Don Juan Chapa, not you Governor—"

The Governor gave a little awkward cough at being tangentially acknowledged and nodded his head.

"—Don Juan, I am told you were educated in Sevilla. Is that true?"

"It is, Your Excellency. Or at least that small amount of formal education I was blessed to obtain before leaving for New Spain."

"Ah, at the *Colegio Santa María de Jesús*?" asked the bishop.

"Yes, Your Excellency."

"Would you believe, Don Juan, that I was educated at the very same university? I was born and raised just fourteen *leguas* away in the humble town of Palma del Rio. And what did you study there, Don Juan? Surely not Theology, as I did?"

"No, Your Excellency. I did not have a mind for such lofty subjects. I began studies in the Law, although they were interrupted by my departure."

"It is fortunate for this new *reino* that you chose it," said the Bishop, "for I am told when you arrived here nearly fifty years ago there was scarcely a man in this *reino* who could read or write, much less with knowledge of the Law. But I have to ask, why did a learned man such as you, who might have risen far in the capital, instead chose this distance place to make your career? Why not the Ciudad?" probed the Bishop, "or even our fair city of Guadalajara? I wonder, did your rumored status as a foreigner have anything to do with your choice?"

Chapa rubbed his hands together with some discomfort, "You may recall, Your Excellency, a claim about ten years ago

198

that I was an illegal *extranjero* here. A claim rebuked by the Royal Court and confirmed by His Majesty himself. I have never denied I was born in Genoa, Your Excellency, but I became a man in Cádiz, in the care of my uncle, who was himself married to a woman from the peninsula. I was a loyal Spanish subject even as a child of fourteen."

"And you came to New Spain via Veracruz?"

Chapa replied, careful with his words, drawing out the narrative until he could get a feel for the focus of the Bishop's interest. The *comisario* may not have been present, but this bishop was proving to be a subtle interrogator, "Yes, that great, dirty port was my first taste of New Spain. And two months of malaria was my first reward for leaving my homeland. So the five-week journey to the capital was a blessing. I traveled with a trade caravan, but every step of the way I imagined myself Cortés, who journeyed by that very same route."

Chapa looked around at his audience, gauging their response, as he leaned into his narrative. "As we climbed away from the swampy coast, the air became cooler and more healthful. The mountains I had seen in my youth were craggy and stony, covered with scrubby pine trees and the aromatic brush of the Mediterranean. Here they were lush and populated with every manner of tree and flower, full of birds and monkeys and frogs. I felt I had entered some sort of antediluvian garden. Genoa, where I was born, is a great city as well, but it is old, as old as the earth it seems. There are few buildings where any living soul can remember who laid the first stone. But this city of México was so very different, more like Cádiz, a gleaming new city still in the making when I lived there.

"You know México, of course, Your Excellency. And so do you, Governor. My children do not, so forgive me if I indulge them a little." Chapa continued, seeking to distract his interrogator with the banal details of his early life in México, "There are the well-known pagan ruins that surprise you around every corner, older than any man can say. But more striking were the myriad new buildings under construction, civilized buildings, rich and decorated with carving and tiles and ironwork. There were workers, Indians, everywhere, filling in the old *México* canals, building churches and convents, palaces and warehouses, many of them constructed with the very stones of the temples of their ancestors.

"Your sons should visit the capital," said the bishop, "You *Norteños* hide away on your *haciendas* and rob yourself of the pleasures of civilization."

"I agree with you, Your Excellency. But these boys don't have the same wanderlust in their blood. They are men who yearn to grow and build and raise a family in peace."

"You and I, Don Juan, we are not so dissimilar," said the bishop, "I too am thousands of *legua* from my homeland. I too came up the road of Cortés from the swamps of Veracruz. I know all too well the shock to the senses and the mind."

Chapa nodded.

"And so, Don Juan, you sought employment in the law?" asked the Bishop, subtly but unmistakably controlling the inquiry as if it were a polite chat.

"If only I could have, Your Excellency," said Chapa. "But I still owed the *consulado* another twelve months of service before I was free. And so I worked in the warehouses of the Ciudad. In truth, I value those months as much as any other. I witnessed the way México served as a waypoint between the Orient and the Occident, how many exotic and wonderful goods came eastward and how Christian civilization traveled westward. Unless the fabled Northwest Passage is discovered or the voyage around the Cape becomes less perilous, there seems no limit to the wealth that will pass through this land."

"But you did not become a merchant," said the bishop.

"No. I am of Genovese blood, and so should have taken to commerce like a duck to water. But for some reason, the push and pull of trade was not for me, and so I sought a different destiny. Deep down I truly am a Spaniard, and love our King as deeply as any man born in Castile."

"Is that so?" asked the Bishop. "Do you recall the year, Don Juan, in which you arrived in the capital?"

"It was 1647, I believe," said Chapa, mystified at the importance of this date.

"The same year our Holy Office of the Inquisition began requiring the booksellers of the city to submit their wares for monthly inspection, is it not?"

"It may have been. I do recall the practice, though I did not know it began only that year."

"And the trouble with that friar, Rodriguez, who peddled heretical works to the so-called intellectuals. Did you ever meet him?"

"I did, once," said Chapa, hoping he would be asked no more on the matter.

"Ah, I hope he did not influence you too greatly," said the bishop. "Young men are so impressionable."

"For better or worse, Your Excellency, he was a comet flying far too high and too fast to singe a poor man like me. I was blessed with a head for letters and for sums, and I knew enough of higher maths and astronomy to use an astrolabe, but beyond that they are a mystery to me. I know the sun comes up in the morning and goes down each evening, and that the location of stars can divine a path through the night—more than that is for wiser men than I to discern."

"It is wisdom indeed to know the limits of what one can know," said the Bishop. "I commend you for avoiding the tail of that troublesome comet."

Chapa nodded and glanced over at his children. They still seemed nervous, sensing that this discussion of the past, harmless as it seemed, was just a prologue to what would come.

"And then this brings me again to the great question," said the Bishop. "Why would a man of letters, with wealthy clients in the city to pay for his bread, a growing bureaucracy serving the Viceroy in which to make a career, and surely friends by that point, even a *novia* perhaps—why leave all that behind to come here to the far north, where hardly any town has more than two-hundred Christian souls?"

"It does seem mad in such a light," said Chapa, "though you overestimate my talents. In a land where men of even modest learning are rare, would I not climb faster and farther than in the crowded lanes of México?"

"Perhaps," said the Bishop.

"Think of it this way, Your Excellency. At the end of my life I sit here, with my children at my side, the guest of the great Bishop of Guadalajara and the Royal Governor of this *reino*. Would I have been blessed with such company had I been one of a thousand men buried in the great administration of the Viceroy? I suspect I would not."

"Why then, Nuevo León, of all places? Why not the rich provinces of Zacatecas or Guanajuato? Or the fertile plains of the Bajío? What lured you to a land best known for its awful climate and annual Indian wars?"

"It was, in the end, Your Excellency, a chance encounter with a great man. Don Alonso de León, the elder, was in the capital on some business. Don Alonso was one of those men that drew others to him almost instinctively—he moved as someone who was never in a hurry, always confident he would arrive when he was most needed. His voice was deep and penetrating, but he never yelled—he was a man who took being listened to for granted. There was a rustic quality about him, certainly, but not the crudeness that one often sees among those who stay too long on the frontier. He discarded the extraneous trappings of the city, but lost none of the polish and sophistication.

"He heard of my love of books and confided that he was writing an *Historia*, a work that related the early years of this *reino*. I read portions of his manuscript and through his prose I started to love this land, even though I had not yet seen it with my own eyes. I felt God himself had revealed his design to me. I offered Don Alonso my service and set out with him for Cadereyta just six days later. With no horse of my own, I walked with the baggage amongst the mules, but, Don Alonso rode alongside me often and we spoke of the history and nature of this strange land we were bound for."

The bishop leaned back and smiled, taking a sip of his wine. "These are fascinating reminiscences, Don Juan. I hope you don't mind indulging me."

"Not at all, Your Excellency," Chapa said with a relaxed smile, "To be quite honest, I had some apprehension you might be accompanied on this visit by a *comisario* of the Holy Office. I assure you this is much more pleasant."

"Oh," said the bishop, "the *comisario* has been here this whole time."

Chapa's heart sank suddenly. Had this bored young secretary truly been examining him since he arrived?

The Bishop continued, "In fact he has been here in your town these three years. Don Juan, gentlemen, let me properly introduce you to the *comisario* of the Holy Office of the Inquisition for the Diocese of Guadalajara: Padre Joseph Guajardo."

Chapa turned to see the pudgy face of Padre Joseph smiling at him, eyes blinking like a cat.

Padre Joseph sat up and spoke for the first time since Chapa arrived, "Your Excellency, would you permit me a question of Don Juan."

"Of course," the Bishop said with a nod.

"Don Juan, you loved Nuevo León from the outset, you say?" asked Padre Joseph.

"Yes, and I do to this day," Chapa replied, unfolding his hands that he found were now damp with sweat.

"That is a notion of great interest to me," said Padre Joseph, "for a letter has come into my possession that is purported to be in your hand. Do you think we ought to hear it?"

Chapa's stomach tightened even further at this news. The priest had opened his letter, after all. Would this be the end of him? He took a deep breath and answered as simply as he could: "If they are my words, I will stand responsible for them."

CHAPTER 16

The Comisario

The Bishop gestured to his secretary, and the younger man dutifully produced a piece of paper with a broken seal. He held it out, but the bishop did not take it.

"Please show the letter to Don Juan so that he may confirm or deny that it is in his hand," said the Bishop.

The secretary walked over to Don Juan and handed him the unsealed letter, now carefully refolded. It had been opened, the letter inside carefully re-folded and returned to its original state. Chapa removed the letter and gazed upon his familiar shaky writing. He nodded soberly.

"Excellent," said the Bishop, "I hope you do not mind if I ask Padre Joseph to read it to us. He is a younger man with a strong voice. I had the pleasure of conducting Mass with him just this morning."

Chapa looked around the small company—all eyes were fixed upon him. "I do not," he said quietly. His heart sank as he looked at the fear in his children's faces.

The secretary handed Joseph the letter and stepped back to his place behind the Bishop. Padre Joseph took the letter in hand and began to read.

***

TO THE RIGHT AND PIOUS FATHER NICOLÒ CHAPA, CÁDIZ, ANDALUCÍA

My dearest Nicolò,

I pray this letter finds you healthy and content. I write this time in full knowledge that this will in all likelihood be my final correspondence to you. I've been overtaken with illness, one that I fear may bring my death.

A mere week ago I might not even have had the chance to write this letter. But with the constant care of my servant, Francisco, I have restored my strength sufficiently to sit behind my desk long enough to write to you. Yet I fear the small hill on which I stand is but a brief way station before the road winds again into the dark valley below.

I write to you now with love and appreciation for the years of our boyhood and your patience with these infrequent correspondences. I do not cling jealously to life. I have always tried to live by the words of Lucretius: Nimirum hac die una plus vixi, mihi quam vivendum fuit.

And yet, here at my life's end, I am vexed with a great dilemma. As you know, brother, my life was given in service of this reino, *bringing order and civilization to the barbaric frontier as best I could. But the culmination of that effort and the sole labor of my later years has been an* Historia, *an extension of the great work begun by my first mentor, Don Alonso de León, which chronicles the years that have transpired since he left off of the task.*

This work of many years is now in jeopardy. When I came to Nuevo León so many years ago, it was a distant island of free thought, a place almost irrelevant to the powers of this world, far from the intolerant minds enforcing discipline in the great cities. Governor Don Martín de Zavala read and discussed openly books and treatises that would have been burned in Ciudad de México. The saving grace of the dangers and discomforts of this rugged territory has been the space it afforded to truly think and to seek truth with an independent mind. However, I fear those times are now coming to a close.

I cannot endanger my family. But you alone know the heartache it will cause me to destroy this Historia. *Part of this anguish is selfish, for it is the work on which I have labored many years. But beyond my own attachment to the work, it exists also as the only thorough record of our Christian civilization here in the northern frontier. I do not claim to have written a work of great brilliance or profound insight, nor have I ever strived to. It is a simple record, nothing more. But still, I fear that generations to come will be poorer without the knowledge of all that transpired here in those early years.*

Think of the Dark Ages from which Christianity has at long last emerged. What wisdom and lessons could we learn if only men had taken the time to write of what transpired in the golden years that preceded it. I fear that our time here in New Spain will become a new Dark Age, where men in this land will pursue only material wealth while forgoing the pursuit of knowledge and wisdom. Ratio et prudential curas, non locus effuse late maris arbiter, aufert.

There is no time to receive your counsel in this matter. I must resolve my course of action soon — likely in a matter of weeks. I only write because there is no one else in whom I can confide. Well, perhaps there is one other, but it is a different situation altogether. My hope is that the the act of writing might itself elucidate the right path.

I love you, Nicolò, now and always. If there is a life hereafter, I hope we are joined there. If there is not, perhaps this love somehow shall outlive us.

May God preserve you,
Giovanni
4 December, 1693
Monterrey, Nuevo León, México - Nueva España

***

Having completed the recitation, Padre Joseph dropped his eyes to his hands—consciously avoiding Chapa's steady gaze—and carefully folded the letter.

"Is that Quintus Horatius Flaccus?" asked the Bishop, "Speaking about the wide views over the sea?"

"I believe so, yes," answered Chapa. It was too much to hope the Bishop could be lured into a long discussion of the Classics.

206

"It pleases me to know," said the Bishop, "that I have not forgotten all my education. Now, Don Juan, we would like to reconcile some things presented in this letter."

"As would I," said Chapa. His fear was gone now, replaced with resignation, but also with a slow anger, and a pricking feeling of pride in the forthrightness of his words.

"You speak of a kind of intolerance in the capital," said Padre Joseph darkly. "I can only take that as a criticism of the Holy Office of the Inquisition and our work. Is there any other possible explanation for such words?"

Chapa could feel the tension rise and looked towards his children. His son Gaspar's hands worked into a tight fist in his lap. His daughter Maria's face was filmy with perspiration, despite the cool weather. Jose Maria's brow was furrowed, while Nicolas was calm, betraying nothing.

"Please correct me if I am mistaken, Your Excellency, but if I understand correctly, in your time as bishop the Holy Office has ended the cruel, abhorrent sports of bullfighting and cockfighting, and closed the lascivious theaters."

"That is correct," said the Bishop.

Chapa turned to the Bishop, searching for the right words to turn the discussion onto more even ground. "Then I would say these are expressions of intolerance that are noble and just. That tolerance of evil things is evil and intolerance of them is good." Chapa didn't have much hope for this line of discussion, but had to look for a way to turn the conversation onto a more benign path.

"You are a clever man, Don Juan," said the bishop, "But you cannot expect me and these good people here to believe you wrote of the Inquisition's intolerance as if you championed it."

"I champion the work of our church in all things, and the Inquisition particularly in its efforts to cleanse New Spain of immorality and heresy. But—"

And at this "but" Chapa could feel the hearts of his children sink. "—as a humble sinner I will admit to you here before God, because I came here to tell the truth and not to lie,

207

that I cannot understand why certain works may not be read. I defer, and I obey, but I do not understand."

"Do you obey, though?" asked Padre Joseph.

"I do, Father. An old man may gripe about the weather but he does not fool himself that he might change it. Such are the sour mutterings in that letter. I apologize for them, but they are not the words of a heretic or a rebel. I destroyed the works of Cartesius that Don Martín de Zavala had asked me to. And I destroyed the beautiful poems of Sor Juana Ines de la Cruz when the Holy Office banned them. And if you so ordered me I would destroy the works of St. Augustine himself, though I hope you do not. But I confess that I would still not understand."

"Do you truly not see how words can be dangerous, Don Juan?" asked the Bishop calmly.

"Words that incite sin, yes. Or, words that intentionally express heresy. But if a man writes of truth as he himself witnessed it, or of abstract matters of geometry, how can that offend God? How could an impartial description of the world He created be a sin in His eyes?"

"I would not think a well-read man such as you," said the Bishop, "would need an example of how words, even if they are the truth, can do grievous harm. But it seems such an example must be made plain to you. Father Mateo, please hand me the next letter."

Chapa found he was unable to swallow, suddenly confused. What letter could this possibly be? Had an old copy somehow become mixed up in the pages of his letter to Nicoló?

The bishop continued, "It is another letter to your brother, it appears. Written forty years ago but still in remarkable shape. I take it this is a copy?"

"A copy?"

"Do you keep a copy of your correspondences in your home?" asked the bishop, "In your trunk, among all of your other papers that you keep locked away? Surely you did not simply write dozens of letters without delivering them? These are copies, are they not?"

Chapa was stunned. "I . . . yes, I always transcribe a copy. It satisfies my drive for order, for completeness."

"It is a curious practice," said the bishop. "You are a most thorough man, and an eccentric one. I will not waste everyone's time with the whole of the letter, though your prose is most pleasant." He placed his spectacles on the end of his nose and scanned the letter for a particular passage. "Ah, here:

> *Today I met the woman who is to be my bride: Beatriz Treviño de Olivares, on the invitation of her father and in preparation for our upcoming marriage. She is eighteen years of age, and according to all reports, has a sweet and forthright nature.* "

"That is nice, isn't it? I am told she was a lovely woman."

"She was, Your Excellency," said Chapa.

The bishop continued:

> *I confess to you (and you alone, dear brother) that there are persistent rumors about this family — baseless, I am sure — relating to what the Spaniards call* limpieza de sangre. *The Treviños are one of several prominent families here in Nuevo León (along with the Garzas and the Benavides) who are whispered to be Judaizers.*

"That is most unfortunate. And, let me see, here:

> *Last spring, during what I calculated to be one of the eight days of Jewish Passover, I was served corn tortillas but no flour ones, nor any bread. And this on a hacienda with a flourmill? Was this a coincidence? My paranoid nature getting the better of me?*

"I should certainly hope so," said the bishop, setting down the letter and removing his glasses. "Now, Don Juan, you were not lying in this letter to your brother, were you?"

"I . . . no."

"You wrote what you thought was the truth. Or the truth of your personal experience," said the Bishop.

"Yes."

"And yet today, spoken publicly, these words stand to do a great deal of harm to your children, don't they?"

"A great deal, yes, Your Excellency."

"Then trust me. Trust in the Church. Trust in the Holy Office. Your papers are dangerous. You tell us you are a loyal Spaniard and yet you write in this letter of Spaniards as if they are a separate people from yourself. You tell us your name is Juan Bautista Chapa and yet you sign your letters 'Giovanni.' You tell us you loved Nuevo León before you even saw her, and yet your letters and journal speak of frustration and loathing for this *reino*. Baseless or no, you impugn the good Christian name of your own wife and, with it, that of your children. And there are darker things still, hinted at in your Journal, that I shall not discuss in the company of your daughter. It is for the general good, and your own particular good, that all these writings be destroyed."

Chapa shook his head slowly, trying to grasp what was happening. The letter intercepted by Joseph he understood, but these other writings. . . "How can you—I apologize, Your Excellency, I must know, how can you know what is in my personal papers? How did you acquire that forty-year-old letter?"

Padre Joseph smiled, "You are too trusting, Chapa. It was merely a matter of placing the Indian slave there in your home. He belongs to the Church, does he not? Anything he read was read by the Church. You welcomed his help, but you must have known that fundamentally he was not his own man, but rather an extension of the parish, which is to say an extension of me, the Church, and our Lord Jesus Christ. By inviting him into your home, you were inviting the Holy Office."

Chapa's head reeled, his mouth filled with saliva. He staggered to his seat, at last finally grasping the extent of his betrayal. "Francisco. Francisco stole my papers."

"He read them, yes, on my instruction," said Padre Joseph, "And brought me the ones of greatest concern. Which, I must say, is a great many of them. By bringing them to me, he fulfills not only his duty, but bestows a great gift on your soul—the chance to confess and make right the wrongs you have committed."

The bishop interjected, "I beg you, Don Juan, informally here, but in the presence of your children and these good men. Destroy them all, and you will spare us all a great deal of anguish. I am an old man myself, Don Juan, and I pray every day that we shall never again see an Inquisitorial Trial in the North. Please help that wish come to pass, my son. The choice, for now, remains with you."

Chapa remained silent, his head still reeling from the revelations of the last few minutes. The careful husbanding of his correspondence, the obsequiousness of the introduction of his *Historia*, the decision to remain anonymous, had all been for nothing. Francisco had exposed him, stripping him naked in front of the eyes of the Inquisition.

His children rose silently and Maria offered him her arm. Together they walked out of the side door of the cloister and out into the dusty squalor of the *traza*.

***

La Historia del Nuevo Reino de León, Introduction

To the Devout Reader

This History is written so that the important journeys made by Captain Alonso de León (may he rest in Glory) will not remain buried in the tomb of oblivion. The captain was a settler who lived in the town of Cadereyta in Nuevo León. Because of his clear understanding of the period, he wanted to leave to posterity a record of his explorations; the reasons for his journeys; the customs, rites, and nature of the Indians; and the events that occurred from the time of his reconnaissances to the year 1649. His chronicle required an extensive effort to secure information from the older residents of the area and from old documents, which, as a careful person, he collected.

The very careful manuscript was dedicated to Dr. Don Juan de Manosca, the Inquisitor of the Ciudad de México, so that it might be printed. This did not take place, however. Although I do not know the reason the work was not published, I attribute it to the fact that soon after the manuscript was completed, the author left México to visit Spain on business for Governor Martín de Zavala. That may have been why the publication of the work was frustrated. I have continued these discourses from the year 1650 to the present year 1689 because of the deep affection I had for the deceased.

I well recognize how difficult and dangerous it is to write histories in these times, because of the disbelief of some and the censorship of others, who boast of censuring others' vigilance. But even if those who read these poor scribblings censure them as other malicious critics do, they shall not be able to point a finger at me, because I am an anonymous author. Since they do not know who I am, they will not have a target at which to fire shots, as the fortune Zoilus did when he criticized the writing of the Prince of Poets, Homer.

I would like, then, to give thanks to him I owe so much (for death does not extinguish the obligation that was contracted in life). In the last analysis, payment is partly an acknowledgement of the debt, even when it is not possible to pay it.

The style will not be lofty, because of my personal inadequacy. Moreover, the concepts will be crude, because those who live in remote areas tend to forget the polite language of the court, even if once they learned it.

The truth shines on all occasions and is pleasing to all. Veritas est ad quatior rei ad intellectum.

I hope the reader will have the good grace to pardon all my shortcomings.

Introduction excerpted directly from the book _La Historia del Nuevo Reino de León,_ by Juan Bautista Chapa

CHAPTER 17

Plato's Allegory

Gaspar and José Maria escorted their father home, their arms locked into his for support. Even on a less eventful day the walk to the *traza* and back would have tired him greatly. As it was, he had to summon every ounce of strength to stay afoot. Such was Chapa's pride that he refused to let Gaspar call for a cart to wheel him home, as if that would have been a final admission of defeat.

When they reached the house, unlocked as always (for what was there to steal?), his sons all but carried him inside to his chair. There on the floor lay Francisco, eyes closed — though if he was truly asleep or feigning Chapa could not tell. Looking at the old *mestizo* curled on the floor, the full force of Francisco's betrayal truly hit home for the first time, hurt and rage coursing through Chapa's veins like a sudden fever. Was there a single thing he could trust from this man, on whom he had come to depend almost like a brother?

"Would you like us to throw this miserable Indian in the gutter, Father?" asked José Maria, his face flushed with fury. "He deserves to die in the streets like a dog."

In that moment Chapa almost assented, thinking about all the days and months the slave had spied on him, rifling through his most intimate papers, all while accepting his confidences, discussing the *Historia* as if he were an equal, a colleague, a friend. His mouth once again filled with saliva, the urge to vomit almost overtaking him. In all his life, despite all the intrigue and power struggles he had witnessed and been victim to, no one had ever delivered a betrayal so complete, so devastating. But this defeat was so total, so final, that it left him without even the strength, the energy to hate the old man lying before him.

"No, let him stay here," said Chapa, flatly. "Moving him now would be the end of him. If he dies here so be it. I have enough sin on my conscience, I don't need to add his death," he said, his voice weak, his throat raspy. "And don't send anyone to care for me – these last days have shown me that I can care for myself, and my mind craves solitude above all else."

Gaspar looked to his brother. "I told you he would be stubborn about it. We will leave you be for the moment, but I will send Doctor Alaniz to look in on you. No doubt he will confirm it for you when he arrives, but I can tell you plainly, the man is dying. I will send someone to look in each day, as they will need to bury him once he dies."

Chapa sat in his chair, pondering the complexity of his own emotions, the extent of his affection for this simple man now suddenly overwhelming him. The human heart was a mystery, and even though he had suffered the most complete betrayal of his life, still he was not sure which struck him harder, the news of Francisco's surreptitious betrayal or this confirmation—he had known, hadn't he?—that the old *mestizo* would soon perish. Francisco, after all, had had no real choice in the matter. Slaves must follow their master's orders, and in his heart he knew that Francisco had done so only under duress. What would Beatriz have said in such a moment?

Chapa turned to his sons, his face concealing the conflicting emotions that roiled under the surface, wanting nothing more at that moment than to be alone with his thoughts.

"All I ask is that you put fresh wood on the fire and leave me in peace. I have had far too much excitement for one day," he said, shivering a little in the room whose fire had dwindled to a few embers.

Gaspar leaned against the doorway, "Father, do not ignore the matter before you."

"And what matter is that?"

"Your papers, father," said José Maria, with somewhat less impatience than his older brother exhibited. "Let us take them now and burn them. Let us take this weight off your mind now. You yourself agreed."

"I agreed that the reasoning of His Excellency was sound. I did not consent, as yet, to any destruction."

"You know in the end you have no real choice in the matter," said Gaspar.

"In the end," said Chapa, "None of us have any choice. You can rest assured that I will do the sensible thing for you and your children. But I must have one last night and day with these papers. They are the warp and weft of my life, you see, my work, my memory of your dear mother, my growth as a man. When these are finally taken from me, there will be nothing left."

"But you *will* let us take them? Tomorrow?" asked Gaspar, urgently, "I must return to my *hacienda* soon."

"Yes, tomorrow. You can come for them after *siesta*. Until then, leave me. Even condemned Socrates was granted a last night of peace with his friends."

Gaspar rolled his eyes at the dramatic reference and stepped away from the wall. He patted his brother on the shoulder, gesturing silently towards the front door. José Maria went to the kitchen to find fresh wood for the fire, and Gaspar brought a blanket to wrap around his father's shoulders and fetched a cup of wine cut with water, while Nicolas ensured that the larder was still well stocked with food. Chapa kissed them all, and soon the men were on their way, leaving him alone again with Francisco.

Chapa sat silent for a moment, watching the flames overtake the fresh piece of kindling. How many times had he gazed into the fire, deep in thought over his labors? How would his life's work look when set aflame? How quickly would the fire consume all that he had ever created?

"Francisco, are you awake?" he asked, softly.

Francisco rolled over, turning his face towards his master. His eyes were open. "Yes, Don Juan."

"You heard my sons? You were awake then?" asked Chapa, pulling his chair closer to the fire and nearer Francisco.

"I awoke sometime after you arrived. I heard much of what you spoke of, yes."

"Gaspar believes you are dying. Are you really that ill?"

"I have never felt weaker. My breath is shallow. I am cold and then I sweat. I pray to God I am not dying. But I am very sick."

"Sit up Francisco. There are things I need to ask you."

"The *comisario* was there after all," said Francisco.

"Yes."

Francisco felt the weight of years of guilt, shame and revulsion wash over him, distilled down to a sharp and piercing pain. "I did only what I was compelled to do, and only under the threat of excommunication and the shaming of my daughter for the crimes to which I confessed. Padre Joseph did not believe my confession and threatened to put my daughter Luisa to trial unless I did what he commanded."

Chapa listened, watching Francisco's anguished face, strangely calm while he listened to the *mestizo*. "I understand. It angered me, of course, when I realized how much I trusted you and how misplaced that trust was. But it is my own fault, I should not have let myself forget what you are, and whom you served"

"I did what I could," said Francisco, unable to remain silent. "For the first time in my life, I measured myself by how little I accomplished. I gave them only the least scraps necessary to satisfy them. But as time went by, he kept demanding more and more."

"I appreciate your efforts," said Chapa, unsure if he meant these words.

"I wish," said Francisco, trying to wet his dry lips with his tongue, "I wish you had not . . . had not . . ."

Chapa stooped out of his chair and knelt down by him on his right knee, bringing his own cup of wine and water to the poor servant's mouth. "Take a sip or two before you continue. There is no rush."

Francisco took a small sip and let the liquid trickle down his throat. The light of the fire played across his face as the room darkened with the waning sun. Seeing him now so helpless stirred pity in Chapa's heart, even though anger was still a bitter taste in his mouth. "I wish you had not woken from your siesta so early that day."

"What?"

"That day in autumn, when you awoke while I read *Los Sueños*. I have often thought, since then, that if you had not witnessed me reading, then you would not have unlocked your trunk for me. And I might not have had my weakness tested by sin."

"The Church itself asked you to do it, so truthfully it was no sin," said Chapa, the old rigor of logic forcing him to acknowledge the truth of Francisco's situation.

"I am not sure," said Francisco.

"We are both now the same, both bound in a hopeless choice," said Chapa. "It is not even a choice. I feel as if I dangle over a great cliff, a single hand holding onto the shelf with diminishing strength. I know what fate awaits me. I will let go—it is only a matter of time. But it's so hard to imagine actually doing it."

Francisco took a deep breath and formulated a thought. He began slowly, "Your letters. Surely they are not too great a loss. For they were all delivered, were they not? Can the destruction of these copies be such a tragedy?"

"Perhaps not," said Chapa, unsure where the meandering mind of his servant sought to lead him.

"And your journal," Francisco continued. "Who did you write it for but yourself? As an old man now, how many more times would you read it? Once? Surely not more than twice. So why not take this night and day to re-read it all once more? And then parting with it will be easier."

"You speak some wisdom, Francisco, about these things. It is petty selfishness that compels me to treasure these papers. I should have strength enough to let them go, and I will. But what about the greatest loss of all, the work that could balance, in some small way, the many sins I have committed; the work that could add a small drop to the cup of knowledge that I have always savored, my *Historia*."

Francisco nodded and tried to speak but could not. He licked his lips again and motioned for the cup; again Chapa brought the cup to the poor man's lips. "I want to tell you something . . . but . . . let me rest just a moment, and drink a little more," said Francisco weakly, sipping again from the cup.

"Sleep," said Chapa.

"No, I am afraid if I sleep I might not wake again. And I have to say something important. Let me just rest, silent, for a moment."

Chapa leaned back in his chair, struck by the old man's frailty, and it reminded him of his tender last moments with Beatriz. The thought softened him, and he asked, quietly. "Would you like me to read to you?"

"Si, Don Juan," said Francisco.

"What will it be? The poem of Garcilaso de la Vega?"

"If you don't mind, *patron*. . . Could you read to me from *Don Quixote* once more?"

Chapa nodded, struggling to rise from his chair, "I will go to my study and fetch it."

Francisco shook his head, "It's here, by my shoulder. I somehow needed to look at it one more time, but I didn't have the strength to hold the book."

"Lay quietly and I will read to you. Should I continue from where you left this scrap of paper here, near the end?" Chapa asked, frowning a little at the choice, his least favorite section of the book. "You know, you never really told me why you love this book so much. What is it that attracts you to Don Quixote?"

218

Francisco thought for a second, and sighed, resting his hands on his stomach and staring up at the low ceiling, "I guess because it lets even a slave like myself dream a little. It lets me laugh at the ridiculousness of life in one part, then lifts my soul somehow a little closer to God in the next passage."

Chapa nodded. It was strange how close their thoughts were, an unlikely friendship for sure. Yes, it had become a true friendship, hadn't it? One that had enlivened these late months. The betrayal stabbed him once again, but he tried to let the thought drift through him, cleared his throat and began to read:

> *As he left Barcelona, Don Quixote turned his gaze upon the spot where he had fallen. "Here Troy was," said he; "here my ill-luck, not my cowardice, robbed me of all the glory I had won; here Fortune made me the victim of her caprices; here the luster of my achievements was dimmed; here, in a word, fell my happiness never to rise again."*
>
> *"Señor," said Sancho on hearing this, "it is the part of brave hearts to be patient in adversity just as much as to be glad in prosperity; I judge by myself, for, if when I was a governor I was glad, now that I am a squire and on foot I am not sad; and I have heard say that she whom commonly they call Fortune is a drunken whimsical jade, and, what is more, blind, and therefore neither sees what she does, nor knows whom she casts down or whom she sets up."*
>
> *"Thou art a great philosopher, Sancho," said Don Quixote; "thou speakest very sensibly; I know not who taught thee. But I can tell thee there is no such thing as Fortune in the world, nor does anything which takes place there, be it good or bad, come about by chance, but by the special preordination of heaven; and hence the common saying that 'each of us is the maker of his own Fortune.' I have been that of mine; but not with the proper amount of prudence, and my self-confidence has therefore made me pay dearly; for I ought to have reflected that Rocinante's feeble strength could not resist the mighty bulk of the Knight of the White*

Moon's horse. In a word, I ventured it, I did my best, I was overthrown, but though I lost my honor I did not lose nor can I lose the virtue of keeping my word. When I was a knight-errant, daring and valiant, I supported my achievements by hand and deed, and now that I am a humble squire I will support my words by keeping the promise I have given. Forward then, Sancho my friend, let us go to keep the year of the novitiate in our own country, and in that seclusion we shall pick up fresh strength to return to the by me never-forgotten calling of arms."

"Señor," returned Sancho, "travelling on foot is not such a pleasant thing that it makes me feel disposed or tempted to make long marches. Let us leave this armor hung up on some tree, instead of some one that has been hanged; and then with me on Dapple's back and my feet off the ground we will arrange the stages as your worship pleases to measure them out; but to suppose that I am going to travel on foot, and make long ones, is to suppose nonsense."

"Thou sayest well, Sancho," said Don Quixote; "let my armor be hung up for a trophy, and under it or round it we will carve on the trees what was inscribed on the trophy of Roland's armour —

These let none move

Who dareth not his might with Roland prove.*"*

"That's the very thing," said Sancho; "and if it was not that we should feel the want of Rocinante on the road, it would be as well to leave him hung up too."

***

Chapa smiled at the image of the poor, ill-fed horse hoisted into the tree and set the book on his lap. He glanced over at Francisco and saw that he was still awake, his eyes trained upwards, listening intently.

"I have always found the end of this book very sad," said Chapa.

220

"Isn't the end of any book a little sad?" asked Francisco, "Any good book, I mean."

"Yes, but this one in particular. And not merely because Don Quixote dies, as all men must. He is old and has been through many adventures so his death itself doesn't seem sad. What bothers me is that he abandons his dreams. In this passage he seems so crestfallen, so resigned. He faced defeat and sorrow so often, but he could always weep and then get up to fight again; but here, he is finally a broken man, one who accepts defeat with his head down. By the very end, he denies all of his adventures and even renounces his very identity, the name of Quixote."

"I understand it differently. Do you really think, Don Juan, that he no longer believed he was a *caballero*?"

"Yes, of course. In the final chapter, he declares that he is no longer Don Quixote but merely humble Alonso Quixano."

"But do you believe he was telling the truth? Could he not have said such a thing without believing it?"

"Why would he tell such a lie, after living as Don Quixote for so many years?"

"He wished his niece to marry, and his renouncing of madness would aid her. And he writes his will in that final chapter. Don't you think he could just be saying what needed to be said? For the good of his heirs?"

Chapa considered Francisco's words, turning over the idea in his head, considering whether he had perhaps missed something crucial about a book he had read and reread so many times. Perhaps in this, as in so many other things, it was time to shift his perspective. "So he spoke the truth, the actual truth, which to him was a lie, because he was still mad?"

"Have you ever known a man who was truly mad to become sane after one night's sleep?"

"I suppose not," said Chapa.

"Then perhaps the Knight of Sorrowful Countenance only feigned sanity and made those gestures as his final act of chivalry," said Francisco.

221

Chapa smiled, "It may be time for me to read this book again, Francisco. These many months of conversation, and the sharpening of perspective that comes with a sense of impending death, have deepened my thinking. Revisiting my *Historia* through the eyes of another has made me take another look at the events of our country and the course of my own life. You have lived the same events, been governed by the same Crown and Church, but you experienced the course of our history quite differently. I will soon be alone with these books, the writings of so many others, but none of my own. I suppose I will have to find my solace in reading old favorites again, looking for new truths in old friends."

"You will still have pen and paper. Perhaps you should write a new *Historia*, written now with the wisdom of someone who has truly faced death. Once your papers are burnt, you could write in peace, without suspicion."

"Write my *Historia* anew? I don't imagine I have that much time left. And I think you are too generous in assessing the tenacity of the Inquisition; I think they would surely take it from me once again. But I have let you talk too much. Should I continue reading?"

Francisco shook his head. "One more sip; I am not finished with what I have to say."

Chapa knelt and for a third time held the cup of wine and water to his servant's mouth. Francisco drank more deeply this time. A little life seemed restored to his eyes, however temporary.

"Thank you. I have a sin to confess to you, if you will hear it."

"I am no priest, Francisco. I might have been once, and perhaps my life would have been better. But you need not confess your sins, to me or to any man. You have lived a hard life, filled with hard choices. You have wronged me, its true, even if it might have been against your will. Confess your sins to God, if you must, but I know you are a good man. Better than many I have known who wear silk and scarlet."

Francisco moved his hand impatiently, cutting Chapa short. "It concerns the *Historia*."

Chapa turned towards Francisco, asking sharply, "Did you give some of the *Historia* to the *comisario*? I thought it was still intact when I looked at it. But at this point, what does it matter? You can't harm a book that I must burn tomorrow."

"No," said Francisco, sitting up now, with more energy than he had shown in days. "It is not that. I would never have given him part of the *Historia*. I gave him letters, journal entries, anything but what I knew was most valuable to you. When I die the *Historia* will remain unread by any living man save you."

"So what then?" asked Chapa.

Francisco hesitated and then finally pushed himself to speak, "I . . . I copied it, using the cache of paper you kept hidden, fastened on the underside of your bed."

"You copied my *Historia*?" Chapa asked, not entirely understanding what Francisco could have meant, "When, while I was meeting with the Bishop? You couldn't possibly."

"No, I started long before this terrible day. For many nights, beginning not long after you gave it to me, I stayed up late, copying faithfully each page of your book. I knew the reach of the Inquisition and knew I would be powerless to resist a request to deliver it. I feared I would have to steal it, or that you would be forced to destroy it."

Chapa sat, stunned. He didn't know how to think about this new piece of information. Part of him was stung anew by the duplicitousness of the old slave, the extent of his secrecy, the way that he treated each discussion of the *Historia* as if he had just read it. Had he ever really known anything about Francisco, what motivated him, who he served? At the same time, there tugged at him a little hope, a small lift. The hopelessness that had drowned him just moments ago parted just a little. "Where is the copy? What have you done with it? Why did you copy it?"

"It is already long gone from here. It sits now in the hands of the Mercedarian friars in Guadalajara."

"What? How? What gave you the right to deliver my *Historia* without my consent?"

"I gave it to the muleteer to deliver. At the end of the day, I had to decide what would happen to it. Seeking your advice would have forced me to disclose my theft, my spying. I couldn't force myself to speak the truth to you, not because I cared for my own life, but for my daughter's sake. I was prisoner to my sins. If I did wrong again, I truly apologize." Francisco said, his face betraying his pain, but his voice steady, "They are not librarians, like the Benedictines, so I don't know what they will do with the document, or whether others beyond their walls will ever read your *Historia*, but they are no friends of the Inquisition and I believe they will keep it safe."

Chapa leaned back in his chair, contemplative and calm once again. Could this possibly be true? Could this old man, part Indian and part *negro*, have truly found time to copy such an enormous manuscript, all while singlehandedly taking care of his sick master and looking after this old house?

Or, as he implied about old Don Quixote, was Francisco speaking a deliberate untruth, searching for a final kindness to deliver as he lay dying? Chapa nodded. It was a lie of compassion, no doubt, to make him feel less aggrieved at the loss of all his works, but a lie all the same. Hadn't Francisco already shown his capacity for lies and deception, made a false confession in order to save his daughter? Chapa felt confused, hope warring with suspicion, both fighting with the calm resignation he had cultivated these past hours.

At the end, though, it was peace that won the day. He added logs to the fire, left Francisco on his mat, covered with one of the soft blankets Beatriz had woven. "Goodnight, friend. I pray you wake tomorrow stronger than today."

Chapa walked to the bedchamber and sat down heavily on the side of his bed. He pulled his boots off, but lay on the bed fully clothed. Sleep fell upon him immediately.

***

I know her well, this cañón, *this* burrone. *I've visited her a hundred times and a hundred times before that. She is so old; she has known many men before me. And she will surely know many after. But, for now, she is mine alone.*

I know the feel of her walls, the echo of my songs through her heart, the steady pulse of the stream that runs through her, the bends and twists of each of her arms and fingers.

I walk forward, effortless, each stride easier than the last. The canyon too, becomes freer. Once narrow it grows wider and wider.

My bare feet fall softly on the moist ground – good, black soil. So rich is the earth beneath me that I cannot even hear my footsteps. All around me is silence. Alongside me is a cool, wide river. The water is clear, rippling across smooth stones as it makes its way towards the distant sea.

Or is it so distant? I find myself emerging from the canyon, the walls peel away into the distance to my left and to my right. The soil gives way to wet sand. A long flat beach lies in front of me. And beyond that? Yes, the sea.

Is this my own tranquil Ligurian sea? Or the great Oçêano Atlantico? *Or is it a body of water even vaster? That great blue water which lies to the west. What do they call it? The Ocean of Peace?*

The tide rolls up to me, the soft foam swirls around my toes. The water is warm; the sun lies low across the horizon, casting a shadow onto the sea. This is my shadow – I own it and I am at peace. Am I all alone here? Or is that a figure I see down the beach? Is he walking towards me, or away from me? Could he be a friend?

Amô.

***

The next morning Chapa rose, still dressed in his clothes from the day before. Stray wisps of last night's dream, another visitation of that haunted walk through the canyon, still floated through his mind. He was reminded of Plato's allegory of the cave, a favorite of his from his studies in Seville. A sense of peace and calm settled over him, realizing now that the nightmares that had haunted him for so long were not real, but instead were cast by mere shadows, events he could not see and could not understand.

He crossed to his study, and sat down at his writing table. Beatriz's mirror winked at him as it always did, resting on the little scrap of velvet. He picked it up, looking into its depths with none of the hesitation he usually felt. His rider had finally mastered the elephant. He was ready; it was time. He looked into the little oval, this time eagerly seeking his last conversation with the man hiding in its depths.

***

He set it down at last, paused a second, then picked it up again, slipping the little mirror in his pocket. He felt for the key around his neck, lying against the little gold ring he had given Beatriz on the birth of their first child. He stood up and tugged at the handles of the old trunk, dragging it slowly and with great difficulty across the rough stones of the patio towards the garden gate.

When Chapa finally reached the little gate next to the kitchen, he started a little when he saw Francisco sitting on a little stool near the *fogón*, taking shallow breaths, sipping a cup of hot broth from the pot that his master had left simmering the night before. He stayed seated, resisting the urge to stand and help, instead watching and gauging Chapa as he stood at the doorway to the kitchen. Chapa smiled gruffly, "So you live to see another day, Francisco. Good, because I need help with this one final task. My arms are tired and I can't finish it alone."

Without a word — for what more was there to say? — Chapa and Francisco hauled the trunk out to the garden and towards the small fire pit at its center. Once they were finished, Francisco stood back, the blanket hanging from his shoulders, watching as Chapa opened the trunk and surveyed its contents. A final hesitation grabbed hold of Chapa and he looked back to

226

Francisco, hoping for some final unexpected sign that might stay his hand. None came.

Turning back to the trunk, Chapa began with the easy ones first, copies of old letters and official records from the *haciendas* forming a solid base. Tidy and careful as ever, he placed each neatly tied bundle of papers precisely in an open grid, knowing that the flames would need air to burn effectively. Next the journals, until one by one, all of his old memories went into the pyre: *Albisola, Genoa, Cádiz, Veracruz, Ciudad de México, Cadereyta, Monterrey,* and *Beatriz.* Finally, he reached for the one last, largest bundle, the *Historia.* He looked back at Francisco, sagging in the doorway. The old servant, face as impassive as ever, only nodded.

Francisco, shivering with fever—or was it emotion—shuffled over to the stove, took a sliver of pitch from the pile, lit it and walked it over to Chapa. Chapa took the pitch and knelt over the pile of papers he had arranged, crisscrossed neatly in their low pyramid, with ample channels for air—the fire would consume it quickly and surely. Chapa stood silently for a little while, then bent to light the fire, before stopping at the last moment. Francisco watched as he pulled the little mirror from his pocket, kissed its rim, crossed himself, and tossed it on the pyramid before setting the paper ablaze. He had pulled all he could from that mirror; the twin worlds of reality and imagination reflected in its depths finally merged into a single, peaceful truth. What was left to discover he would find only in his heart.

Chapa stood and watched the flames grow, watching as the first sheets of white paper turned first yellow, then brown and finally black. The flames leapt higher and higher up the pyramid, casting flickering shadows that played and danced, flickering first over his face, then Francisco, the warmth of the blaze flushing their cheeks and the light reflected in their eyes. As each little bundle caught fire, another piece of his life's work dissolved into gray ash, little fragments rising slowly into the sky, snowflakes that rose instead of fell.

Francisco stood impassively, a few steps behind Chapa, watching as his shoulders shook with silent sobs, until finally, the mirror shattered with a loud crack, the sounds echoing against the garden wall and rousing them both from their reveries.

The shattering of the mirror served as a marker, the moment at which the past ended and the world became clear and still. The sun rose above the Cerro de la Silla and the shadows of the early morning were gone. A few moments later, Francisco stepped to Chapa's side and reached out his hand, delicately pulling out a tiny sliver of glass from Chapa's cheek, the little drop of blood mixing with his tears as he watched the last few licks of flame die into the ash.

EPILOGUE

Francisco died just a few weeks later, on New Year's Day 1694.

Chapa drafted his last will and testament on January 8th of that same year. He named his sons Gaspar and José Maria executors. His vineyard in Albisola was left to his uncle Giovanni, if surviving. His Spanish and Italian books were left to Gaspar, and his Latin books were to be sold to purchase a funeral Mass. Against the protests of all present, he left one quarter of a lot in Monterrey to Francisco's daughter, Luisa.

Chapa never again picked up a pen after Francisco's death. He lived another year in peaceful solitude, surrounded by his books and cared for by his sons and daughters. He died on 20 April, 1695, his children and grandchildren by his bedside.

A manuscript copy of Juan Bautista Chapa's work, *La Historia del Nuevo Reino de León*, was finally discovered by the noted historian Genaro Garcia and published in 1909 as the first history of Nuevo León. The identity of its author, however, remained a mystery until 1961, when another historian, Israel Cavazos Garza, conclusively determined that the author could be none other than Juan Bautista Chapa.

Made in the USA
Charleston, SC
04 February 2016